T H E
M U S I C
O F
T H E
D E E P

OTHER BOOKS BY
ELIZABETH HALL

Miramont's Ghost
In the Blue Hour

THE
MUSIC
OF
THE
DEEP

ELIZABETH HALL

LAKE UNION
PUBLISHING

Text copyright © 2018 by Elizabeth Hall
All rights reserved.

Published by Lake Union Publishing, Seattle

www.apub.com

Amazon, the Amazon logo, and Lake Union Publishing are trademarks of Amazon.com, Inc., or its affiliates.

ISBN-13: 9781503954687
ISBN-10: 1503954684

Cover design by PEPE *nymi*

Printed in the United States of America

For Misa and Marcos

PROLOGUE

The sky was the color of a bruise, dramatic shades of gray and purple and lavender, feathery tinges of soft gold. A storm loomed on the western horizon, just beginning to rattle the edge of the island. Wind tossed the branches of the cedars and hemlocks and firs, bending them into dramatic poses. In the deep blue-gray water of Haro Strait, waves skipped and jumped, kicking up sprays of white. Seagulls rode on the swells of air; an eagle called out from the heights.

The sign for the Buena Vista Cemetery danced in the wind, chains creaking and moaning. Just outside the cemetery gates, Emmie stopped and shivered, watching the coming storm. It seeped into her bones; her joints scraped and sighed, a combination of winter storm and the accumulated wear and tear of sixty-five years on the planet.

From here, she had just enough height to look down on the main street of town, two blocks long, filled with various businesses of the tourist trade, or at least filled when the economy was good. She looked down there now, admiring the way the Christmas lights managed to soften the threatening storm. Lights filled every window, some lit only with white, others boasting every color of the rainbow. They managed to bring a feeling of warmth to the bleak, short days of winter. Like stepping into a Norman Rockwell painting, they made life in this town look pretty and perfect and charming. With lights like those, it was almost possible to believe that nothing bad could ever happen here.

Almost possible, but the lights did not deceive her. Even as she stood, looking down at that picturesque little town, sparkling and twinkling like a child's favorite dream, she could feel the gusts, moving through the trees and the stones of the cemetery. Wind moaned, like the voices of the long dead. Leaves picked up, swirling away in the squall. Something was stirring in those stones. Stirring up the past, stirring up memories and ghosts that were best left quiet.

"Hush now," she whispered over the graves of the dead. As if her quiet command had any purchase. As if she could stop the wind and rain and storm. As if she had the power to stop the spirits from whirling up into the present, wreaking havoc on them all.

She turned to continue her way up the hill to her home, and that's when it hit her. She grabbed her left arm, doubled over in pain, as if she'd been kicked. For one moment, stars filled her vision, multicolored bursts of light, similar to the Christmas lights in town. She leaned against the cemetery fence, hung her head, and waited for the dizziness to pass.

Her old dog, Pete, stood close to her, watching intently. The dog was attuned to every movement Emmie made, to every subtle change in her eyes or her voice, or the occasional tremor that crept into her hands. He watched her as if he were her guardian angel and not the other way around. She lowered herself to a bench, forced herself to breathe. After a long minute, her breathing returned to normal, and she reached to rub the dog's ears.

"It's okay, boy. I'm okay." Emmie leaned back against the bench, and the dog sat down next to her leg, both of them surveying the gravestones in front of them and the storm-tossed sea beyond.

Emmie had long been ultrasensitive to every ripple of energy around her. But now, combined with her advancing age, she wasn't always sure just which energy, just whose pain she was feeling. When she was younger, she could always sense whatever it was out there that was hurting: a horse or a dog or a coyote with its foot in a trap. Somehow, she knew, and always managed to find the creature that was radiating pain and needed the healing touch that Emmie had to offer.

But lately, when the waves of hurting washed over her like this, she couldn't always tell where it was coming from. Could be animals, could be humans. Could even be something going on in her own body. And lately, there had been times when she had also been feeling the pain of the dead.

Emmie sat still, gazing over the gravestones and the eternally green grass, past the cedars on the edge of the graveyard, out to the purple sky and pewter waves. She had always found it odd that the founders of the tiny town of Copper Cove had seen fit to place the cemetery just exactly here. It was on a rise of land, with breathtaking views of the waters of both Copper Cove to the south and Haro Strait to the west, the village spreading out below. *The best view in town*, Emmie thought, yet again. As if the dead could appreciate such a thing.

As she sat there now, surveying the town and the water and the storm, she thought that maybe this cemetery's location was not some random miscalculation on the part of the founding fathers. Certainly, the dead had the best view in this town, the prime piece of real estate. But for the first time in the nearly fifty years that she had lived here, Emmie thought maybe there was a good reason for that. Maybe they used this vantage point to keep an eye on the living. As if the dead were the ones in charge.

ONE

The smell of cedar permeated every molecule of air, and Alexandra inhaled it like tonic. She was driving off the ferry, her first such encounter with the Washington State ferry system, and onto Saratoga Island, a place she had never been before and knew next to nothing about. The only thing that mattered, right at this moment, was that she had managed to put two thousand miles and a one-hour ferry ride between herself and her old life. She was as far north as she could possibly go without leaving the country, and Alex hoped it was far enough.

The aroma of cedar wrapped around her, and she let herself take her first real breath since leaving Albuquerque three days before. The tension of the drive had lodged in her shoulder blades, and she leaned forward in the seat, trying to stretch her back and navigate her surroundings at the same time. Rain had started, yet again, and she flipped on the wipers and the headlights, staring into the murkiness of the road that led her from this quaint tourist town where the ferry emptied, into the northern, rural reaches of the island.

Dusk came early this far north. The sun was gone and the light was dim, despite the fact that it was not yet four o'clock. Eight miles later, down a twisty, two-lane road that wound through huge stands of

Douglas fir and cedar and hemlock, she pulled into the tiny town of Copper Cove, population 514.

Tapping the brake, she drove slowly down the main street. A smattering of businesses clung to two blocks, staring out at the water of Haro Strait to the west. The buildings were old, a New England painting of 1870s homes and businesses. She reached the end of the street and curved to the left, and then turned left again, heading back north through a few blocks of Victorian-era houses. Everything was dressed for Christmas. Twinkling lights decorated all the lampposts and trees and swooped down lengths of fence. Windows and yards glowed with rainbow-colored twinkle lights. She stopped the car, staring at the street and the lights and the reflections of lights on the wet pavement. To her right, a few boats sat moored in the marina of Copper Cove, also bedecked with Christmas lights, as if this whole place were lifted straight from a Hallmark card.

Alex exhaled. The trip was a blur of highways and rest stops; she had not stopped at a motel but had simply pulled off the road and slept in the car when exhaustion overtook her. Her sleep was fitful and brief, whether she was in a real bed or tipped back in the front seat of the car, and so she had not counted it as much of a sacrifice. But now, three days later, she needed a shower and a good night's sleep in a real bed. And at this moment, she really needed to eat. Alex had not eaten a real meal since before leaving Albuquerque—nothing but fast food and gas station junk. Her brain was fuzzy with exhaustion; her body craved nourishment and rest.

She grabbed the three pages of magazine article that had prompted her northern journey, taken from the pages of a recent edition of *Nature* magazine. Alex had known, as soon as she saw the article and the picture of the woman who had written it, that this was information she needed to keep.

She tucked the folded pages into her bag and headed into the Drift Inn for a meal. The café, like the town around it, was cozy and quaint and teeming with Christmas lights. They decorated every post, every beam in the ceiling, and ran along the backs of each knotty pine booth. Alex slipped into a booth by the window and glanced around. A bar ran down one entire wall of the café, and it, too, was flooded with Christmas lights, doubled by the mirror behind them. A few people were seated, but it was early for the dinner hour, and Alex was grateful for the quiet.

The waitress brought a menu and a glass of water. Her eyes lingered, for a moment, on Alexandra's face. Alex swallowed and dropped her gaze to the menu. She hated being scrutinized like that, hated the feeling of sticking out.

"Special tonight is polenta with spicy shrimp. Can I get you a drink or anything, to get you started?" The woman's face had changed slightly. She was back to doing her job, not so intently focused on the facial features of this stranger before her.

"The special sounds good. And some hot tea."

Alex turned and stared out the window, drawn to the sight of the water.

"Up for a visit?" the waitress asked when she returned with a cup of tea.

Alex met her eyes. "Actually, I was thinking I might stay awhile."

"It's a great place, for sure. If you can get used to rain and clouds and short, dark days. Gray, gray, gray. Where you from?"

"New Mexico. No rain. No short, dark days." As soon as the words left her mouth, Alex felt a moment of panic. She did not want to answer questions, and now that it was too late, she wished she had lied about where she was from.

The waitress smiled and nodded. "Looks like you go for extremes."

Alex took the folded pages of the magazine article out of her purse and opened them, pressing the creases with her finger. "Would you happen to know where I could find this woman? Dr. Margaret Edwards?"

The waitress cocked her head to look at the small picture of the gray-haired doctor of biology who had authored the article. "Maggie?" she asked, straightening her neck. "Sure. She's sitting at the booth right behind you."

Alex turned. Dr. Margaret Edwards looked very much like the picture in the magazine article that Alex held in her hand. Late seventies, with a severe short haircut, her thick gray hair obviously not something she spent time worrying about. Her eyes were a keen and piercing blue, even behind the thick glasses. Alex stood for a moment, taking in the real woman, the cup of coffee on the table before her, and a pile of reading material, which consisted of several scientific journals.

"Dr. Edwards?"

The woman looked up, taking in Alex from head to toe. "Nobody around here calls me that. Where are you from?"

"Albuquerque."

"No, that's not what I meant. Which news crew sent you? Because you should know right off the bat that I refuse to do any more interviews."

Alex shook her head. "I'm not from any news crew. I spoke to you about a week ago. About the archival work you need done? I'm Alexandra Fra . . . Turner."

"Ah." Maggie Edwards indicated the seat across from her, and Alex slipped into the booth.

Dr. Edwards appraised the face of the woman in front of her. "I wasn't expecting you until after Christmas."

Alex pressed her lips together. "There was a break in the weather, so I decided to go ahead and leave."

"You didn't want to spend Christmas with your family?"

Alex forced a slow exhale, trying to keep herself steady. She shook her head. "The weather report predicted a storm front. I didn't want to spend three days on the road, fighting snow and ice the whole drive."

"Ah." Maggie took a swig of her coffee and continued to examine Alex Turner.

"How'd you get that shiner?"

Alex looked away. She had hoped that the bruises had faded enough to be unnoticeable. "It's a crazy story, really. No one would believe it."

"Try me."

"I work at the University library, archival research. As you know," Alex added, glancing at the woman across from her for a second before her gaze flittered away. "And last week, I was moving boxes of material that I'd been sorting and scanning. Anyway, I pushed open this heavy door to the storage unit—temperature regulated, you know—and then leaned down to pick up the box. By the time I had it in my arms, the door was swinging closed. Caught me right in the eye, just as I was standing up." Alex brought her eyes back to her questioner.

Dr. Edwards took a deep breath. "That's quite a story."

Alex tipped her head slightly. "I told you no one would believe me."

"A job at the University is a good job, just about any way you cut it." Maggie ran her finger around the rim of her coffee cup. "I'm still a little confused as to why you would leave a good job to come up here to the end of nowhere in the dead of winter, just for a few months of work for me. I don't pay very well."

Alex shrugged. "I took a leave of absence." She turned and looked out the window at the water. "I just needed a change, I guess. A break from routine. And when I read about your work, I thought this might be a good place for it."

Maggie Edwards leaned back in the booth. "Well, the grant will pay for about two months of your time. That's it. There's a mountain of work, but not a mountain of money." She began to gather her papers to leave. "The truth is . . . I am very far behind with cataloging and sorting and entering things into the database. My office is piled with data that's not helping anyone. Totally inaccessible to researchers in its current condition." She stopped and gazed at Alex again. "I've been overwhelmed with information for a long time now."

Alex nodded. "That's my specialty. Organizing information."

Maggie stood and pulled on her coat and hat. "Where are you staying tonight?"

"I don't know. I just got into town. I guess I'll look for a hotel."

Maggie laughed. "A hotel? The week before Christmas? Not hardly. We're on the islands, you know. Tourist season up here is all summer and every holiday. Thanksgiving, Christmas, New Years. Spring vacation. You aren't likely to find anything available right now."

"Oh. I hadn't thought. It's not that much of an issue in Albuquerque."

"And if you did find something, it would cost an arm and a leg." Maggie finished gathering her papers and closed her satchel. "As I said, I don't pay that well."

She stood and wrapped a wool scarf around her throat.

"I had planned on putting you in the big house in a week anyway, so I guess it won't make any difference that you're here early. All I need to do is get some heat on. Eat your dinner and come up to the house. Turn left at the end of Main Street and head up the hill. I'm in the little cabin on the cove. First driveway after the cemetery." Maggie threw a twenty-dollar bill on the table, then turned and left before Alex could respond, her steps firm and quick on the hardwood floor of the café.

Alex leaned back in the booth and took another deep breath. The waitress arrived with her dinner and set it on the table. Alex looked at the polenta and shrimp, and her stomach rumbled. She could not remember the last time she had eaten an actual meal. It felt like weeks.

"Need anything else right now?"

Alex shook her head. "No, I don't think so."

The waitress looked toward the door that Maggie Edwards had just exited, and then she leaned down a little, as if picking something up off the floor. "You going to work for Maggie?"

"For a bit."

"Staying at her place?"

Alex nodded.

The waitress looked from side to side, and then leaned forward to wipe the table. "Don't let her put you in the captain's house," she whispered. "That place is haunted, you know." She turned and walked away.

TWO

Alex pulled into the driveway to Maggie's cabin. She felt better already: breathing the sweet smell of the cedar, the biting scent of salt water providing the perfect base note to the perfume of green. She was here, safe and sound. She'd met Maggie Edwards and had at least temporary employment. And she'd just finished one of the best meals she could remember eating in months.

The cabin was set back in the woods to her left, still visible from the road, but not exactly on it. Despite the fact that the rest of the town was decked out in a lavish display of Christmas lights, the cabin belonging to Maggie Edwards radiated only the harsh glare from the porch light and a pale glow of lamplight from inside. Alex walked up the wood steps and had just raised her hand to knock when the door whooshed open and Maggie stepped out, pulling it closed behind her.

"This way," she muttered, heading down the steps and back down the driveway. She turned and headed into the dark.

Alex, at five feet one inch, had to move fast to keep up with Maggie, who was a good six inches taller. She hadn't realized that there was a larger house across the driveway from the cabin. Trees towered over the two-storied giant, completely shrouding it in darkness.

"I'm putting you in the main house. I use it for interns or visiting scientists. May not be perfect, but it is available." They climbed the four steps to another porch, and Maggie pushed open the front door.

Alex stepped into a foyer area, lavishly finished in the old-fashioned woodwork of another time. An ornate oak banister ran up the staircase to her left, but instead of curving to a landing on the second floor, it ended abruptly, near the top of the stairs. A door had been built, obviously added after the initial construction. It blocked the stairs at the top; she could see nothing of the second floor above.

Dr. Edwards followed her gaze and answered the unspoken question. "This old house is huge, much too big for one person. Built in the 1870s, when they didn't seem to understand the benefits of insulation. Costs a small fortune to heat the whole thing. Normally, I only have one or two interns in the summer, maybe a colleague or two for short stays in the winter. There are two bedrooms downstairs, and that's where I put guests. I had that door built several years ago to try to keep the heat in."

Alex nodded, pulling her gaze away from the abrupt ending of the staircase at that strange door. She followed Maggie into the room on the right, a living room area, about fourteen feet square. There was an energy-efficient woodstove inserted in the old brick fireplace, and it radiated warmth into the room. A sofa sat against the front window, and in the corner across from that was an old-fashioned armchair. Antique furniture, most of it a golden oak color, filled many of the spaces. Windows at the front and sides of the room stared out at the darkness.

Directly behind the living room was a dining room, filled with an old oak table and six chairs. A massive oak buffet stood against the far wall, the mirror grown hazy with age. The kitchen was across from that. It had obviously been remodeled at some point. Wood cabinets, painted white, and a relatively new refrigerator and stove made the place up-to-date, and surprisingly cozy. Behind those rooms, Maggie led her down the hallway to two bedrooms and a bath.

"The bedroom in the middle is the warmest, of course. That one at the end of the hall catches all the breezes off the water." Maggie opened the door to that back bedroom, and cold air swooped out around her. Alex took a quick step backward. "Old windows. No insulation."

Maggie closed the door and moved to another door at the end of the hallway. "This is the back porch. There's a washer and dryer and a back door. You can pull the car up behind there." She indicated the back of the house with a tip of her head. "Also cold, as you can see. The middle of the house is definitely the place to be."

"This is a big house," Alex said.

"Yes. Exactly why I wanted to live in the cabin. The drafts here are awful." Maggie grimaced, and added, "But like I said. Stick to the middle rooms; you'll be warm enough."

Alex nodded and let out a long, exhausted sigh.

Maggie turned to her. "You know how to feed a fire?"

"I think I can manage it."

"Wood's on the front porch. Might even be coffee in the kitchen cupboard. I had a colleague up just a few weeks ago, so it's been cleaned semirecently."

"Thank you, Dr. Edwards. I appreciate this."

Maggie stopped at the door. "I wasn't expecting you this soon, but since you're here, we might as well go ahead and get started. Come up to the cabin in the morning. We can take a look at the work I need done, and then you can get groceries and settle in before everything closes for the holiday."

Alex nodded. "Sounds good."

"I don't celebrate Christmas, so you're on your own."

"I don't really celebrate it, either," Alex murmured. She moved to the window in the living room, looking out at the lights of town down below. The water reflected those colorful lights, broad moving bands of red and blue and green. Her eyes traveled the distance from those twinkling lights to the room she was in, and she drew in a sharp breath.

The ornate wrought-iron spires of the cemetery fence were just a few feet away from the window where she stood. She had not realized just how close the house was to the edge of the graveyard.

"That cemetery is so close," Alex said. "Almost the perfect setting for a haunted house."

Maggie's eyes flared for a moment. "You believe in ghosts, do you?"

Alex turned, and their eyes met. She shrugged. "I've never seen one. But the waitress did say something about . . ." She stopped herself just in time. "Haunted houses."

Maggie snorted and shook her head. "If you get to know her better, you will find that Caroline has an absolute flair for drama. She really ought to be in the theater."

Alex watched the woman in front of her.

"And this is the most haunted town in Washington. Or hadn't you heard?"

Alex shook her head.

"Brings in lots of money—those old ghosts. Paranormal conference in October. Ghost hunters. Ghost tours. Our general store even sells some of that ghost-hunting equipment—electronic voice recorders, electronic meters. Ghosts mean money."

Maggie moved to the window, looking out at the cemetery.

"You'll hear quite a bit, if you stick around here. It's one of the more annoying traits of living in a small town. But we'll get along a lot better if you ignore all that gossip." Maggie walked to the door, and then turned to look at Alex once more.

"Besides. We're all haunted by something. Isn't that so, Alexandra?"

Alex moved her car to the back of the house, grateful that she'd been instructed to leave it here, away from the street, surrounded by bushes and towering cedars. She grabbed her bag and headed inside. It had been more than three days since she had last had a shower, and she was keen to wash away the sweat of the past few days, the scents of her own body, with the pheromones of fear and pain and tension. Standing next to the shower a few minutes later, waiting for the water to warm up, she wished there was a way to wash away all the effects of the past eleven years with Daniel Frazier. If only it were that easy—to turn on the water and step inside and let all of the trauma of the past flow onto the floor and down the drain.

Alex leaned into the mirror over the sink, examining the color around her eye. At least she could see out of it; at least it stayed open now. She stripped off her sweatpants and T-shirt and turned slightly. The mirror reflected it back to her, one huge storm system of bruises running down her hip and thigh and up into the small of her back. The colors ran purple and blue, with tinges of yellow, and Alex felt slightly sickened by the sight. Her memories of that last fight, just three days ago, were tattered, as if all she had were the scraps left over after a fire. She could not remember being hit; she could not remember what had started the whole ordeal; she could not remember how it had ended. It had happened before, where the pain obliterated the memories. But there was always something about those blank spaces that pursued her, chased her, staying close, like a shadow. She swallowed, fighting the fears that were buried just under the surface, fighting to keep herself upright, fighting to stay focused on the next thing that needed to be done.

She looked at her bruises in the mirror and let out a long breath. *Thank God Dr. Margaret Edwards can't see that*, she thought as she stepped into the water.

THREE

Branches scratched against the window, and the sound reached through the fog of sleep, scraping against her brain. It was still dark when Alex opened her eyes, and she lay still, trying to remember where she was. In that first moment of consciousness, everything was still blurry around the edges; she had to really concentrate to bring it all into focus. She stared at the sky outside the window, a slightly lighter shade of black, just pale enough that she could see the outlines of the trees. She watched as the branches of a giant cedar swayed back and forth, as if signaling to her that she was no longer in New Mexico.

Instinctively, she reached for her cell phone, wondering whether it was morning or midnight, and that's when it came back to her—all the ways that her life had changed in the past three days. She no longer had a cell phone. That, along with her wedding ring, now lay mired in the muddy waters of the Rio Grande, pitched out the window of her car as she drove away.

The table next to the bed held an old vintage lamp, the shade trimmed with fuzzy ball fringe. Underneath it was an old-fashioned alarm clock, the kind that must be wound to keep going. No electricity, no battery required. It was ticking away, as if nothing unusual had occurred in any part of the world, and the glow-in-the-dark hands told her it was now six o'clock. That meant it was seven a.m. back home.

Home. Now that was an interesting concept. All those Christmas songs and stories and movies, with the "I'll Be Home for Christmas" theme, all those commercials about warmth and love and family. Did it really exist, anywhere? For anyone? Because it certainly wasn't a place that Alex had experienced—not in the recent past, at any rate.

She pushed those thoughts away. Everything here was different, including the longer nights. Not a glimmer of coming daylight could be seen in the sky.

Alex pulled on her socks and a sweater and padded into the kitchen. She found a coffee maker, a sugar bowl with paper packets, and even a bag of Seattle's Best in the cupboard. She started a pot of coffee and let herself breathe for a few moments. Just breathe—inhale, exhale. Just breathe, as if nothing in the world were wrong, as if her whole life were just as it should be.

She carried the mug of steaming brown warmth over to the dining room and stood at the bay window, cup warming her hands, as she stared at the sparkle of gray water out there in the sound. The rain was steady, a relentless stream of drops that hit the glass and slid down, racing each other to the bottom of the windowpane.

The clouds were thick and low, backlit by the pale radiance of an almost full moon, not yet set in the western horizon. As she watched, the clouds scuttled away, and for just a moment, the light of the moon came through and bathed the landscape in an eerie white glow. She could see the blocks of town down below, most of the buildings still dark.

Her gaze pulled in closer, to the cemetery just a few yards away from the house. With the advantage of moonlight, Alex could make out a smattering of the stones. It was so close to the house, the fence no more than twenty feet away from the window where she now stood. Fingers of tree branches brushed against the dark sky. The clouds moved swiftly, racing on the marine currents of air. They swallowed the moon, and the landscape went dark once again. Alex could see nothing but the vague reflection of her own face in the glass.

That brief glimpse of the cemetery brought it all back to her in a rush. It was still too soon, the loss too fresh, and her stomach clenched. Not even three months had passed since she had stood at the cemetery in the small town of Edgewood, New Mexico, watching as they lowered her mother's body into the ground.

Frances Turner had been lucky, if that was the correct term, that the cancer had claimed her so quickly. She was in the hospital only briefly, sent home to die as soon as they discovered that it had already spread to most of her organs. Alex spent the next three weeks sitting by her mother's bedside, watching as a parade of nurses and volunteers from hospice tried to keep Frances drugged enough to keep the pain at bay. She'd slipped away so quickly that Alex hadn't really had time to process the whole ordeal.

The next thing she knew, she was standing next to the grave as the mourners came up and squeezed her arm or her hand, most of them repeating the same tired phrases that everyone did at such times. "So sorry for your loss." "If there's anything I can do." "At least she's not in pain anymore." They were people her mother had grown up with; Alex knew only one or two in the whole group.

She pressed her lips in a grim line. They'd meant well, she knew that, but those phrases seemed so empty at that moment. Everything was empty. Her mind, her heart, the words that floated in the air around her. Empty, empty, empty.

Frances Turner was the one person who understood Alex, the one person who loved her, no matter what. And Alex hadn't really appreciated that until after the woman was gone.

For most of her life, Alex had been the rogue electron, that weird anomaly that orbited just outside the nucleus of the rest of humanity.

She'd been different for as long as she could remember, starting with her first year in the Albuquerque public school system. It became apparent after only an hour of kindergarten. While the other children were struggling to learn the letter *a*, Alex took one of the small readers from a corner shelf and read the entire book, obviously bored by what kindergarten had to offer.

Her intelligence was rabid; she devoured everything the teachers in the public school could throw at her. Her parents supported that keen intelligence in their only child, and her mother took her on weekly trips to the bookmobile, an outpost of the downtown library that visited their neighborhood every Tuesday evening. Alex always checked out eight or ten books and read them all before the week had passed.

But to the other children, this made her a peculiar creature that they would rather avoid. Winning spelling bees and math flashcard games and finishing her worksheets faster than anyone else only made that division deeper. They found her vaguely threatening, almost repellent, like some smelly bug. She spent most of her school days, including recess and lunch, with her nose pressed in a book.

In the fourth grade, she began practicing another form of intelligence, one not taught in the regular school curriculum. It involved reading the emotional vibe in the room, particularly when her father didn't come home for dinner and her mother sat at the table staring into space, their food growing cold. By the end of that fourth grade year, her father had moved out of the house and in with his secretary, who was pregnant with their coming baby.

She and her mother had been forced to downsize to an older, two-bedroom home, while her father and his replacement family relocated to sunny southern California. It was about that same time that Alex's vision first began to grow fuzzy, as if she could not bear to watch what was happening in her life. By the time fifth grade was over, and she was about to enter middle school, she had glasses on her nose and a few extra pounds on her small frame, that bit of extra weight putting a little padding between her heart and all the rejection in the world. Her hair was an unremarkable brown and too curly to control, her eyes an unremarkable shade of gray that faded to invisible behind her glass lenses.

Being alone and outside felt normal. On some level, she had always known that she was a misfit. She remembered the way her father used to take apart engines in the garage. Always, always, when he had them reassembled, there was a part or two left over, lying on the concrete of the garage floor. She had asked him once, when she was no more than five, "What about those pieces?"

He had smiled and ruffled her too-curly hair. "Don't worry, baby. We don't need them anymore." No longer necessary for the successful operation of apparatus. Just like Alex.

By the time she started middle school, the feeling of separateness was embedded in her psyche. While all the other girls discussed shades of fingernail polish, or which boy they would like to catch in a game of spin the bottle, Alex pushed her glasses up on her nose, ran her fingers through her short, thick curls, and went back to her book, where none of the characters cared what she looked like or felt threatened by how smart she was.

Instead, she came to rely more and more on the friendship of her mother. Given their mutual understanding of rejection, they became more like friends than mother and daughter, each of them secretly trying to help the other survive this shake-up to their lives. Each of them keenly sensitive to every nuance of mood, every subtle scent of sad or lonely or scared that lingered in the air around them, like the delicate whiff of expensive perfume.

When it came time for college, Alex knew she would not move too far away. She had grown more independent during high school, but she knew that she could not really leave her mother, and she chose the University of New Mexico because it was nearby.

She found library science her second year. After all those years of being an outcast, she was not prepared for the wondrous feeling of finding a place where she truly belonged. It was in categorizing and sorting information that she finally found her place in the cosmos. She loved pulling together the papers for her master's work, and she spent many happy weekends devoted to finding out everything she could on a variety of different topics. The PCB levels in birds and fish of Lake Superior. Geologic formations of the desert southwest. The benefits of grass-fed cattle on western rangeland. She was endlessly fascinated by the information she could find, about all kinds of subjects, and by her ability to catalog and assemble mountains of data into usable references.

She started working for the University library part-time in her junior year, and she never left. Just as soon as she had her Master's of Library Science, a position in archives opened, and Alex was right there waiting for it. She loved her work, loved everything about it—the interesting subjects that floated across her desk in the form of newspaper and magazine articles, old photographs, reports from various scientific disciplines. She loved organizing it, cataloging it, making it accessible for researchers. And she loved working by herself, back in the archival office, next to the temperature-regulated museum safe. A rogue electron, still off on her own, but finally comfortable in her own orbit.

That was the life she was living when, at twenty-eight years old, Alex went to the University Christmas party, an event, just like junior high school lunch, that she loathed. She never knew what to wear or how to do her hair, and usually ended up in a broom skirt and sweater, hair loose and messy, eating holiday goodies and looking at whatever reading material was to be found in the current venue. She despised the parties but understood that universities are highly political animals, and that if she wished to remain in her position, she had to at least make an appearance.

By that time, her social circle had broadened to include not just her mother but also a handful of friends from college and colleagues at the University, where being smart was acceptable. She had even had a boyfriend or two, a few nights of totally forgettable sex. None of that had prepared her for Daniel Frazier.

Of course she had noticed him. Who wouldn't? At six foot one, with his dark wavy hair and brown eyes and three days' growth of beard stubble, he was quite striking. He worked as a geologist for an oil company, and had started teaching one class at the University just that fall. His two most attractive traits were that he was single and still new enough that no one had started to complain about him yet.

At the Christmas party, he was caught in the middle of a web of female spiders, most of them older, many of them professors or the wives of professors. Alex had watched them all for a moment, like a scientist observing the behavior of a group of rhesus monkeys, and then plopped down on a couch, reaching for one of the books arrayed on the table before her, firmly entrenched in the judgments that she had already made about Daniel Frazier.

She looked up again when he sat down in a chair nearby.

"Hey."

Alex glanced behind her, as if there was something she was missing, as if he couldn't possibly be speaking to her. She turned back to him. "Have you run out of beautiful females to talk to?"

He laughed. "Not yet." His eyes locked on her.

Alex felt a blush coming from somewhere, and she pushed her glasses up on her nose and tilted her head back.

He glanced at the book in her hand. "I just had to find out what you were reading that was so fascinating. Forsaking the wonders of the Christmas party for a book?"

"I'm in library science. It's an occupational hazard."

He laughed again, displaying a formidable set of brilliantly white teeth. "Daniel Frazier. Geology. Always interested in scratching the surface." He held out his hand.

Alex stared at it for a moment, slightly befuddled, before lowering her book and extending her own hand. "Alexandra Turner. Always interested in digging deeper."

"So what are you reading? Romance?" He ran a thumb down the side of his mustache, trying to hide a flicker of amusement.

Alex made a face. "Oh, God no. Life's too short for that garbage."

He laughed. "You don't believe in romance?"

She paused for a moment and pushed her glasses up on her nose. "In the abstract, maybe. For other people. Cinderella. Snow White. Haven't observed much of it in real life."

He sat back in his chair, looking at her as if he were appraising the value of a rare antique.

For someone who prided herself on her ability to read emotional conditions, Alex completely missed in this situation. She didn't realize it at the time, but what she had just said was exactly the type of challenge that a man like Daniel Frazier could not resist, something like the thrill mountain climbers find in attaining the top of Mount Everest. It didn't matter that she wasn't a great beauty. It didn't matter that she didn't dress to draw attention. The fact that she wasn't interested in him was more enticing than any perfume or low-cut gown or fluttering fake lashes could ever be.

"I thought that's what all women wanted. Romance."

"Not this one," she quipped. She had to force herself not to look away, as if those brown eyes directed at her so intently were stirring up the mud in the depths of her being. Male attention had been a very rare commodity in her life, especially since her father had moved away. She had forgotten what it felt like. He was looking directly *at her*, speaking to her, paying attention to her, laughing at her humor. All her judgments about this man began to shift and slide and tumble into a heap of broken rubble.

"So what are you interested in, Alexandra Turner?"

"History. Botany. Architecture. Archaeology. Anything but romance."

"Even geology? We're the redheaded stepchildren of the sciences, you know. Not nearly as exciting as black holes and supernovas. Not nearly as lovable as butterflies and baby polar bears, or pine trees and flowers. Physicists, biologists, ornithologists—now those are the ones who get all the glory."

"Oh, I don't know. Baby polar bears are pretty cute, that's true. But there's nothing like an earthquake or a volcano to really shake things up, make you think about the wonders of geologic construction."

He laughed, a full-on genuine laugh, and a few people turned to look at the two of them, a small tremor of attention reverberating in their direction, something akin to a low-level tectonic event. "Some people see us as the Antichrist, you know. Out looking for suitable places to drill oil wells."

"I don't have a photographic memory, but I don't recall a mention of oil wells anywhere in the Bible." She could not believe the things she was saying to him, but something in her rose to the challenge of being smart and funny and maybe even a tad more approving of the drilling of oil wells than she would have been under other circumstances. The bright glare of his attention made her sit a little straighter.

"Daniel Frazier, there you are!"

They both looked up to see Dr. Dixon, the head of the geology department, standing nearby.

"Come and meet my wife."

Daniel stood and took one step, so that he was standing next to the couch where Alex sat. He put a hand on her shoulder. "Nice to meet you, Alex."

She nodded. "Yeah. Same here."

He squeezed her shoulder, one gentle touch, and moved away.

He had barely disappeared before Rachel Medina plopped down next to Alex, a smile playing at the corners of her normally cool exterior.

Rachel was the assistant librarian, and she and Alex worked together. "I think he likes you," she whispered.

"Oh, please." Alex reached for her wine.

"No, really. I was watching. He couldn't take his eyes off you."

"Then I must have spinach dip stuck in my teeth." She turned to her colleague and curled her lips away from her teeth, for inspection.

Rachel gave her an exasperated look. "I know you like to hide behind those glasses and those oversized sweaters, but really. You're quite the catch, you know."

"Only if someone is trying to land a whale."

"Alex, stop it. You are not nearly as unattractive as you seem to believe you are. And besides, anyone of substance isn't going to care about looks. You're the smartest person I know, and that's saying something. We work at a university, for Pete's sake."

Alex pushed her glasses up on her nose and took another sip of her wine. "You're only saying that because you hired me."

Rachel looked out at the crowd of professors and their wives, scattered around the room like small clusters of crystals. "Around here, brains usually go hand in hand with ego. I mean, really. What kind of person will get up in front of a packed hall every day and pontificate for hours? They love to hear themselves utter. Like failed actors, they need sole control of the stage and a captive audience. Totally full of themselves."

Alex laughed. "Harsh, but maybe true about a few of these people." She ran her finger around the rim of her glass. "So, is that a polite way of saying I'm fat? Kind of like that 'she's got such good skin' thing?"

Rachel turned slightly and gave Alex a sharp look. "If he wants tall and thin and blonde, then he can go to California. If he wants a woman who knows how to listen, who can offer an intelligent opinion without getting pushy or arrogant, then he doesn't need to look any further. You are one of the best employees I've ever had. Loyal, hardworking, easy to get along with. So quit with all the fat comments, would you?"

Apparently, those were exactly the qualities that Daniel appreciated.

Alex was sitting at her desk in the museum office on Monday morning when she heard a flutter of activity outside her door. The instant-messaging bar on her computer flashed on her screen: **Geologist and assistant professor just entered the building.** The message was from Rachel, whose office sat on the mezzanine, with a view of all the comings and goings on the library floor below her.

One of the student aides came to the door and said, "Alex? There's someone here to see you." Her eyebrows went up in a provocative question mark.

Alex had just taken a bite of her morning scone when Daniel stepped into the room. He held a bouquet of flowers in his hand.

"These are for that very attractive and intelligent archivist I met the other evening."

Alex swallowed her bite of scone and brushed crumbs from her lap. "Huh. I wonder who that would be?"

He laughed. "I believe you are the *only* archivist I met the other evening."

"Oh, right. So that would be me, then."

He smiled and nodded, holding the flowers out to her. The bouquet held pine boughs and white baby's breath, interspersed with red roses and tiny loops of glass beads. "I hope you like roses."

Alex stared at the flowers a moment, as if they were some strange species of lizard that she had never seen before. She did not take them from his hand, but leaned back in her chair and moved her glasses down her nose a fraction, looking at him over the tops. "Okay. I get it. You need a list of research materials dating from"— she shook her head back and forth—"oh, the nineteen fifties or so, on some obscure paleo-geology topic, and you need it in thirty minutes. Right?"

"Do people really do that to you?"

Alex nodded. "At least once a week. And very few of them actually bother to send flowers. The exact number would be . . . let me think . . . zero?"

He smiled at her, continuing to hold his hand out in front of him. "No research required. I just wanted to bring you something you're interested in, and I believe you mentioned botany. I picked up a few botanical specimens."

Their eyes met.

"Are you going to take these? Or are you waiting for my arm to fall off?"

Alex swallowed and reached out to take the flowers. She put her nose into the bouquet. "Thank you." A blush crawled up her arms and neck and face, and for a moment she felt slightly light-headed.

He leaned his backside against the desk and looked at her. "Any chance I could talk you into having dinner with me?"

Alex leaned slightly to the side, examining the clock on the wall in the main part of the library, clearly ticking off the time of twenty minutes after ten. "It's a little early for dinner, isn't it? Not exactly the fashionable hour."

He laughed again, and Alex felt just a twinkle of confidence. That made what? Two or three times now that he had laughed at something she said?

"Actually, I'm on my way to Deming for a few days. But I was hoping that when I got back on Friday, you would agree to have dinner." He looked at her. "I know you didn't mention food, specifically, as one of your interests. But I do know of a restaurant in a historic building. You did mention history, right? And architecture?"

Alex shook her head, as if trying to dislodge a marble. "You were listening?"

He nodded.

Outside the window to her museum office, she could see two of the student interns watching them intently. Alex turned back to look at Daniel.

"I'll pick you up at six," he said. It wasn't really a question. "Care to give me a phone number? So I know how to find you?"

Stunned by the events of the last few minutes, Alex was slow to respond. "Sure. I guess."

Rachel, of course, had jumped immediately into the stew of possibilities. She insisted that they go shopping. Spending time at the mall was never Alex's idea of a good time, and shopping for clothes, with all the trying on and looking in mirrors and confrontation with the reality of the way she looked, was in the farthest galaxy away from what Alex found pleasant. "Absolutely not," Alex responded. "Dressing rooms are nothing but torture chambers. That would completely kill any excitement for Friday."

"Then let's go get your hair done. A new cut and style?" Rachel fingered the unruly curls around Alex's face. "I know a great hairdresser. Just down the block."

She let herself be led to the beauty parlor, and watched as the young man in a black shirt and black pants turned her hair into something quite attractive, wispy waves that she was certain she would never be able to duplicate on her own. When she put her glasses back on at the end of the 'do, she stared at the person in the mirror. "Huh."

"You look fabulous." Rachel beamed.

"Do they pay you to do the cheerleading around here?"

And though Alex steadfastly refused to go to a mall two weeks before Christmas, Rachel was able to maneuver her into a small boutique, two blocks away from the library. Rachel wandered the racks, choosing two or three tops for Alex to try on, and Alex ended up leaving with a silk blouse in a deep forest green, slightly more fitted and with a lower neckline than she might have picked if left to her own devices.

"This is ridiculous," she murmured as they walked back to the office. "I can't possibly be comfortable like this." But despite her refusal to be openly excited, some kind of underground seismic shift was taking place in her psyche.

Friday evening finally arrived, and there he was, standing on her doorstep, with those dark eyes and that flash of smile. He stood still for a moment, taking in the new hair, the silk blouse. "Wow. You look great."

"It's the low light," Alex stammered. "December evenings are kind to everyone."

He laughed and whisked her away to an enchanted fairy tale of an evening. They went to Old Town, the collection of shops and restaurants and buildings that had been part of the original Albuquerque settlement. At that time of year, every tree and building and walkway was lit with Christmas lights and *farolitos*, the traditional Mexican lanterns. They strolled through the plaza and some of the side streets, and then ended up at the Hotel Albuquerque. "I made reservations at the Tablao Flamenco," he told her. "Have you been?"

Alex shook her head. "I've heard of it."

Daniel held the door for her, and they stepped into a small bar area with a stage at one end. "They serve tapas and cocktails and sangria, and the music and dancing are some of the finest flamenco ever. Some people say even better than what you would find in Spain."

Two guitarists sat on the stage, and immediately Alex fell under the spell of the classical Spanish guitar. They were served an array of appetizers as they watched the dancing and stomping feet and swirling dresses. The dancers who were not involved in a dancing capacity for any particular number added their clapping syncopation to those who were. Each time the waiter appeared with another dish, Daniel slid his chair just slightly closer to Alex. By the end of the first round of dances, he had his arm around the back of her chair. By the end of the second round, and another round of sangria, he had placed one hand lightly on her thigh.

If there had ever been something resembling "normal" in Alex's dating life, this certainly wasn't it. She had had a few dates in college, mostly with boys who were just as awkward and clumsy as she was herself. There had been an assistant professor of zoology a little over a year ago, but their connection had never approached anything even vaguely romantic. He was much too interested in his own research to pay any attention to Alex, and they had stopped dating about two dates after their first sexual encounter. She shuddered to remember it.

The flamenco bar was not the type of place conducive to conversation. It was not the kind of place that encouraged staring into one another's eyes. But the music and the dancing were hypnotic. And the sangria and the candlelight certainly didn't hurt.

When they left the venue, around ten thirty, walking out into the fairy-tale lights of Old Town at Christmas, Daniel wrapped his arm around her. By the time he stopped, beneath one spectacularly lit oak tree, and turned her face up for a long, slow kiss, she was completely enchanted. Every kiss she had ever experienced, until that night, was an awkward and bumbling attempt to avoid knocking teeth. Not so with Daniel Frazier. When he pulled back and suggested a nightcap at his apartment, she nodded. And an hour later, when he slipped that new silk blouse off her shoulders and leaned in to kiss her and tell her how beautiful she was, Alex was hooked. The drug of his attention was potent; her addiction to it was assured.

The first date was two weeks before Christmas, and it never really ended. She spent the night at his apartment; the next day he took her to Santa Fe. For the four-week period that the University was closed for winter break, unless he was out in the field on a job, they spent every moment together.

On New Year's Eve, he rolled onto his side, next to her in bed, and ran his hand down her collarbone. "Maybe we should get married," he whispered into the dark.

Alex's diaphragm contracted sharply. Had she heard him correctly? "But . . . we've only known each other what? Not quite a month?"

He continued to run his finger gently over her neck and shoulders and breasts. "Alex, I'm thirty-seven years old. Old enough to know what I want when I find it."

Her body was responding to the touch of his hand, and her eyes fluttered. She took a breath and looked at him. "So what was the question?"

He moved on top of her, his eyes locked on her. "Will you marry me, Alex?"

She couldn't stop thinking about him, wanting him, in every way possible, far too often. The many fascinating subjects covered in *Scientific American* lost a bit of their appeal. His attention was intoxicating, and it went straight to that part of Alex that had always believed she did not belong, that she was not good enough. Suddenly, here she was, Alex Turner, being courted by this good-looking man.

For the first time in her life, other women were looking at her in a completely different way. She was no longer unacceptable Alex with the thick glasses and her head in a book. Her status as an outlier was changed. Now she was the woman on Daniel Frazier's arm.

By the end of January, less than six weeks later, Alex had given up her own apartment, the one just a few blocks away from her mother, and moved in with Daniel. They set a date to get married—on Valentine's Day—as if that would totally disprove Alex's initial refusal of anything to do with romance.

"It's all happening so quickly," her mother had fretted.

"A whirlwind romance." Alex smiled. Romance. She had actually used that word.

"Whirlwind. Gale force. Tornado. Hurricane. It does appear that many things that move that fast are associated with storm systems."

Frances sat down on the edge of Alex's bed, stripped of sheets and blankets, since it would soon be tossed to the street as she abandoned her old, solitary, far-too-peaceful life. "How well do you really know him, Alex? You met him less than two months ago."

"You think he's really Jack the Ripper?"

Her mother pressed her lips together. She shrugged. "Have you followed him when he goes out at night?"

Alex let out a humph. "Oh, Mom, relax. I know what I'm doing." She had always been, after all, the smartest girl in her class, the one who could look at a problem and figure it out almost instantaneously. From the big picture to the smallest details, Alex had always been quick and sharp, and usually correct.

"Any man can act a part for a few months, Alex. You don't really know what kind of man you have until you've had a chance to observe him in many situations, over a much longer period of time." Her mother ran her thumb up and down the bare mattress.

"Is that the recipe for marital success?" Alex regretted the words instantly; they lodged in her mother's physique in a subtle but unmistakable jerk.

Frances drew back slightly and squared her shoulders. "Have you stopped to wonder why he needs to move so fast? This is 2005. People who get married these days have been together for years. They already have a child or two."

Her mother's objections were easy to explain away. Alex swiftly and silently assigned the ulterior motives of a woman who had lost her own husband (sour grapes) and did not want to lose the friendship that she and Alex enjoyed (jealousy). Obviously, her mother did not trust men, any men, after the lies and deceit she had endured from Alex's father. And just like that, Alex cast aside her mother's fears, like erasing the chalkboard in a school classroom.

Alex sat down and patted her mother on the knee. "Don't worry, Mom. I know what I'm doing." She had still believed that intelligence was enough, that she knew as much about relationships as she did about organizing information. That she was much too smart for anything bad to happen to her.

She'd been wrong, more wrong than she could ever have imagined. She didn't really know him at that point in time; she didn't really know what kind of man she had married. And standing next to her mother's coffin, just a few months ago, she knew the truth of what her mother had tried to tell her.

Alex had turned, and there he was, her husband, off in the distance, talking on his cell phone and smiling. *Smiling.* As if none of the events of the past few weeks touched him in any way; as if the service at the church, and the line of cars going out to the cemetery, as if that box covered with flowers and about to be lowered into the ground, had nothing to do with him.

He wasn't standing next to his wife, his hand on the small of her back, offering physical stability and emotional support. He was off in the trees, talking on the phone and *smiling.*

In that moment, she knew. It flashed in her mind like a neon sign. Over the past eleven years, she had experienced a myriad of emotion, a roller-coaster ride of highs and lows in that weird arrangement called marriage. But just then, standing next to her mother's coffin, looking at her husband talking on the phone and *smiling,* Alex knew that what she really felt, and had never admitted until that very moment, was the one emotion she had always tried to avoid. Hatred. She hated Daniel Frazier. Hated him with a bitter surge of feeling, as if she had just swallowed acid.

Alex exhaled again, trying to shake her mind away from the memories of all that pain. She forced herself back to the present, standing at the window in Copper Cove, looking out on the cemetery just below the house. A small white light skittered through the stones, bouncing up and down, moving from side to side. Alex gasped. For one brief instant, she almost thought her mother was out there, in the cemetery of this tiny town on a remote island in Washington, a ghostly light dancing over the stones. As if her mother had had no trouble tracking her down.

Alex watched, waiting, until the light stopped moving. She exhaled, finally, when she saw that the light was a camping headlight, clamped on the forehead of a woman out there in the darkness of the cemetery. She wore a long duster coat, down to her shins. Her white hair glowed in the darkness.

Alex watched as the woman stopped, moving through the gravestones in fits and starts, sometimes stopping for longer periods of time. The light bounced on the ground in front of her, and Alex could see a dog, sniffing and straining on a leash. She swallowed and let herself relax. Of course it wasn't the ghost of her mother, and Alex felt silly that she had given the idea any attention at all. As if the ghosts of the past were anything more than her own imagination, as if they could actually follow her all this distance.

It was at that very moment that the headlamp turned in Alex's direction, the shaft of light blazing across the ground and through the window and directly into Alex's eyes. She raised her hand quickly, blinded by the beam of light that tore through the glass and caught her, like a deer in the headlights.

FOUR

"It's open."

Alex was standing on the porch of Maggie's cabin and had just raised her hand to knock when Maggie's voice reached her. She opened the door and stepped into a small mudroom, cluttered with boots and slip-on shoes. Jackets hung from hooks against the wall; several rag rugs lay scattered about, in varying shades of wet and muddy. She hung up her coat and turned.

The main part of the cabin was roughly twenty feet square. Alex could see a bedroom in a far back corner. The kitchen was located in the other back corner, just behind the mudroom. In the front room, a potbellied stove was radiating heat, tingeing the air with the smell of wood smoke and coffee. Maggie sat in a corner, directly across from the front door, at a desk piled high with papers. She pushed her glasses up and appraised Alex.

"Ghosts keep you awake?"

Alex brought her head up sharply. It was hard to read anything in Maggie's face. She let out a nervous huff. "Didn't hear a thing. Slept like the dead."

A smile played at the corners of Maggie's mouth. "There's a bowl of oatmeal in the kitchen. Coffee's on the stove. Get yourself some breakfast, and we'll get started."

Alex nodded and headed to the little kitchen area. She took oatmeal from a pan on the stove and dished it into a bowl. Before she could even think to ask, she heard Maggie's voice. "Milk, syrup, blueberries—all in the fridge. Decorate that mush however you please."

Alex brought the bowl into the front room. "Thank you. I was getting a little hungry."

Maggie looked at her over the tops of her glasses. "I figured. Nothing's open this early. We'll work half a day or so, and then you can go down and buy some groceries. Get settled."

Alex lowered her body into one of the chairs by the fire. There wasn't much in the way of furniture in the front room, just three mission style chairs with red leather cushions, arranged around the potbelly stove. Along the walls were numerous bookshelves, every inch stuffed with books and papers.

Maggie tipped her head toward a worktable, directly across the room from her own desk. "You can work right there. That computer is old and slow, but I think it can handle the essentials."

Alex nodded and carried her oatmeal over to the work space. She turned on the computer and sat down in an old, beat-up office chair, eating oatmeal as she waited for the machine to wake up.

Maggie pushed her own chair back. "So. This stack of boxes." She indicated a tower of cardboard storage boxes, stacked five or six high, against the wall. "That's your job for the next few months." Maggie took her coffee cup and poured from the blue enamel coffeepot on the stove. "And I should warn you right now that what I'm asking you to do is almost certainly impossible."

"Oh?"

Maggie took her coffee and stood by the front window, looking out at the water of the strait. "I got my degree in marine biology back in 1960. You could count on one hand all the women in that field back then."

Alex located a coffee cup and poured. She moved over to the window and stood beside Maggie.

"There are several of us—scientists, that is, not women—who are located up and down the west coast here. A few in British Columbia and a few of us in the States, spread out through these waters, all the way down to Seattle. And several of us have been studying the orcas, and their habitat, for forty or fifty years now. This group of orcas? The Southern Residents?" She nodded toward the waters out the window. "They are the most studied group of orcas in the world. Most of what we know about killer whales comes from the scientists in these waters."

Alex examined photos hanging on the walls. There were terrific shots of the orcas, flying through the air, turned sideways, as if they were playing.

"How much do you know about them?"

Alex shook her head. "I didn't actually do any homework—other than the one article I showed you."

"There are orcas all over the world, but they are all a bit different in the way they do things. We have two kinds of orcas in these waters. Transients, or Biggs killer whales—they hunt mammals. They are the ones who eat seals and sea lions, an occasional moose or deer that is out swimming from one island to another. Transients move around a lot, in and out of the waters of Puget Sound. Tend not to vocalize as much, since they have to sneak up on their prey. And they usually travel in small numbers. Less than five, most of the time.

"The other group is the Southern Resident Killer Whales—SRKW. They eat fish, mostly Chinook salmon." Maggie picked up binoculars and scanned the waters below them. "They travel in groups of ten or so, sometimes more. Stay together in families their entire lives.

"They are the ones that most people think of when they think of orcas. Shamu, *Free Willy*, the spectacle at the marine parks. Fish eaters, all of them." Maggie took the glasses from her eyes and looked at Alex.

"Be a little difficult to put on a show in front of the kiddos and feed the orca a baby seal, now wouldn't it?"

Alex shuddered.

"But the two groups don't mix. Residents have not mated with the transients for more than seven hundred thousand years. Longer than mankind has been around. Everything about the two groups is different, the way they hunt, the way they vocalize—everything. Except, of course, that they are both black and white. Both are orcas—killer whales.

"The transients are doing fine; their numbers are steady and increasing. But the residents? The fish eaters? They're not doing so well."

Alex said nothing, but she met Maggie's eyes.

Maggie tipped her head toward the wall of boxes behind them. "I've kept a copy of everything over the years. All the reports, all the sightings. Everything. There is one scientist who has photo identified every whale in the pod. They have distinctive dorsal fins, distinctive patches near the fin. Like a fingerprint. And he's taken pictures of every one. Given them numbers, according to the family and pod that they're in, and names. If the babies live long enough, they get names, too. So in these boxes you will find the family trees for each one of those whales that is still living.

"Another guy has studied the sounds they make, looking for language patterns. He's made a dictionary of their vocalizations.

"And then there's me. I'm a habitat biologist, so I study everything that affects the places where they live. Pollution, ocean acidification, global warming, Navy sonar, all the ship and boat noise out there in the water. The list of things that affect the orcas, and their habitat, is mind-boggling. And the worst?"

Alex met her eyes again.

"They're having a hard time finding enough food. Salmon have been on the decline for . . . oh, I suppose since white men first reached this area." Maggie turned toward the window again. "Did you know they used to have wild salmon in Europe? And on the East Coast?" She took a deep breath. "The Pacific Northwest is the only place left where you can still find wild salmon now, and it's getting harder every year. Seems to me that man, as a species, is bent on destruction. Everywhere man shows up—white men, anyway—all the natural systems go to hell."

Maggie took a swig from her coffee cup.

"As far as I know, there is no one place where all the different information is gathered. The salmon people and the whale people and the ones studying pollutants and boat noise. No one central location for accessing all that material. I really wanted to come up with a way to organize all of it—my own work and theirs."

Alex nodded.

Maggie exhaled, a sound that seemed profoundly tired. "I'm on the downhill slide to eighty, and I'm not going to live forever. And if there's anything else I can do to help protect those blackfish . . . I want to do it."

"Sounds like a good plan. It's a problem I've seen so often—people doing all this great research and no really good way to access everything. Is the University of Washington willing to help?"

Maggie turned and gave Alex a long look. "Probably. I haven't asked."

"Oh?"

Maggie grimaced. "It's been my experience that if you want a project done right, you need to do it yourself. Or at least oversee it yourself."

Alex waited.

"So." Maggie turned toward the stack of boxes and picked one off the top. She set it on the table with the computer and pulled off the lid. "You're going to find all kinds of stuff in these. Some of it will not look related to the orcas at all. But it is.

"I've got reports on salmon populations, in all the streams up and down the West Coast. I've got reports on what's happened in the waters since they started salmon farming in British Columbia. Since they built those dams on the Snake River, and the Fraser, and the Columbia. There's a dam on almost every river system out here, sometimes more than one. Those dams have had a huge impact on the salmon populations."

Maggie moved back. "I've got reports on ship noise. Oil spills. Chemicals and pollution that have been dumped in these waters over the last hundred years. Did you know that the Canadian government is looking at shipping tons of that tar-sands oil out of Vancouver? They've got a pipeline from Alberta carrying that sludge, mixed with all kinds of chemicals, and they want to load it on ships and go right through these waters." Maggie shook her head. "Sometimes, the thought of all the idiocy in the world is more than I can handle."

Maggie's shoulders slumped for a moment, as if someone had let all the air out of her body. She tapped her hand on the box.

"We have reams of data, from this group of scientists up and down this area who have been studying the whales for forty years." She turned to Alex again. "What we don't have? Is a way to save them from our own stupidity."

Maggie looked out the window again. "I hear it all the time—the orcas are not as smart as people. They can't speak the way we do; they can't make tools and technology. As if that makes us smarter. As if that somehow gives us the right to destroy them—to destroy the life they depend on. To destroy the waters they live in.

"But they are the top of the food chain in the oceans, and they've been around six million years. Humankind has been around about two hundred thousand. We think we are so smart. And with all our brains and science and technology and tools, we've just about managed to destroy the planet. The orcas were managing just fine, until we showed up.

"Now the A Pod in Alaska? Hasn't had a baby since the Exxon Valdez oil spill in 1989. The Southern Residents? J, K, L Pods? We put them on the endangered species list in 2005, with a population of less than eighty. And in the last eleven years, when we're supposed to be protecting them? Helping the population recover? You want to know how much progress we've made?"

Maggie stopped speaking for a moment, her jaw clenched. "None. We have seventy-six orcas right now. That's it. The chances of saving this group grow dimmer every day.

"I'm an old woman. I've been watching these orcas since I was a little girl." She turned back to stare at the waters. "I just hope I die before I have to see a world without them in it."

FIVE

It was just after two when Alex left Maggie's cabin and walked down the hill to the main street of Copper Cove. The rain was falling softly, but it wasn't far, and Alex had no intention of driving that car with the New Mexico license plate in this small town. As if the license plate glowed, advertising exactly where she was from. She wanted, instead, to blend into the landscape, into the gray clouds and rain. Unnoticeable. Unremarkable in any way.

She pulled the hood of her fleece jacket up over her head; raindrops clung to the fleece like tiny glass beads. Despite the rain, it felt good to move a little, after three days in the car, and she walked up one side of Main Street, intending to get a better feel for the town before she went back down the block to the grocery store. On the other side of the street, meandering slowly down the boardwalk, was the same woman she had seen walking in the cemetery earlier that morning. She was in the same dark gray duster, her white hair visible beneath her hat, her glasses misty with water. She was walking another dog, a smaller one this time, and a tiger-striped cat followed just a step behind, stopping whenever the woman did.

Alex was watching her so intently she nearly bumped into the waitress from the Drift Inn. Her eyes shot back to the red-haired woman in front of her, and Caroline reached for Alex's arms, trying to avoid a complete collision.

"Whoa! You'd get arrested if you were driving like that." Caroline laughed. "Hey! Don't you own a raincoat?"

Alex refocused her attention and shook her head. "No need for a raincoat where I come from. You just stand under a door and wait ten minutes. Might have to do that once a year or so."

Caroline snickered. "Well, you need one out here. Or maybe two, or three, or six. One for town, one for walking the dog, one for working in the muck . . ."

Alex nodded. "Guess I need to go shopping, then."

"How was your first night at Mad Maggie's?"

"Mad Maggie? As in mad insane?"

Caroline shrugged. "Not exactly insane. But she is forceful. And very . . . I don't know what the word would be . . . inflexible? Determined? She's a force to be reckoned with, that Maggie. Kind of like a thunderstorm."

Alex nodded, still too distracted by the woman with the white hair to really absorb what Caroline was saying. "I slept fine. Didn't hear any chains rattling or doors slamming. No ghost that I noticed. Woke up too early. I think I'm still on Mountain time."

"Well, it won't take long to adjust. Around here, we sleep ten hours a night in the wintertime and only six or so in the summer. Kind of like the light. Except, of course, that we have way more darkness than ten hours right now."

Alex followed the woman across the street with her eyes, watching as she stooped to gather dog waste. "Who is that?"

Caroline looked where Alex was looking. "Her name's Emmie Porter." Caroline leaned closer to Alex, and her voice dropped to a whisper. "Some folks call her the village witch."

Alex turned quickly. "Oh?"

Caroline tipped her head. "And some folks call her the most talented healer they've ever seen. Two hundred years ago, that would have been the same thing."

"I saw her early this morning, in the cemetery. Walking a dog—a different dog."

Caroline nodded. "You'll see her out walking quite a bit. She's kind of a dog whisperer. Always has an animal she's working on. Dogs, cats, horses. I've even heard of her working on an alpaca at a little farm up the road."

Alex looked at Caroline. "Dog whisperer?"

"They say she's really sensitive. That she can feel energy. An empath. Kind of like Reiki or something. I've heard that she can look at an animal, put her hands on it, and she can tell where the animal is hurting. She can figure out what's wrong."

They both watched as Emmie Porter shuffled down the street with her animals.

"A lot of folks are a little afraid of her. There are even a few people who say she can read minds."

Caroline watched Emmie for a few moments. "Sometimes, she seems normal enough. If you watch her, it looks like she's talking to herself all the time. But then you might notice a bird, or a cat, or a dog. Sometimes she talks to the trees." Caroline turned back to Alex. "Some people even say that she talks to the dead. The ghosts."

Alex swallowed. "Oh?"

Caroline shrugged. "That's what they say, anyway. You know the whole town is haunted, don't you? Every single building. Even some of the places outside the buildings. We have ghost tours and paranormal conferences. It's a big business, you know. Ghosts."

"I heard that," Alex murmured.

Caroline turned and caught Alex's eye. "People say that the whole place is filled with spirits. And that if the spirits want you to stay, you stay. And if they don't want you to stay, then . . ." Caroline raised her hands to her sides.

"Wow. You believe all that?"

Caroline smiled and shrugged. "I don't know. But I came here ten years ago, with my boyfriend. I'm still here. He's not."

"He didn't like island life?"

Caroline pulled her bottom lip under her teeth. She shook her head. "Nope. We were here two weeks when he ran off with someone else. To California, I think."

"I'm sorry. That's . . ."

Caroline paused. "I guess the spirits didn't want him to stay." A moment passed before she spoke again. "They must not have liked him at all. He sure cleared out of here quick. Rotten bum. Left me holding the bag on the lease we'd just signed."

They stood together for a moment, neither one of them speaking. "Lots of folks around here say that Emmie's the one who has kept their horses or their dogs or cats alive. We have horses on this island that are over thirty years old. Cats that live to be twenty or more. That's not normal, you know."

The two women watched as Emmie Porter continued her way down the street on the opposite side.

"I'm not sure I believe everything they say about her. Seems pretty far-fetched, a lot of it." Caroline turned and met Alex's eye. "She seems nice enough, any time I've been around her. Just a little—different, you know? But I can tell you one thing. I sure get nervous if she turns and looks at me for too long. It's almost as if she can see right through me. Right down to every secret I ever had."

It was at that very moment, as if the entire scene were scripted by some omniscient director with a perfect sense of timing, that Emmie Porter stopped and turned in the direction of the two women. Caroline, however, was not the object of her attentions. She looked directly at Alex. Their eyes locked, for one brief moment. Alex turned away and shivered.

SIX

Emmeline Porter was a slender thread of a woman. Five foot seven in her stocking feet, still slim like a young girl, despite her sixty-five years. She added bulk to her frame with clothing, and she had a signature look that everyone on the island recognized: oversized sweater, jeans, and a long dark gray duster made of waxed canvas to shed the rain and keep her pants dry when she was out in the weather. As it happened, she was out in the weather quite often.

Her hair had silvered in her late thirties, almost overnight, but Emmie had never attempted to dye it. Thick and wavy, dark coffee brown when she was younger, she had kept it long her entire life, and wasn't about to change that now, despite what any fashion guru might say about appropriate hairstyles for women her age. As a child, her hair had been tamed into a thick braid, out of her face so that she could ride horses across the pastures of her father's ranch. She loved the feel of the wind in her face, loved the warmth of the sun on her shoulders. She loved swinging up on the back of her pony, bareback, and racing her brother, feeling her long braid hitting against her back, feeling herself at one with the animal beneath her.

Growing up on her father's cattle ranch in Dalton, Montana, had been the perfect school for the study of human and animal nature. She and her older brother, Ethan, had spent most of the daylight hours outside, when they weren't in school, and Emmie had developed the skill of quiet observation. Born into a man's world, at a man's time, and surrounded by the good old boys of her father and his generation, she learned to keep her thoughts to herself. But she watched—everything—from the births of kittens and puppies and cattle and horses, to the ways in which they could suffer and die. She had observed the keen intelligence of the horses, had learned to pay attention to every subtle change in their behavior. The horses always seemed to know, long before she did, if there was a coyote or a rattlesnake or a mountain lion nearby. Their ears would lie back against their heads; she could sense the alertness of the animal traveling up through her legs, even if she rode with a saddle. She learned to avoid being thrown off or surprised, simply by tuning in to the subtle clues of the horse.

The ranching world was a hard-knock school for someone with such extreme sensitivities, and Emmie was considered something of an odd duck. She hated hearing about the men going out to shoot coyotes or setting traps for foxes outside the chicken coop. She couldn't watch the news on television; she never reached for the newspaper that her parents shared over breakfast every morning. There was enough death and destruction on the ranch itself without borrowing any from other places. And while most of the people she knew were stoic and accepting of all the death around them, Emmie was not.

It wasn't, as her father believed, that she was too softhearted. It wasn't sympathy, which implied feeling sorry for the creature or person that was suffering. What Emmie felt was the *actual pain* the animal felt. She could feel the sharp teeth of a trap, clamped around her own ankle. She could feel the rifle bullet, as if it were entering her own back, when the boys went out shooting coyotes.

At seven years old, she had awakened one night, feeling an incredible pain in her abdomen, a pain so severe she could barely breathe. She lay in bed for a few moments, trying to figure out if the pain belonged to her own body, or to something else. And then she scrambled from bed and went to her parents' bedroom.

It was calving season, and her father kept all the cows that were about to give birth in the corrals and barn close to the house. That allowed him to get up every two hours and check on them, to make sure there were no cows or calves in trouble. He'd been outside just thirty minutes before, and all was well.

"Daddy?" Emmie said, not too loudly but not whispering, either. Her father was exhausted, getting up so often every night.

"Hmmm." He rolled over in bed, forcing himself to wake up, yet again.

"I can hear a cow," Emmie said. "I can hear her . . . screaming, kind of." Even at seven years old, Emmie knew better than to say that she could *feel* a cow in trouble.

Her dad blinked for a minute, and then threw back the covers and pulled his Carhartts on over his long underwear. He never completely undressed during calving season; that would have been pointless.

There was, indeed, a cow in trouble, and her father had to wrap chains around the calf's legs, inside the womb, and pull. This wasn't the first time, nor would it be the last, and Emmie, from her bedroom inside the house, could feel every spasm and shooting pain that the cow went through. She lay in her own bed, tears streaming down her face and into the pillow, clutching the blankets as the pain ripped through her own body.

But they survived, both cow and calf, and at breakfast the next morning, her father put his hand on top of her head and whispered, "Good job, Emmie." That was just about the full range of emotion for Frank Porter, and she knew that he was proud of her.

This was Montana ranching in the fifties and sixties, and Emmie learned quickly that there was no room for intense sensitivity. When confronted with the pain and suffering of the humans and animals around her, she learned to minimize her reaction. She flinched. A shudder ran down her spine. And she turned away, distracting herself with some other activity so that she wouldn't have to think about it. She learned how to block out any of the feelings that tried to lodge in her own body.

Though she'd spent her whole life turning away, trying to avoid it, the pain caught her in its trap when she was a junior in high school. Her brother, Ethan, had joined the Marines and headed to Vietnam the summer before. It was 1967; Vietnam had taken over the news, another dark wave of stories that she tried hard to evade.

Emmie hated the whole idea—the thought of war, the thought of Ethan in a jungle on the other side of the world. Though she had avoided the news in all its forms until Ethan left, afterward she developed a fascination with the protests against the war. She watched on their old black-and-white console television as people marched the streets in San Francisco, and Washington, DC, and college campuses across the country. She watched as Jane Fonda made impassioned speeches.

Her father walked into the living room and turned off the television, shooting Emmie a look that made his viewpoint clear. Frank Porter had no tolerance for people who protested against their own government, or Hollywood actresses who questioned the sanctity of America's decisions. But some part of Emmie hoped that those protestors could somehow magically end the war and bring Ethan home safe and sound.

Ethan did come home, that spring of 1968. His body, what had been recovered of it, arrived in a plain box, covered with an American flag.

Emmie vibrated with her own pain, but the pain of her mother and father was so strong she could barely manage being in the house. It radiated from their bodies, like the shafts of moonlight behind a patch of clouds. Her mother grew quiet. She never sang anymore, the way she had always done when she was cooking or working in the garden. She lost weight; her face grew gaunt and angular, as if all the life had been sucked out of her. She often sat in a chair by the front window, staring out at the day, knitting needles clutched in her hands but no progress being made.

Her father spent more time outside than he ever had, looking for almost any excuse to stay out of the house where Ethan's memory still permeated the air like the scent of a cigar, where the echo of his laughter still reverberated in the corners. Frank worked with the horses and cows; he spent hours chopping wood. When he had more than enough wood cut and split for two Montana winters, he began to tinker with machinery, taking things apart and putting them back together again. Anything to avoid remembering. Anything to avoid feeling. Anything to avoid the pain.

Dustin Curtis showed up the following spring, when Emmie was a senior in high school. Her father always hired five or six cowboys in the spring to help him move the cattle to the high country, to the land they leased from the forest service in the mountains. A few of those cowboys were local men, but every year there would be a stranger or two in the bunch, someone from outside the town of Dalton and the confines of the Chugwater Valley.

Dusty could ride and rope and manage a fence post as well as any of the others. But he was one of the few cowboys who actually stood taller than Emmie when they were all out in the corral. She couldn't take her eyes off him. Emmie had never before ventured into the world of romance, partly because she had been constantly under the watchful eyes of her older brother and her father, but also because she'd never met anyone who would qualify as even slightly more interesting than her horse. Dalton, Montana, was a town of less than two hundred souls, and not one of the boys under thirty was able to look her in those dark brown eyes and carry on a conversation. Something about her caused every one of them to freeze up, to lose their ability to speak.

Dusty had several admirable qualities, the least of which was being tall enough to look up to. He had seen more of the world than Helena and Butte, which made him much more interesting than any of the local boys. And he wasn't completely tongue-tied when she was in his presence. A shiver ran through her every time she stepped into the corral and he looked at her and said, "Mornin', Emmeline."

And then one day, she watched Dusty working with the horses, and it changed everything. Tom Holfield, one of the regular boys, had been trying to load a mare into the horse trailer. Emmie always hated it; she would walk away, if she could, so that she didn't have to watch. This horse was young and very skittish. Emmie knew in her bones that the mare was deathly afraid of the trailer, of the metallic noises when she was going in, and the dark feeling of confinement, of the way the boys always yelled and whipped her to get her inside.

Tom was losing his temper. His face was crimson, and he was snapping his whip, ready to haul back and teach that horse a lesson. Dusty stepped up and said quietly, "Let me give it a go."

Tom dropped the reins and stepped away, anger still flooding his face, and they all watched as Dusty kneeled down on the ground, about ten feet away from the mare. Her reins dangled on the ground, and Dusty made no attempt to grab them. He just sat there, scrunched down on top of his heels, and looked at her.

Dusty didn't move for what seemed like ages, and neither did the mare. When he did stand, he did it in slow motion, fluid and soft. The mare watched him for a few moments longer, and then walked right over to him, as if she had known him her whole life. He walked her around the pasture a bit, and stood next to her, holding her reins loosely in his hand, as they walked toward the horse trailer.

He didn't get her in all at once. Dusty took a few steps and stopped, waiting for the mare to adjust. Then a few steps more. It might have taken thirty minutes, but the mare was in the trailer, with no neighing or crashing against the sides, no stomping a foot or pulling her head back. No whipping or yelling involved.

Emmie was spellbound. She had never seen anyone who used such a gentle approach with the animals. She met Dusty's eyes and asked, "What were you doing? Staring into her eyes like that?"

Dusty slapped his hat against his leg and met her gaze. "It's called 'hooking on.' I was waiting for the horse to hook on to my energy. To get us in sync. Working together, instead of pulling apart." He stared at her another moment.

She watched him walk away, back to working the horses that were left in the corral. He had looked in her eyes just long enough that she could feel almost exactly what that horse had felt. Hooking on. She was hooking on to the energy in that blue-eyed cowboy.

Her restlessness that summer only added to the spell he cast. She was eighteen; she had just graduated from high school. Ethan's death had filled the house with a stifling darkness; her pores were overflowing with the ache of loss. Dusty crouched down and looked at a horse, and suddenly Emmie felt as if everything inside her had been stirred up, the way the dust kicked up in the corral when they were out working the wild ones.

When her father caught them behind the barn, kissing in a way that left not a flicker of daylight between their two bodies, he did what any reasonable father would do. He told Dusty to get his things and get out. Dusty picked up his hat and knocked it against his pants. "Yes, sir," he murmured, but his eyes met Emmie's before he turned away, and in that look, she knew.

Emmie didn't scream, or make a scene or shed a tear, or beg her father to reconsider. Some part of her knew that what her father was doing was opening the door, allowing her to have the perfect excuse to run off with this slender cowboy who wanted to head west. She watched, without a word, as Dusty walked away. She met her father's eyes before he turned and went back to his truck.

By the time Dusty had gathered his things from the bunkhouse, she had gathered a few of her own, and at dusk, she climbed out her bedroom window, shimmied down the side porch, and ran through a tapestry sunset to meet him at the road.

Emmie turned and looked in the eyes of that woman, the one who had just moved in at Maggie's. Pain radiated from her body like the northern lights, colors flaming off her skin and hair and pouring from her eyes. But as Emmie met the woman's eyes, she knew there was more than just pain involved.

Emmie could look at an animal and see almost immediately where the trouble was. She would notice a glow, or feel the heat from a shoulder or the stomach, or wherever the problem happened to be.

This young woman across the street was a seething mass of color and heat, the energy so mixed up that it was almost like looking into a mud puddle. Emmie had spent most of her life trying to help, and she had been able to do that with so many of the animals. But people? That was a completely different story.

The dog pulled on his leash, and Emmie's attention came back to him. He was old, and getting wet, and ready to go home. She turned and headed uphill, forcing herself not to look at that young woman again.

SEVEN

Alex sat at the table in the dining room, a single guest at a table for six. In front of her was a TV dinner, cooked in the microwave. Christmas dinner. She heaved a sigh and pushed the plate away from her, staring out the window at the relentless clouds, the relentless rain. The ever-present gray.

Christmas Day. She was thirty-nine years old, and this was the first Christmas that she had ever spent completely alone. Growing up, at least after her father left, Christmas had been a rather solitary affair, usually just she and her mother. Even so, her mother always cooked too much food; they had a few traditions, just the two of them, like walking to church at midnight, and opening one present on Christmas Eve. While that had never seemed like a proper Christmas, the Jimmy Stewart / Donna Reed / *It's a Wonderful Life* kind of Christmas that they show in the movies, it had only become worse after she met Daniel. It seemed to Alex that every significant event in their relationship had come right around Christmastime.

By the time her first Christmas as Daniel's wife rolled around, all the fairy dust of their whirlwind romance was gone. Truthfully, they hadn't even made it to the altar, back in February, before the sparkle had started to tarnish.

They were just little things really. Nothing to get all worked up about. It had started a week before their marriage, when they had gone to the county licensing office to apply for a marriage license. Both of them had to give their answers to the clerk, and she filled everything out. The question seemed innocuous. *Have you ever been married before?*

Alex smiled and answered, "No."

Daniel smiled, too, and answered, "Divorced. October 2005."

Alex felt her face fall. Her eyes jumped from Daniel's face to the form on the counter. Her mind rushed to process this: just two months before they started dating, he had been married to someone else? She didn't want to start anything in front of the clerk, so she acted as if none of this information was new to her. But when they had finished, and been given their license to wed, and were back in Daniel's Volvo, Alex turned to him as he backed out of the parking space. "You were married before?"

He had his sunglasses on, and though he turned toward her for one brief second, she could see nothing but her own reflection, minimized to the size of a bug. He turned his attention to the traffic. "I told you that, Alex. I distinctly remember telling you about that."

She waited. "I guess I don't remember."

"You guess?" He humphed into the air. "Christina. We divorced after less than a year. I know I told you this. Don't be silly." He looked at her. "You really don't remember?"

Alex shook her head and said nothing, not wanting to argue. She was certain it was the kind of information she would remember; she was almost certain that he had never mentioned it.

"I can tolerate many things, Alexandra. But not a woman who lies. Not a woman who cheats." He trained his eyes straight ahead, focused on the road, lost behind the mirror lenses. "That would be wife number one. She lied. She cheated. And now she's gone."

Alex watched as his jaw tightened; his Adam's apple bobbed as he spoke. He reached over to touch her hand, on the seat between them.

"It's one of the many reasons I'm glad I found you, Alex. I know you're not like that." He rubbed his thumb back and forth on top of her hand.

She exhaled, and with that breath, all her questions and doubts about whether or not he had actually told her escaped into the ethers. The wound was obviously still sensitive to him. She let it go, knowing that she would never be like wife number one, knowing that lying and cheating were not part of her make-up. Knowing that together, they could move beyond the wounds of the past, that her love was strong enough to fix whatever parts of him were still broken.

That was exactly the place where her intelligence and emotional sensitivity worked in his favor. Alex could understand; she could see his viewpoint. She could see where he might not have been as direct as strictly necessary in divulging those details—not out of a desire to hide this from her but out of a need to protect himself and his fragile ego. That made perfect sense to her. And so she gave him a pass, wrote him an excuse that was much more elaborate than anything he had strictly *said*. She herself would not be quick to share a story that put her as the object of lying and cheating.

It didn't stop there, with the marriage license. Some part of her had understood that marriage was a compact of compromise, that she would have to adjust to things she didn't totally support. One after another, she found herself giving in to his demands, without much in the way of conversation.

She had not planned on changing her name after their marriage. It was 2006, Alex Turner was an educated woman with her own career, and most of the women in her acquaintance were opting to keep their own names. She had never really given it a thought.

One night at dinner, alone in their condo, he asked her about it. "Have you finished the paperwork to become Alexandra Frazier yet?"

She must have let her jaw drop open, stunned by this expectation that she had not seen coming.

"I take it that's a no? You look completely surprised, Alex."

"I guess I am. I just thought—" She never had a chance to finish her sentence.

His hand came down on the table next to his plate, and the dishes jumped. "Damn it, Alex! What's the problem here? I thought you wanted to be my wife."

She flinched. Blindsided, once again, she sat at the table, her mouth open slightly. A sliver of fear lodged in her body, the way his hand had come down so hard and fast.

He stopped and sat quietly for a minute, his breath hard. After a moment, the energy of that slap on the table still echoing in the room, he reached for her hand. He swallowed hard and murmured, "I'm not trying to be mean. It's just that . . . I love you so much, Alex. I just want the world to know that you're mine now."

Mine? You're mine now? As if she were his possession? Her brain was shouting at her, screaming out about the way he had just used his size and force and the threat of violence to make her afraid. But the other part of her thinking went immediately to his defense, as if he were a little boy. A little boy, afraid of losing the person he cared about, just the way he had with his first wife. A little boy who had been hurt and was simply trying to protect himself.

She had witnessed what didn't work in a marriage—her parents—and she was determined to do whatever it took to make her own marriage a success. Her mother had maintained her own name, her own credit, her own identity. And Alex had seen just exactly how well that worked.

So she did it again. She ignored any of those little twitches that asked, "What about me? What about what I want?" and went ahead and changed her name. With each act of giving in, his demands seemed to grow bigger, like a child testing the boundaries. But he was not a child, and every time he slapped the table or leaned in over her, the first thing that always invaded her awareness was his size. He was a head taller, and sixty pounds heavier, and much, much stronger, and it was almost as if he knew exactly how threatening even those subtle behaviors could be.

It felt odd, becoming Alexandra Frazier after twenty-eight years of being Alex Turner. There were more steps involved than she had anticipated—changing her social security card, her credit cards, her bank accounts, her driver's license. But she did it, knowing that it was important to Daniel, that it would give him reassurance about her love.

They'd been married about five weeks when he did it again, taking the wind right out of her sails. She was at work, back in her private office by the museum, and one of the student interns came to her door.

"He's here, Alex."

Alex looked at her, pushing her glasses up. "Who's here?"

"Your husband." The girl smiled. "You never told me he was so good-looking."

Alex stood up and straightened her skirt and headed out to the front counter. Daniel was leaning against it, one arm propped on the granite, smiling and talking to another student intern. He turned to Alex, a big smile on his face. "Ready?"

"Ready?" she repeated, not having any idea what he was talking about.

His smile grew slightly larger, but his eyes flashed at her. "For lunch? Don't tell me you forgot." He smiled again, directed at the student aide with the low-cut T-shirt, and shook his head. "Head in the clouds sometimes, I guess."

"Oh. Yeah. Let me get my bag." Alex did not remember, but she wasn't about to say anything in front of those young girls, hanging close to Daniel like he was some kind of rock star.

His demeanor had completely changed by the time they reached his car. He was silent, none of the smiles and teasing and laughing that she had witnessed just a few moments ago, in front of the students. His jaw was set, the look in his eyes a mystery behind those mirror lenses.

Alex turned and watched out the passenger window as they drove away. Her attention came zooming back when he pulled up in the parking lot of Bank of America. She turned and looked at him. "I thought we were going to lunch."

He killed the engine and turned to her, pulling his glasses down enough to meet her eyes. "We are. Alex, are you okay? Because it sure seems like you're forgetting things a lot lately."

She wasn't quite sure what to say, and she wasn't quite sure what she was forgetting. That comment deflected her, for a moment. She immediately started searching her brain for clues, for some forgotten detail that she now needed to find.

"Let's take care of business, and then we'll grab some lunch."

He put his arm around her as they walked into the bank. Daniel was greeted by one of the account representatives, who ushered the two of them back into his cubicle. "I have the paperwork ready, Mr. Frazier. Please, have a seat."

Alex sank into one of the leather chairs, and Daniel sat down next to her, staying slightly on the edge of the seat.

"Mrs. Frazier, we just need your signature here." He placed papers in front of her, marked with a sticky note. "And here."

Alex glanced at the papers and licked her lips. "What is this again?"

Daniel let out a huff of exasperation and shook his head. "You really don't remember?" he asked incredulously.

Alex shook her head slowly.

The clerk stepped in. "This is to change your account. So that your paycheck will go directly into this checking account . . ." The clerk indicated an account number. "Automatic deposit."

She saw the names at the top of the account—Daniel Frazier. Alexandra Frazier. She exhaled slowly, trying to hide her discomfort, her absolute shock. She did not remember having a discussion about this. She did not remember agreeing to the idea of putting her paycheck into a joint account. She sat there, staring at the paperwork, searching her mind for some snippet of conversation that she had overlooked.

Daniel sat forward in his chair and put his hand on top of hers, resting on the desk. His voice low and soft, he whispered, "You really don't remember, do you?"

She raised her eyes to his face and shook her head slowly.

Daniel glanced at the clerk, and then back at her. He let out a long sigh, as if gathering all his patience. "It's okay, Alex. If you don't want to do this, I understand. I just thought we'd be able to save some money now. Health insurance, car insurance, all of that. Cheaper when we do it together. That's what marriage is all about, isn't it?" He smiled at her and at the clerk. "But this is up to you."

The words made it sound like she had a choice. The clerk would swear that Daniel Frazier was not forcing anything. But as she sat there, looking in Daniel's eyes, his hand over hers, his fingers tightening just slightly, it did not really feel like a choice. It felt as if the whole thing had been orchestrated—that she'd been put in a position where she would not be able to say no.

He pulled his hand away. "We're a team now, isn't that right, Alex?"

She waited for a moment. In slow motion, she took the pen out of the holder in front of her. She signed the forms, what seemed like far too many of them. The clerk told her she would get a debit card for their joint checking account within the next ten days. "And of course, you can write a check at any time, since we now have your signature." He smiled at her and tapped the papers into a neat line.

She told herself that this was fine, that it was indeed a normal thing for a married couple to do. It was true, what Daniel said. They would save money on insurance. They would work as a team.

It didn't take long to find out that teamwork was not really what Daniel had in mind. Two weeks later, she sat curled up in her favorite chair in their condo, reading the latest issue of *The Atlantic*. Daniel sat at the desk in the corner, working at the computer.

He turned around and looked at her. "Alex, what is this?"

"What is what?"

"All these charges on the account. Starbucks, $8.50. Starbucks, $11.87." He met her eyes again. "I thought they had coffee at your office."

"They do. But sometimes a few of us go out for coffee and a scone. Just to get out of the office. A Friday treat—for surviving another week." She lowered her magazine and pushed her glasses up on her nose.

"A coffee and a scone?" Daniel repeated. He looked at her body, curled up in the chair. "Do you really think you need a coffee and a scone?"

She couldn't speak. She felt her face flush; she could feel every pound of her short frame. His words, his look, were like a mirror, reflecting everything about herself that she had never liked. *He's right. I'm too chubby. How could anyone ever want to be with someone who looks like me?*

He turned back around to the computer. "And this? At the bookstore? Eighty-six dollars? What is that for?"

For a moment, she froze. Her throat felt as if it were stuffed with cotton; her words came out slowly. "I was just paying the bill for my account."

"You bought eighty-six dollars' worth of books and magazines?"

She nodded. Her fingers grew sweaty, holding the magazine she'd been reading.

"You work in a library, for Christ's sake. Don't you have access to all of that at work?"

"Yes, but I'm working. I don't have time to read everything . . ."

Daniel's face flamed. "You can damn sure check it out, can't you? Or is that not allowed? To borrow from a library?"

She didn't say anything.

He leaned back in his chair, like a principal with an unruly student. "I'm not trying to be mean, Alex. It just doesn't make sense to me, spending money on things like that."

He spun around to the computer and turned it off. "We want to buy a house someday, don't we? Have a child? If we can cut out all these unnecessary expenditures . . . we can get there a lot quicker, don't you think?"

Her thoughts swooped and flitted, like bats in the twilight. She earned a good living from the University and had a right to spend some of it on whatever she wanted. Didn't she? Did marriage mean that she no longer had those rights? That her own needs and wants had to be pushed aside for the greater good of the marriage?

Before that night, she had not paid any attention to how he spent money. He made a good living, too, and she just didn't bother with thinking about it. But now she began to watch. His words did not match his own actions. He didn't want her to spend money going out to coffee, but he went out to lunch, almost every day. His car often had coffee cups and wrappers from the bakery. And not two days after he had chastised her for buying books, he came home from work wearing a new camel-hair coat.

He modeled it for her and turned away from the mirror. "Makes me look more professional, don't you think?"

Inch-by-inch, step-by-step, he took control of her life, draining her of any power she had, taking her name, taking her money, taking her ability to make her own decisions.

Like mold, it had crept in, starting with one tiny spot. Easy to ignore, easy to forget when not looking directly at it. Until one day, the mold covered everything, the walls and the ceiling, creeping in and taking over.

Alex looked again at the TV dinner in front of her, at the empty chairs at the table around her. Maybe Christmas Day alone wasn't so bad, after all.

EIGHT

Caroline Baker had reddish-brownish-golden hair, in the color formerly known as "dishwater blonde" or, if someone was feeling particularly generous, "strawberry blonde." She didn't like to mess with it, and so she usually twisted it into a knot at the top of her head and secured it with whatever stick-like material was close at hand: quite often a pencil or a chopstick.

Caroline had a raspy voice, full of squeaks and rough spots, and when she sang, she belted out the song as if her life depended on it, which, in a way, it did. Singing was her answer to living in this dark, rainy country, producing roughly the same results for her that meditation or antidepressants did for other people. It did seem, though, that the effects of her singing on said other people were not quite the same as those she experienced herself.

For her, the singing was calming, similar to the feeling one could get from inhaling large quantities of marijuana, which you could now buy locally, at the marijuana store, and pay taxes on, just like liquor. Occasionally she did that, but more often than not she just started singing. Somehow it managed to chase away her blues or fears or lonelies or too-much-of-this-particular-boyfriend, or pretty much any negative emotion that snaked its way up into her brain. "I Am the Walrus" could fix just about anything, and you didn't have to have actual cash, which they did require at the marijuana store. Caroline was fifty years old, and to survive on this island, she worked whatever job was currently available, except for babysitting. Absolutely a "no" on anything to do with kids. They moved fast and they smelled funny, and she was certain even the marijuana dispensary did not have anything strong enough to allow her to deal with children, no matter how much THC they managed to produce with modern growing methods.

So she filled in at the Drift Inn, whenever the regular waitress or bartender was out of town or if there was some big wedding reception. She fished for salmon with Rusty Grable, whom she called "Rusty Gable" behind his back, since it was obvious that what was upstairs in that man's head was not in perfect working order. She chopped firewood, painted houses, inside and out, rewired old cabins, and could tape-and-texture a wall better than anyone in Copper Cove. The trouble was that most of those activities had limited lucrative value in the dark damp of winter.

Her favorite work, the thing she came back to again and again, was throwing pots out of stoneware clay, creating wild teapots and vases and coffee cups, pieces that quite often spouted a creature coming up out of the lid or the handle or the base, something half orca and half raven. The tourists loved them.

In the Pacific Northwest in the wintertime, it made more sense to be a glassblower, which required fire to do the work. Glassblowers could at least manage to stay warm. But there's no accounting for life's passions, and playing in the mud seemed to be Caroline's. So she sat at her wheel, her hands wet with clay, the woodstove in the corner of her studio chugging away, trying to keep her from freezing solid while handling this wet, muddy mess. The current piece of pottery had her on a Dusty Springfield kick, and she was belting out the words to "I Only Want to Be With You."

She had just finished moving the new piece to a shelf to dry when she turned and saw Alexandra Turner standing outside the studio, staring at the pottery pieces in the window. She appeared to be nibbling on a chocolate croissant.

Caroline smiled and strode to the door, yanking it open before she had completely finished the last chorus. "I see you've managed to find the back alley of Copper Cove. We're off the beaten path back here. In the projects."

Alex looked at the pastry in her hand. "I followed my nose. Sure hadn't smelled anything like this before now."

"Yeah, Brewed Awakenings. Our local coffee and pastry guru. You've discovered the key to surviving life in the drippy northwest."

"What's that?"

"Coffee and baked goods. The whole Seattle area is known for how well we do those two things. We get downright snobbish about it. Probably no one could live here in this weather without coffee and baked goods." Caroline ran her messy hands on her apron. "Starbucks began in Seattle, you know."

"Well, it definitely made my morning brighter. Is this you?" Alex asked, indicating the pottery in the window and eyeing the smock Caroline wore, streaked with clay and muck. A wood sign hung over the pieces in the window, painted in bright purple. **MUDD PUPPIES.**

"Yep, that's me. Mudd puppy extraordinaire. Come in. I'll show you around."

Alex stepped through the door into the room, roughly fourteen feet square.

Caroline pointed to the woodstove. "Over there is the heating system. Kitchen," she said, pointing to a small three-foot countertop, sporting a tiny sink and an electric teapot. "Work area," indicating her pottery wheel. "Display," she finished, holding her arm out to the window that Alex had been admiring. "My bedroom is in the back." She pointed to a beaded curtain at the back of the room.

Alex smiled. "Nice. It's got a great feel in here."

"I can't believe you're still here," Caroline said just as Alex popped in the last bite of her pastry. "That makes what, a week? That you've been working for Maggie?"

"Not quite. We had Christmas yesterday, so officially, I have now worked two days."

"That's pretty close to a world record, working for Maggie. She runs through interns like some people burn through firewood. Last summer, she had one girl from U Dub who went to lunch on her first day and never came back."

Alex murmured, "U Dub?"

"University of Washington. No one around here says *u double u*. Ridiculous waste of syllables."

Alex smiled weakly. "Well, I'm glad to hear it isn't just me. I was beginning to think that I had become completely stupid and inept since leaving New Mexico."

Caroline shook her head. "Naw. That's pretty much Maggie's assessment of everyone."

Alex stood still, looking at the newly thrown pieces on a shelf. Her face fell, her shoulders slumped, like a puppet with slack strings.

"It's tough, huh? All this gray and rain and darkness?" Caroline started washing her hands. "You got here at the worst time of year, you know. Worst weather. Short days, long nights. Wet, wet, wet. This is the darkest time, around the solstice. That alone is a big enough adjustment, and then add in that you work for Mad Maggie."

Alex nodded. "Yeah."

Caroline finished cleaning the mud off her hands and arms and hung her apron on a hook. "When I got here, ten years ago, all I could do was sleep."

Alex looked at her.

"Dark and rainy. About seven hours of daylight. If that's what you can call this," Caroline said, tipping her head toward the gray skies outside the window. "And then my boyfriend, the one I'd moved up here with, that dirty double-crossing no-good son of a sailor, ran off with some woman he met at Strait Up."

"Strait Up?"

Carolyn lifted her nose and indicated a building out on the main street. "The bar-slash-distillery. After that, I *really* wanted to sleep."

Caroline stared out the window a moment, and then sighed and turned to Alex.

"You'll adjust. Although even the old-timers sleep more in the wintertime. Coffee, baked goods, sleeping. It's a wonder we don't all weigh nine hundred pounds by the time summer gets here."

Alex smiled and wiped her fingers on her jeans.

Caroline looked around, out to the alley, and then leaned in a little and lowered her voice. "I don't tell this to very many people, but . . ." She leaned back, stretching to make sure there was no one in the back. "Sometimes I go sit with the spinsters."

"The spinsters?"

"It's this small group of people who get together and spin or knit. Shoot the bull. Mostly a bunch of old ladies. They call themselves the spinsters." Caroline looked Alex in the eye. "But don't tell anybody. I don't want to ruin my sullied reputation."

Alex laughed.

Caroline pulled on a jacket and a knit cap. "What do you say? Want to give it a try?"

"Now?" Alex felt prickles of ice crawling on her skin. She began to shake her head. "Ah . . . I don't know, Caroline. I really don't feel up to socializing."

Caroline took her by the elbow and steered Alex toward the door. "It helps, believe me. To get out a little bit, talk to other human beings. I can't imagine how I would survive without those spinster people. Come on. I'll introduce you."

❖

Caroline steered her to a house on the water side of Main Street, near the end of the block. It was three stories high, a beautiful old Victorian. When Alex had walked past it in the daylight, it gave off an aura of sad and neglected. On this gray, rainy afternoon, the house looked different. Lit from within, lamplight fell through the windows and onto the soggy green grass outside. Somehow those lights made it seem more like a refuge from the weather.

"Nice house," Alex muttered.

"This is the old Hadley place. The city owns it now. Different groups rent it for meetings, and art fairs, and such." Caroline opened the door.

They went through an arched doorway, framed by elaborate woodwork from another century, and entered a parlor. There was a fire burning in the fireplace, and several people sat in chairs in a small semicircle around it. Windows curved in an arc along one wall, looking out on the gray waters of Haro Strait.

"Hey, everybody," Caroline called out. "Got a new victim for your little fiber web. Fresh blood."

A man stood by the fireplace. He was tall and solid, with white hair that stood in short spikes and bright blue glasses that brought out the blue of his eyes.

Caroline started with him. "This is David Hill. Spinster extraordinaire."

David held out his hand. "She thinks she's funny. I am not a spinster. I've been partnered up for quite some time. But I am a spinner. Nice to meet you . . ." He raised his eyebrows, waiting for a name.

"Alex. Alex Turner." She shook his hand.

"Younger than our average spinster," David said. "Demographically, this place is ninety-nine percent retirees. You know the joke about Copper Cove, don't you?"

Alex shook her head.

"Copper Cove is the place where people come to die," he continued. "I think the average age here is, like, eighty-seven or something."

Alex let her breath out slowly. "I don't think I'm quite ready to die yet."

"No. Me, neither. Do you spin? Or knit?" he asked, retaking his seat nearby and picking up a pile of knitting, needles carefully rubber-banded together.

Alex shook her head.

"Well, we'll teach you. You'll love it," he said, wrinkling his nose.

"The words of a true pusher," Caroline cautioned. "Careful, Alex. Knitting is a gateway drug. Starts with one pair of knitting needles and one ball of yarn. And before you know it, you have three spinning wheels and two weaving looms, and you can't find a place to eat your dinner, because every available surface in your house is covered with fiber."

"Surely you jest, Caroline?" David made a face.

"And then you die, and your next of kin comes in and throws all that yarn in the trash, not realizing that their inheritance is all wrapped up in the thousands of dollars' worth of hand-dyed merino and cashmere that they think looks like cat barf."

Alex laughed.

"You laugh now. Just wait. Goodbye to sanity. Pretty soon you'll be sniffing out every yarn shop in the Pacific Northwest, just like a true addict in need of a fix."

"She's right about that." A dark-haired beauty stopped her spinning wheel and held her hand out to Alex. "Aditi Bannerjee. Nice to meet you, Alex. It is addictive. But also very . . . calming. Kind of like meditation."

"Aditi is a software engineer for Boeing. She lives in Seattle and only comes up when she has a few days off. We see her three or four times a year."

"My parents retired here, so I come up when I can. I need this spinning drug, let me tell you. That commute on I-5 is awful. Spinning brings me back to earth. Makes me human again," Aditi continued. "Very Zen."

Alex turned to the next person in the circle and inhaled sharply. It was the white-haired woman she had seen a few times now, walking by the cemetery. The one Caroline had described as the village witch.

"This is Emmie Porter," Caroline continued.

Emmie dipped her head toward Alex. "Hello." She met Alex's eye for just a moment, and then bent her head to watch the fibers running smoothly between her thumb and finger and onto the spinning wheel in front of her.

"And this is Grace," Caroline finished. "Grace Wheeler has a little sheep and alpaca farm just outside of town."

"Nice to meet you, Alex," Grace said quietly. Grace was another slender, gray-haired beauty. She sat next to Emmie in the back corner of the room, and the two of them looked like they could be sisters.

Alex took a seat at the edge of the circle and watched all the busy hands around her.

Caroline kept up her running commentary. "David runs the newspaper. *The Strait Scoop*. Strait as in Haro Strait, not the straight and narrow."

"Well, if it were the *Straight* g-h-t *Scoop*, I couldn't be the editor, now, could I? Never been straight a day in my life."

Caroline leaned forward, as if she were divulging a state secret. "Every issue ends with, 'And that's the news from Copper Cove. Where all the women are single, all the men are gay or alcoholic, and all the dead still walk the streets.'"

Alex stared at Caroline.

"As if I would ever print that," David said. "There are one or two married women around here. And I always do my best to print the truth." He picked up his knitting needles, and then stopped and turned to Caroline, examining her latest hairdo. "Caroline, is that a piece of driftwood in your hair?"

Caroline turned slightly, showing off the messy bun of hair, wrapped through with a small stick. "You like it? It's not easy to find driftwood that has just the right size and curvature to it."

"When did you pick that up?"

"This morning."

"So it's not yet dry?" David asked.

Caroline gave him a very stern look. "This is the Pacific Northwest. How strict is your definition of *dry*?"

David exhaled heavily and began knitting. "Well, you smell like a dead sturgeon, so if you're in the market for a boyfriend this year, I'd lose the hair ornament."

Caroline made a face. Her eyes dropped to the basket of knitting David held in his lap. "Why don't you take your mossy green balls and go sit somewhere else?"

"Ahhh!" David gasped dramatically as he leaned away from her. He straightened his shoulders and held the basket a little closer to Caroline's line of sight. "I'll have you know that these balls are a blend of silk and kid mohair, hand-dyed in a lovely shade called emerald sea." He held his head high.

Caroline stared at him, a perfect straight face. "That is far more than I need to know about your balls, Mr. Hill."

Caroline turned to Alex. "David is a one-man machine at the newspaper—writes and prints and distributes. But he's also the one who does all the ghost tours around here. The encyclopedia of haunted houses in Copper Cove."

"Doesn't seem quite right, does it?" Aditi laughed. "That we should get all our news from the same guy who sells ghost stories for a living."

In the back corner, Grace spoke softly. "So where are you from, Alex? What brings you to Copper Cove?"

Alex turned to look at Grace. "I'm up here to do a little work for Maggie Edwards."

Grace raised her eyes from her spinning, but she did not look at Alex. Instead, she directed her gaze to Emmie Porter, sitting next to her. Emmie did not look up; she seemed completely absorbed in her spinning. Grace turned back to Alex, her gaze coming to rest on the faded colors around Alex's eye.

Alex felt the unspoken question, and she turned away, back toward David Hill. "Is it true? That all the houses are haunted?"

"Well, that would depend on your definition of truth," David said, throwing a pointed look in Caroline's direction. "Just like the definition of dry. Never an absolute, in my experience." He paused a moment. "Truth is . . . fluid. The story changes depending on who is telling it, don't you think?"

He sat back and began knitting again, his eyes on the wool in his hands. "Two things that keep this town alive, pardon my pun. Orcas and ghosts. Orcas bring in the tourists by the droves in the summer, and scientists, too. And ghosts keep the businesses afloat after the orcas move out. Around Halloween, we get all the paranormal fans. The folks who want to spend the night in a haunted hotel, or stay up all night looking for blips on electromagnetic meters. And when it's not pouring down rain, I take groups of people on a walking ghost tour of the town, tell them about all the ghostly activity."

"What kinds of ghostly activity?" Alex asked, her voice quiet, barely audible over the musical sound of the spinning wheels.

David lowered his knitting needles and met her eyes. "Do you believe in ghosts, Alex?"

The dead had never been a part of her life, not until quite recently, and until David asked, she had not ever considered the question. She wasn't sure she really wanted to find out. "I don't know. I've never really had an encounter, I guess."

"Well if you stick around here long enough, you will." David dropped his gaze and began knitting again. "The little bookshop? Moby Dickens? Next to the bakery?"

Alex shook her head. She hadn't noticed that yet.

"Lots of people ask about the shop cat. The one sleeping in the back room, or sometimes on a shelf, sometimes in one of the chairs. Kids want to know if they can play with it. One lady said she was highly allergic, but that one wasn't making her sneeze, for some reason." David sat back and raised his eyebrows dramatically. Then he leaned forward, his voice low. "Because there is no shop cat. Not one that's alive at this moment, anyway."

Grace didn't stop her spinning, but murmured quietly, "David does have a flair for this, doesn't he? You can see why he runs the ghost tours. Just remember this when you read the next issue of the *Strait Rumor* . . . I mean, the *Strait Scoop*."

David scowled at her. "And that little organic market and sandwich shop? Turnip the Beet? People who work there say they can hear footsteps on the stairs and overhead on the second floor. But usually only when the store is quiet, or after closing. We even had one of those Hollywood TV shows come and do a program on that store. They caught orbs of lights on the camera and sounds on their tapes."

Alex felt a shiver run down her spine.

"This place? The old Hadley house." David leaned forward in his seat, his voice dropping, his eyes fluttering up to the ceiling, and the second floor above them, for a second. "The town has tried to rent this place over the years. Either as a home or a business. But people never stay. They complain about loud thumps and doors banging closed. Pockets of cold air." He leaned in even closer. "I can tell you this. We love having our little spinners group here. But we always make sure that no one is stuck leaving here alone." He arched his eyebrows dramatically.

Alex watched him, the library-science part of her brain going immediately to the history of the house. "Do you have any idea who lived here? Or what happened?"

David shook his head. "These places were built a hundred and sixty years ago. I'm sure there have been many people who lived here over the years. And probably a few who have died here, too. I mean . . . all you have to do is walk through that cemetery and look at the dates on the stones. People died young back then. No antibiotics. No Occupational Safety and Health Administration." He knit a few stitches. "This was a mill town, you know. Lots of accidents at the sawmill or out on that water. A thousand ways to die young."

Emmie stopped moving her feet on her wheel. She leaned back in her chair and raised her head to look at Alex.

Their eyes met.

"It doesn't necessarily have to be death. Something bad that happened," Grace murmured.

All spinning and knitting stopped, and everyone waited for Grace to continue.

"We all seem to believe that there is a huge separation between the world of the living and the world of the dead. But what if there isn't? What if the only thing that separates us is much more . . . fluid? What if it's like a gauze curtain? We've all heard of the veil between the worlds. And what if that's all it is? You can still see through it. As if the two worlds are floating in and around and over and through us, all the time. Overlapping. Always there."

Everyone in the room was completely silent.

Grace stopped, her gaze going to the window that overlooked the water. "It's not my idea, you know. Einstein came up with it over a hundred years ago. That the dividing line between past and present and future is an illusion. That time as we know it is an illusion."

David leaned forward. "You're starting to scare me, Grace."

She sat back in her chair and took a deep breath. "I've lived here my whole life, you know. My husband and I bought our little house more than fifty years ago. After he died, there were times when I would look up from doing something, like washing dishes at the sink or spinning at my wheel." Grace looked down at the wheel in front of her feet. "And I would swear that I had just seen him, walking out to the barn. It was something I saw a million times when he was alive. Him rounding the corner to the barn."

She looked up and let her eyes go to each of the people in the circle. "Maybe the fact that he had done it so often left some kind of . . . oh, I don't know. Some kind of energetic footprint. Like a shadow. That could explain that cat so many people see in the bookstore. Or the sound of footsteps on the stairs at the market."

Grace let her eyes drift to the window, staring out at the gray water of the strait, the gray clouds pressing down on it. "It makes sense to me. Like tennis elbow or carpal tunnel syndrome. One action, repeated over and over again, and pretty soon you will get these little spaces where there are problems. Where the energy gets stuck."

Grace turned to Emmie. "Wouldn't you say so, Emmie?"

Emmie shrugged her shoulders and kept her eyes on the roving in her hands. "I have seen that happen with animals. Kick a dog once or twice and he'll cower every time you come around. They hold the memory of everything that ever happened to them—maybe not in their minds but in their cells. In their bodies."

Grace continued, "So maybe not a ghost, but an energy shadow. A memory. A pocket of energy. That could explain that cat in the bookshop."

David spoke up. "Or that captain, at the house you're staying in, Alex."

Alex looked up sharply, her attention riveted on David.

"Have you heard about that, Alex?" David asked. "The captain?"

Alex glanced at Caroline for a moment, and then shook her head. "No."

"He built that house, back in 1860-something," David said. "Lived in it for years. Had a wife and four children. His oldest son took over the house after the captain died. It was in his family for quite a long time."

Grace nodded. "Exactly. He loved that house. People would see him, standing in the windows, looking out to sea. Or looking out to town, as the case may be."

"Huh. Is that why Maggie has had so many interns leave? They see the captain?" Alex asked.

There was rustling from the back corner. Emmie gathered her fiber in a bag and folded her spinning wheel, packing it into a cloth bag. She stood quickly, her face flushed, her movements hurried. Her hands shook. "Excuse me," she whispered. She maneuvered through the circle, and when she got to the door, she stopped. Without turning to look at anyone, or say anything, she left.

They all listened to the sound of the door closing.

Grace watched the door, watched as Emmie walked down the sidewalk and turned the corner. She sighed. "Don't mind her, Alex. She isn't trying to be rude. Emmie is . . . extra sensitive. That's what makes her such a great healer with the animals. But being that sensitive can be a problem. Sometimes being in a group is just really difficult for her. Almost like a diabetic, when their blood sugar gets too high. She gets this . . . I don't know . . . sensory overload. Five of us—especially if two of them are David and Caroline—can just be too much. And we all know that when she needs to leave, she needs to leave."

Alex nodded and let out a long sigh.

Caroline shivered. "Okay, then. I think I've had enough of you spinsters with all your ghosts and energy shadows and phantom cats. I'm headed to Strait Up for an oatmeal stout. Anyone want to come along?" Caroline rose and slipped her coat up over her shoulders.

The other three shook their heads and moved back to their knitting and spinning. Alex shuddered, dislodging herself from the quiet of the stories and stood up. "I don't think I'll go to the bar, but I am going to head home. It was nice to meet you all."

"We're here every weekend. Sundays at two. Like church. The church of fiber. You should join us," David said. "But we also show up down here almost any afternoon. If the light is on, a few of us are here. If you're working for Maggie, you will find you crave contact with a few sane people."

Caroline laughed. "As if she's gonna find any of them here."

David took Alex's hand. "Whatever. Come back again. We'd love to see you."

NINE

"Sure you don't want to join me, Alex? Copper Cove is one of the few places where you don't have to worry about driving while intoxicated. Although walking while intoxicated has its own set of dangers." Caroline and Alex stood outside the Hadley house; Caroline was wrapping a scarf around her neck.

Alex's eyebrows lifted.

"We are on an island. Surrounded by water. You do have to retain enough sense to stay out of the drink. Pun intended."

Alex smiled. "Thanks for asking, Caroline. But I'm going to head home."

Caroline gave her a long look. "Okay, if you're sure. It's the holiday crowd in there. Might be some PBMs."

"PBMs?"

"Potential boyfriend material." Caroline grinned and turned toward the tavern on the corner. Alex could hear the voices, the energy of a vacation crowd, as Caroline opened the door and disappeared inside.

Alex stood on the main street of Copper Cove for a moment, drinking in the sea air. She gazed at the town, at the hundreds of twinkle lights wrapping the trees and fences and homes. The waters of Haro Strait lapped gently against the sea wall, just behind and below the businesses. She absorbed it all for a moment, the calm, the quiet, the beauty, the lulling sound of the water. Then she turned and headed up the hill.

The sounds of town grew softer as she climbed. It was only four in the afternoon, but dusk had dimmed the landscape to a dark ice blue. Alex stopped at the gate to the cemetery and gazed into the fenced grounds. Stones leaned at precarious angles, some of them having already toppled; others dangerously tipped, bowing to the effects of time. They were the color of old iron, blackened by time and weather and too many seasons of rain. She thought of what David had said earlier, that there were a thousand ways to die young back then.

Before now, Alex had never really thought about the idea of ghosts, or energy shadows, whatever they were called. Until recently, she had never had a reason to even think about the dead. But the loss of her mother had changed all that, and she wondered if it were true—what Grace had said about the overlap between past and present. It gave her comfort, to think her mother might still be around somewhere, that she might be with her, even now, separated by only the most ephemeral gauze.

She stepped inside the gate and wandered slowly up and down the rows of stones. Louisa Victoria Henderson, aged twenty-six years, seven months. Jefferson Myers, aged two years, four months. Henry Black, aged eighteen years, four months, two days. The stones were so precise in marking exactly how much life each person had accumulated. The dates were old; many of the deaths had occurred more than a hundred years ago. At the end of one row, she stopped and looked out at the water.

Fog had swallowed the far horizon, and it was now swirling across the water and winding through town, snaking its way up the hill and through the trees. It blurred all the edges, made parts of the landscape disappear. Sounds were muffled, as if buried under a blanket. The fog over Main Street took on an eerie glow, a vague reflection of the lights below. Curls of mist pooled around the gravestones, reaching to absorb her feet. For a moment she watched, as if waiting for the fog to swallow her. To make her disappear, the way the landscape around her was. She took a breath and turned to leave.

Somewhere in the trees up ahead, a dog barked. She started up the hill toward the captain's house. The fog was playing with sound, creating an echo effect, almost as if there were more than one set of footsteps headed up the hill. Alex stopped, listening carefully, her head tipped slightly. When she stopped, so did the sound. She took a breath and moved farther up the hill, her shoes clicking on the pavement of the street. There it was again—the sound of footsteps, hitting the pavement just a fraction of a second after her own steps. A shudder ran down her spine. She stopped again, turning to scan the street behind her.

She could see nothing but the curves of fog, weaving through the trees. The sounds had stopped exactly when she had. Perhaps she should look this up, do a little research on the phenomena of what happens to sound when it is filtered through fog.

Turning back to the hill, she gazed into the towering cedars that surrounded the captain's house. The house was dark, and it was hard to spot through the thick mass of branches. She had not anticipated being gone this long and had not left on any lights. As the fog rolled in, she caught the reflection of dim light in the windows upstairs, just enough pale light to see where the house stood. She stared at those windows, waiting, but if the captain were inside, he did not make an appearance.

Silly, she thought. All she had done was listen to a few ghost stories, and now she was staring into the twilight, looking for things that could not possibly be there.

And that was when she heard it—a woman's voice, talking in low tones somewhere in the trees. Alex turned and scanned the landscape around her. Shadows were thick, particularly around the trees and bushes. Thick vegetation framed every space, every corner of the cemetery, even the sides of the road she was on, and all of it was swirling with fog, like the way watercolor paints would churn and mix on canvas.

A gleam of white caught her attention—white hair almost glowing in the dim light. Emmie Porter stood in the far back corner of the cemetery, in a clump of trees. She spoke softly and waited, as if listening to a reply. As if she were having a conversation. Alex could see no one else in the dark. She could not hear the words being said, only the rise and fall, the soft murmur of Emmie's voice, a one-sided exchange.

Alex shivered and hurried back to the house, moving fast enough to block out any other sounds.

TEN

When Emmie climbed on the back of Dusty's Indian motorcycle that sunset evening in 1969, she had no idea where they were going. As it turned out, Dusty didn't, either.

It wasn't until their first night together, at a hotel in Missoula, Montana, that reality started to seep into their headlong rush to escape Dalton. After the flames of passion had been quenched, at least temporarily, Emmie began to feel the tiniest sliver of misgiving. For the years that Dusty had been out on his own, he'd been working cattle ranches, mostly through the spring and summer and fall. He slept in a bunkhouse, shared with the other cowboys doing the same thing. Emmie could not very well sleep in a bunkhouse with a room full of cowboys. And Dusty wasn't sure how to make a living any other way.

"Don't worry," he whispered into her hair. "We'll figure it out." And when she was cradled in his arms, she wanted very much to believe him. In his arms, she found all the comfort and connection that had been missing at that sad, quiet house in Dalton. He made her feel as if they were a team, as if whatever happened now, they would face it together.

They found temporary work on a ranch in Idaho, Dusty working the cattle and Emmie helping the cook. When that work ran out, they kept moving west, into Eastern Washington, and then toward the Cascade Mountains. September found them finishing up a cattle drive at a ranch in Ellensburg. They collected their pay, and Dusty leaned against the motorcycle, thumbing through the bills in his wallet.

"Winter's headed in," he said, lifting his nose toward the mountain peaks. "Not a good time to be on a bike. And not a whole lot of work for a cowboy. What do you say we go live on an island for a while?"

They pulled out a map, picked an island in the north end of Puget Sound, and started riding.

Doc Taylor was the veterinarian on the north end of Saratoga Island. He and his wife, Kate, owned a small ranch, where they were raising organic grass-fed beef long before most people had even heard of such a thing. They had two colts that needed training, and they provided a cottage on the property for Dusty and Emmie to live in. It was the first time, in the few months since they had run off together, that they actually had a small place to themselves and time together without a coterie of cowboys at every turn.

In some ways, it was not much different from the life Emmie had left. She lived on the small ranch, smelled the horses and the cows every morning when she made coffee. She took a job in town at the Drift Inn, waiting tables, and so she also had a daily dose of the sight of the water, and the dramatic displays of emotion that crossed the sky and the water and the horizon. Her first few months on the island, she felt as if she had been dropped into the best possible world, a perfect cocktail of the ranching and animals that she loved, and the water that called to her like the serenade of a lover. October passed with a brilliant display of leaves turning.

The trouble started in November, when they got their first real taste of life in the Pacific Northwest. The rains started on All Saints' Day and didn't let up. Both she and Dusty had to ditch their cowboy boots and don the ugly monstrosities called mud boots. By the end of November, it didn't appear that even those knee-high mud boots would be enough to navigate the muck around the barns.

Those short days and long nights and eternally gray skies affected the two of them in completely opposite ways. For Emmie, the darkness and damp made her want to nest, to snuggle into the little cottage that the Taylors had provided. She found knitting needles and yarn, and started making afghans and hats and scarves. Kate Taylor taught her to spin.

But just as Emmie settled in deeper with each passing day, Dusty grew more restless and irritable. He stood on the porch in the evening, watching the rain come down in sheets, smoking cigarette after cigarette and running his hands through his hair. He didn't sleep well when he did come to bed, and Emmie would often wake to hear him pacing.

The charms of that quiet cowboy that she had found so enticing back in the summer—being taller than she was and not struck dumb in her presence—turned out to be not quite enough for long-term relationship success.

She knew he was going, sensed it in the coolness of the air between them, in the space that had developed between their bodies in the bed. In her innermost being, she was preparing herself for that—for the day she would come home from work at the café and find him gone, shirts and cowboy boots packed onto his motorcycle, mud boots left behind.

What she hadn't anticipated was the way in which he would do it. She came home from the café, footsore, her back aching from all the standing and bending, to find Ms. Taylor sitting on the porch of the cottage she shared with Dusty. Kate Taylor was composed, but Emmie took one look in her eyes and knew that her whole world had just reversed direction. There was something about the eyes that always revealed painful news, even before words were actually spoken. It was worse than just Dusty clearing out and leaving her behind.

He had been hit by a car, riding his motorcycle on a rain-slick highway, the gray and the water and the slap of windshield wipers making him invisible to the driver who hit him. He was on the highway, headed toward Sea Rose Harbor, the place where the ferry landed. The accident left a trail of litter in its wake, a bumper from the motorcycle, shattered glass and pieces of metal, and the spilled contents of his suitcase: every shirt, every pair of socks and Levi's. It was a messy trail of crumbs that led to his body, which had flipped up in the air and landed on the side of the road in a horrible tangle of limbs. Kate did not supply those details, but somehow, they popped into Emmie's mind, a sickening portrait of the word *accident*.

Emmie sat down on the edge of a rocking chair, all her air escaping in one thick rush. There were no tears. She had been expecting him to go—but not like this. She had not expected this. Her shock at the news kept her quiet and still for a very long stretch, and Kate Taylor, feeling the discomfort in every inch of her ample bosom, leaned forward and patted Emmie on the knee. "Shall I call someone?"

Emmie looked up at her, totally lost for an answer. She did not even know his next of kin—had no idea who or where his family might be or if they even existed. She would have to leave it to the sheriff's office to track down his mother, wherever she was.

"What about you?" Ms. Taylor continued. "I imagine you'll want to be going home yourself, given your . . . situation?"

The question snapped her back into real time. How had the woman known? Emmie had only recently discovered that she was pregnant; she had not yet shared the news with Dusty. The last thing she wanted was for Dusty to stay with her out of guilt or obligation.

From the moment she first suspected she was pregnant, Emmie had sensed that the baby was a girl. She had imagined scenes of mother and daughter; she could see herself caring for that child.

What she could not imagine was heading back to Montana to do it.

Emmie sat gazing at the intense green grass of this little spread, at the blanket of silver-gray clouds hiding the tops of the trees. She tried to picture packing her things and going back to the ranch. She knew that her father would forgive her, that he would take her in, along with the child she carried. She would have a roof over her head, and food on the table, and would not have to be on her feet for hours every day, working at the café.

There had been moments in the past few months when she had missed them—her family, the ranch, her mother's biscuits. The soft noises of the horses in the early morning. It was the life she knew, the life she'd grown up with, the only life she had ever known until recently. She had even called her mother a few times, to let her know where she was and how she was doing.

But living there? Raising a child there? She sat on the edge of the chair, dry-eyed despite the fact that her hormones were completely awash with new-baby chemicals and the horrifying news about Dusty. She just couldn't picture going back. With Dusty, with this move to the far west, her life had expanded, had burst out of the tight seams that had bound her. She could not imagine trying to shrink it back to what it had been just a few months before. When he'd showed up at her father's ranch barely a half year ago, she had glimpsed, for the first time, a life *outside*.

Her thoughts fell into place, lining up like clean dishes in the drying rack. She had no idea how she was going to do it, how she was going to support this baby on her own. But she knew she had to find a way. She turned to the woman sitting beside her.

"Actually, Ms. Taylor, I think I'd like to stay."

It was around that same time that the rumors about Emmie started to circulate in the town of Copper Cove. Emmie did not know what was being said, and she sure didn't know the reasons why, but she sensed something. People looked at her, just a fraction of a second too long. She walked into the general store or the post office, and could hear the change of tone in the room, the sudden dead spaces in conversation, as if everyone had been talking about her. It was a little unnerving.

She mentioned it to Kate Taylor one evening, when Kate had come to the cottage bearing potato soup and homemade bread. "I made too much for just me and John," she told Emmie when she walked in the door.

Emmie was collapsed in a rocking chair, staring out into the gray, rainy evening. She was five months along in the pregnancy, enough that even with her tall, slender frame, it was obvious that she carried a child. She sat with her hand on her belly, absentmindedly stroking that baby bump. She turned to Kate Taylor, tears in her eyes. "I'm not sure what's wrong with me lately. I cry at just about anything."

Kate moved to the footstool at Emmie's feet. She unlaced and removed the girl's shoes, and then began to slowly rub her feet. "I'd say you've got all kinds of reasons to cry. Baby hormones. Boyfriend de . . . gone." Kate modified her words, but they both felt the reverberation of the word *dead* in the air, as if it had actually been spoken. "Having a baby is difficult in the best of circumstances. It can't be easy, trying to do all this by yourself."

Emmie nodded. "This is going to sound crazy," she continued. "But it feels like everyone is talking about me."

"They are," Kate replied flatly.

Emmie's eyes went wide.

"This is a small town, honey. They talk about everybody. And you've given them a few things to chew on since you got here."

"The baby?" Emmie asked, rubbing her stomach.

"The baby is part of it. And Dusty's . . . accident." Kate continued to rub the bottoms of the girl's feet. She didn't say it, but by now everyone knew that Dusty had been packed to leave when he had that accident. Clothes strewn all over the highway suggested much more than a trip to Sea Rose Harbor. "But the main thing that got their attention?"

Emmie shrugged.

"You're pretty. Too pretty by half. Men look. The women notice. Causes all kinds of trouble, especially if you're pretty and the quiet type." Kate picked up Emmie's left foot. "Quiet gets reshaped into arrogant. Stuck-up. Pretty and quiet and a boyfriend who gets killed? All kinds of possibilities in that story."

Emmie took a deep breath. "I thought I was just being too sensitive."

"Too sensitive? Is there something wrong with that?" Kate responded. "Because I happen to think that being sensitive is the most valuable form of intelligence there is."

Emmie's shoulders went back against the cushions of the chair. That was an opinion she'd never heard on the ranch in Montana.

"I've been watching the animals my entire life," Kate continued. "They have to be sensitive—to everything around them. Survival depends on it. It used to be the same for humans. The only ones who survived were the ones who were sensitive enough to pick up on all the dangers. Every noise, every smell, every flicker of movement. And even more than that . . . something deeper. A feeling. The way the animals seem to know before there is an earthquake. They *feel* something."

Emmie was completely still. She had never thought of it like this, had spent her entire nineteen years on the planet trying to ignore all those signals that were going off in her brain.

Kate looked up at Emmie and repeated her statement. "There's no such thing as *too* sensitive.

"Most people have learned to turn it off, to tune it out. Little kids, some of them anyway, still have that. But as they get older, they learn that it's not okay. Somebody, somewhere along the line, tells them to buck up. Quit being such a crybaby. Quit being so sensitive." She put Emmie's foot down and took a breath. "So they block it out. Quit listening to their senses. Quit trusting their own feelings."

Emmie could barely breathe. It was as if Kate were describing her own life on the ranch, the way she had learned to look away from the pain.

"There's a reason why you're here, you know. On this island at the end of nowhere. Here on the ranch with me and John."

Emmie waited.

"John works on the physical side of things. He knows what to do for infection or cuts and scrapes. Broken bones. Foals or calves that are turned the wrong way."

Unconsciously, Emmie put her hand on the mound of her baby.

Kate stopped, her face composed. "But most of the real wounds in the world, most of the real sickness, isn't caused by the physical." She waited, as if gauging Emmie's reaction.

"We all seem to think that once the bone has mended, or the infection is gone, or the physical wound has healed . . . then everything is great, right? All fixed up, back to work. But emotional trauma, emotional wounds . . . they may not be visible, but the effects can last a lifetime. And they can be lethal."

Emmie swallowed. "Lethal?"

"Have you ever seen a married couple, together a long time, and one partner dies, and then just a few months . . . maybe a year . . . later, the other one dies, too?"

Emmie nodded.

"That's not physical. They may develop some kind of physical ailment, but it started with emotion. It started with sadness, or loss, or fear. Sometimes I'll see a woman in a bad marriage, and she has back pain. From feeling unsupported." Kate looked outside for a moment, and then brought her eyes back to Emmie. "Our bodies keep score. Every grief, every heartache, every fear, every trauma. They're just as severe as a knife wound. Just as bad, maybe worse, as being stabbed. The body remembers, even when the mind blocks it out."

Emmie stared at the woman. She had never met anyone who talked like that, who held opinions like that.

Kate pressed her lips together. "I can feel it. Those places where energy is stuck. Those places where emotion is getting in the way of health. It gives off . . . heat. And sometimes, I can see it. Like a ball of colored light."

She waited a long beat. "And I think you can, too."

Emmie took a huge breath and started to shake her head. "I—"

Kate held up her hand. "You don't have to agree with me. I just want you to pay attention. Tomorrow, when you go to the café, just watch. Let yourself really *see* the people who are coming in. Let yourself really *see* the animals that cross your path. That's all you have to do right now. Just let yourself *see*. Let yourself feel the energy that's out there."

Kate stood up and smoothed her skirt. "Better eat before it's cold."

After that night, Emmie felt as if she had been awakened from a deep sleep. She remembered those times as a young girl, when she could feel what the horses were feeling. As soon as she focused on it again, as soon as Kate gave her permission to be sensitive, she found that it returned, only even larger and more powerful than anything she had sensed as a child. Almost as if the act of carrying her own baby was helping to magnify the sensitivity.

It happened the very next day, waiting tables at the café. "Morning, Mr. Griffith," she said when an elderly gentleman slipped into his booth by the window. She knew a few of the locals, and he was a regular, especially since his wife had died eight months before. That morning, after her talk with Kate, she brought his coffee, and she looked at him, really looked at him. It hit her so hard she inhaled sharply and nearly stumbled.

"Something wrong, Emmie?" He looked her in the eye.

For a moment she just stared, her mouth slightly open. Loneliness radiated from his body, like morning mist on the water. Even through the denim jacket that he wore, she could see red light, glowing right over his heart. She felt a stab in her own chest, as if her heart might explode; her left arm was throbbing with pain right down to the fingers.

She swallowed hard and shook her head. "No. I'm fine." Subconsciously, she was pressing her hand against her chest. "How are you feeling, Mr. Griffith?"

He nodded and tried to give her a weak smile. "Pretty good for an old man."

"Good. Glad to hear it." She tried not to focus on that bright red energy in his chest, tried not to give in to the pain she was feeling in her own body. "The usual?" she croaked.

He nodded. "Biscuits and gravy. Egg on top. How about you scramble it today?"

"Will do," she said and turned toward the kitchen.

The two women who worked the general store were sitting at the long bar of the café, finishing their coffee. But they had noted every movement she made when talking to Ben Griffith. They had noticed the way she grabbed her own chest, the way she had shaken her left arm as she walked away from him.

Not four hours later, the old man was dead from a massive heart attack. And what the two women had witnessed went rabid.

A week later, Emmie was walking home from the café, passing the yard of the house that belonged to the Thomas family. Their dog was a curly, ragged-haired gray mutt, and it was out in the yard now, barking as Emmie walked past. She stopped and gazed at the dog. There was a brownish-red glow, near the stomach and the hips. As if the dog had been kicked repeatedly.

Emmie looked up at the Thomas' youngest son, Chester. He was eight years old, generally unkempt, and usually moving a million miles an hour. At that moment, he was in the crotch of a black locust tree, climbing to the next branch. "Shame on you, Chester," Emmie hissed. "Stop kicking that dog."

He glared at her, his mouth hanging open.

"It comes back to you, you know," she whispered. "Someday you will get kicked yourself."

She turned to continue her walk home and nearly bumped into Agnes Pettigrew, the postmistress, who had heard the whole exchange.

Those stories got around, and the next time she walked into the general store, there was no mistaking the energy. The whole room went quiet. She could hear the click of her boots on the wood floor; she could feel the stares of the people standing near the woodstove and the clerk behind the counter, like the barrels of guns, all aimed at her back. When she walked out the door, she knew they were talking about her. She knew they were spreading the stories. And this time, their talk included the word *witch*.

ELEVEN

Alex bolted up in bed, her heart bursting out of her chest like the sudden boom of a firecracker. Someone was pounding on the front door. Her first reaction was panic; she had to force herself to breathe. The green hands of the alarm clock by the bed showed her it was not quite seven in the morning. The sky outside was still completely dark. She waited a moment, wondering if she had only dreamt the sound. The pounding returned, loud and insistent.

"Alex, open up. It's Maggie."

Alex exhaled, threw back the covers, and grabbed her sweater. She hurried to the front door and opened the dead bolt. Maggie stormed in, as if there were nothing at all unusual about walking in on your employee at seven in the morning the Sunday after Christmas. She turned and looked at Alex, standing by the door.

"Get dressed. We're going out." Maggie's voice was commanding.

"Out?" Alex blinked. She had not bothered to grab her glasses when she jumped out of bed.

Maggie was dressed in a puffy Carhartt coverall, a wool hat pulled low on her forehead. "Here. You can wear these. They're not as long as mine; maybe you won't trip over them." She held out a similar pair of coveralls.

Alex took them in her hand, on autopilot, but she was not quite fully awake, and she continued to stare at Maggie's face.

Maggie caught her eye. "Get moving. They'll be here soon."

For one brief, crazy second, Alex felt a wave of panic start to tip her off her feet. Dizziness swarmed upward, and she focused all her energies on staying upright. "They?" Her voice croaked.

"Orcas." Maggie walked over to the front window and stared out at the dark water. "I heard them on the hydrophone. Part of J Pod is out there, headed this way, I think. You might as well get a look at the creatures, since they are the reason you're here. Come on, snap to."

"J Pod." She repeated the words, her mind still fighting to understand.

"Let's go! Hustle."

Alex headed toward the bedroom and began to dress.

"Do you have any long underwear?" Maggie called from the front window.

"I'm from Albuquerque."

"That's not an answer." Maggie humphed impatiently. "They have winter in Albuquerque, don't they?"

"Not winter that would require spending money on long underwear."

"Yeah, I didn't expect you would be prepared for this. I stuffed a pair into the leg of that jumpsuit. You need to layer up. It's pretty chilly on the water. And hurry."

The screen door slammed behind them, and Alex followed Maggie as she headed down a path behind the house. It plunged into thick woods, and Alex was certain that Maggie was about to lead her right over a cliff. The path was steep; Alex struggled to maintain her footing and keep up. Maggie wore a camping headlight clamped on her forehead;

the light bounced off rocks and trees on their way down the slope. Alex felt bulky and uncoordinated in her layers of clothing, like the Abominable Snowman. The path took them directly to the water of the cove, down to a small dock. A boat moved against the pilings in the near dark. They reached it just as the sky began to pale, a deep purple gray over black water.

Alex sucked in air, her heart racing at the sight of the small boat. It had an undersized cover, just over the middle of the boat where the steering wheel and driver's seat were located, but for the most part, the boat was open to the elements. "We're going out in that?"

"Would you prefer to swim?" Maggie had already dropped a duffel bag of equipment on the floor of the boat and was untying one of the mooring ropes. "This thing is older than you are, I'm certain. But it still floats. Montauk. Seventeen-footer. Almost unsinkable." She held a rope in one hand. "They are known for being very stable in the water."

She looked at Alex, standing like a zombie on the dock. "Get in."

Alex met her eyes and forced herself to take a breath. She lifted one overclad leg and stepped into the boat. It lurched slightly; she reached to grab the sides. She heard the slap of water against the hull of the vessel. Her stomach dropped and her throat constricted.

Alex hated water; she had avoided it her entire life. She stayed away from swimming pools, refused to join the rafting trips of her coworkers at the University. She never even put her face under the water when she stood in the shower. And here she was, about to head out in a seventeen-foot piece of wood, or maybe fiberglass, heading into the dark, cold waters of Haro Strait, on a freezing cold day in late December. This boat could only be considered a splinter of protection in the whole huge scheme of things.

Maggie stepped into the boat, and Alex reached to grab both sides at the rocking motion that ensued. Maggie shot her a quick glance and threw a life preserver in her direction. "If you're scared, put this on. If you can get it over that coverall."

Alex fumbled with the catches on the vest.

"Not that it really matters, out here. In these waters, hypothermia takes over in a matter of minutes. Doesn't allow much time for rescue, provided there is anyone else out here who'd be close enough." Maggie turned the key. The motor started easily, and they puttered out of the cove. When they reached the open waters of Haro Strait, Maggie revved the engine, and they lurched forward, Alex grabbing the side of the boat again, her gloved hands clenched tight.

It hit her in the face like a slap from the past, an ill-behaved ghost of memory that she had managed to bury all these years. Water. The last time she had been on a boat. She and Daniel had been married about six months when he informed her that they were spending four days on a houseboat on Lake Navajo with Daniel's boss and his wife.

Alex had stopped where she was, turning slowly. All her life, avoiding even the water of the shower, and now out on a boat? "But . . . I don't own a swimsuit."

Daniel turned and looked at her, his eyes sweeping her five-foot-one-inch frame, a shape that was much more like a rock than a willow. She had put on a few extra pounds after they married. "That's probably for the best."

The words cut, like a knife to the stomach. She had never imagined herself to be anything other than what she was, but those words, that *appraisal*, coming from the man she had only recently married and still believed that she loved, hurt worse than if he had actually stabbed her. She felt as if the blood were draining from her body, pouring out of the wound he had just torn in her psyche.

The long weekend went downhill from there. Daniel looked like a chiseled Greek god in his swimming trunks, like a Michelangelo sculpture that dove into the water and swam and smiled, most often flashing those pearly whites at the other two females on the houseboat with them. Alex felt ignored and completely out of place. She started taking a book with her whenever they were out on deck, so that she wouldn't have to watch her husband of less than a year as he cut through the water, laughing and splashing and playing with the wife of the boss. Bettina wore a bikini that was held on with strings, and everyone on the boat was silently keeping track of the ability of the garment to stay on her body. It was only a matter of time, really. So they were all attentive when she took that one fateful dive off the side of the boat that managed to render her topless. Daniel was floating nearby, a lazy smile on his face.

"Whoops!" Bettina laughed, all wet hair and bare breasts and Farrah Fawcett teeth, as she climbed out of the water and into the towel that her husband held open for her.

Frederick, the boss' recently divorced brother, sat near Alex on the deck, and he turned to her, his eyes hidden behind the dark lenses of his sunglasses. "Ah. Now I know what my brother sees in her. I knew it wasn't her ability to converse."

Alex laughed, for the first time since they had boarded the boat three days before. She and Frederick chatted for a while, her book forgotten in the glare of human attention.

Daniel was quiet when he got out of the water and plopped into the chair next to her, water dripping around him. She was still naive enough not to read the danger in that quiet. He put one wet hand on her leg and sat silently.

It wasn't until they were in their cabin that night after dinner that she got her first lesson in just what Daniel's moody silences might mean. She had slipped off her sweater and was standing by the dresser in her tank top and capris, when he came at her, grabbing both arms in his hands, and pushing her backward, through the glass door that opened onto their own small deck.

"Wha . . ." She was caught completely unawares by that move and was now caught between his body, looming like an angry giant against her, and the railing of the boat pressing into her back, the only thing that separated her from the dark water below.

"See this latch?" he hissed into her face. She glanced down, and there was a small latch, like the kind often used on a garden gate. She swallowed, and her eyes flicked from the latch to his face. "One flick of my thumb, and you would be in the water."

His hands pressed into her upper arms. "And let's see . . . I had too much to drink, everyone would know that. Passed out. Slept through the whole thing. Maybe you got up in the night, and maybe you went out on the deck to look at the moonlight, and leaned against the railing, and . . . well. It wouldn't be hard to conclude that you must have fallen in, while the rest of us slept."

Alex could feel his breath in her face, thick with the whiskey he'd been drinking.

Suddenly he brought a knee up, between her legs, and lifted her off the deck. "I saw the way you looked at him, you little slut. Don't embarrass me, Alex. I won't stand for it. You understand?"

"But, I didn't . . . ," Alex sputtered, knowing she hadn't done anything wrong. Daniel's hands moved up her arms, over her bare shoulders. One hand circled her neck from the front, the other wrapped around the back of her shoulders, pulling her in closer. She could barely breathe. He put his mouth over hers, thrusting his tongue into her. She could feel his erection, pressing against her stomach. His grip on her was forceful, constricting.

He bent and swooped her into his arms, like a child, and for one brief, terrifying moment, she thought he was going to drop her over the railing. She grasped at his shoulders, and he laughed. Then he turned and carried her to their bed, where he didn't even attempt to keep his passion quiet, as if he were purposely making as much noise as possible. Sending a message to Frederick, wherever he might be on this boat. Alex was *his* wife; she belonged to Daniel. And she had the marks to prove it, small bruises on her throat and the backs of her arms. Love bites on her neck and shoulders. As if love had anything to do with it.

Maggie killed the engine, and they bobbed in the water. She lowered a hydrophone, flicked a switch, and said, "Listen. That's them. Part of J Pod."

Alex listened to a whole series of clicks and whistles and high-pitched squeals bouncing back and forth under the water. "It sounds as if they're talking to each other."

"They are." Maggie stared out at the dark water. "I don't know how many different orca pods exist in the world, but they inhabit every ocean. Each pod has its own language, its own distinct way of communicating. Each pod has its own culture, its own way of being in the world.

"Some of those whistles and clicks? That's the orcas, talking to each other. One scientist in Canada has cataloged a dictionary of some of their sounds. As if they're saying, 'Hey, John, over here.'"

Alex sat still, listening to the hydrophone, trying not to let her teeth chatter.

"Some of it? All those rapid-fire clicks?"

Alex nodded.

"That's echolocation. Sonar. The most sophisticated sonar system in the world. One orca can send out clicks in front of her, trying to detect whatever is out in the water, even when it is too dark to see. And from the sounds that bounce back to her, she can tell if there are salmon and which way they're headed. She can tell that we're out here, sitting on top of the water. And from just her clicks? All the other orcas know where things are, too. Even if there's a youngster, following the fish and not paying attention, the sound that bounces back to mom also bounces back to everyone else in the pod. They all know where everybody is, where the fish are. Where there's something else that they need to be aware of. Just from the echolocation clicks of one orca."

They sat, bobbing in the dark water, listening as the orcas talked to each other, the sounds getting closer and louder. A few streaks of pale gray splashed the sky, making it easier to distinguish sky from water.

And then Alex heard it—movement in the water around them. She heard a *whoosh* as one orca came up for air, and water spouted in the gray dawn air around them. The sound was followed by another, and another, *whoosh, whoosh*, as if they were all putting on a show for this water-fearing stranger from landlocked New Mexico.

Alex smiled, a huge grin covering her face. She felt the urge to giggle.

"That was the sound that hooked me, that *whoosh* as they come up for air. The first time I heard it, I was nine years old. We were living in that house in Copper Cove, the one you're in right now, and I was lying in bed, with the windows open. It was summer—the days went on forever. And I heard them. I jumped up and stood at the window, watching the orcas going by out in the water." Maggie turned and caught Alex's eye. "I knew it, right then. That I was going to spend my life studying these creatures. One *whoosh*, and I was hooked."

Alex nodded. "They're incredible."

One orca swam directly underneath them. Alex reached for the sides of the boat again, afraid the giant blackfish might tip them over. It swam to the side where Alex was sitting and rolled slightly in the water. Alex and the orca were looking directly at each other, eye to eye. The look she saw there went straight through her, penetrating her multiple layers of clothing, piercing right through every story, every lie, every decision that she had made in order to survive this so-called life of hers.

It was as if that orca could see it all, the whole mess, and yet could still look Alex in the eye and not cast judgment. As if that orca actually *understood*. As if that orca could actually see every bruise she carried, inside and out. As if that orca could read her pain and despair. They looked at one another for a long moment.

The blackfish rolled away and dove under, and Alex exhaled. Her breath whooshed out in a huge fountain of air, just as the whales were doing.

"Amazing, isn't it? That connection?" Maggie studied the girl for a moment. "Their brains are four times as large as ours, much more elaborate. Highly intelligent creatures. I even know a scientist or two who would venture to say *more* intelligent than we are.

"What they can do, with that sophisticated sonar of theirs, goes beyond just communicating."

Maggie looked out at the water.

"In the sixties and during the Cold War, the Navy had a program where they trained dolphins to locate bombs—land mines under the sea. Even if the bombs were hidden inside a container. And there were times when the dolphins would indicate a bomb, when the Navy was not aware of having planted any at that particular site. When they investigated, the dolphins had detected unexploded material that had been in the water since the Second World War.

"They were able to find things that even the US Navy did not know about. I find that rather remarkable." Maggie was still sitting in her seat, watching the darkened water. "Dolphins and orcas are the same family, you know. The orcas have an even greater sonar capacity.

"It doesn't matter how dark and murky the water is. It doesn't matter how hidden something might be. They can see through things— see what's inside. Like ultrasound—you know those tests that doctors use to take pictures of babies in the womb?"

Alex swallowed, tingles running down her arms, and nodded slightly.

"Same idea. Send sound waves through the skin and the muscle, and see what's going on inside the womb. That's what the orcas can do. They can see inside. There are stories—not science experiments, you understand—but anecdotal stories of trainers, working with captured orcas. And the orcas began to act differently—protectively—around a trainer as soon as they sensed that the woman was pregnant. Sometimes before the woman herself knew."

Alex stared into the water, watching as the pod moved away from them, into the growing light of the day.

Maggie watched them, too. She took a deep breath.

"I'm a scientist, first and foremost. But there's something to these creatures that goes beyond anything I've ever seen." Maggie waited a moment, and whispered, "They have a capacity to understand, to empathize, that is unlike anything I've ever seen with humans.

"How do they do it? Staying together, with their mother, for as long as the mother lives. Staying together in families. Helping each other, helping the new babies. And we haven't seen any sign of violence or anger or disagreements. That's a pretty amazing social structure, if you ask me."

Maggie took a breath. "Sure puts our human culture to shame."

Their eyes met, one tiny flicker of connection. Then Maggie turned away and started the engine, heading them back to land.

TWELVE

Maggie was seventy-six years old, and age had done nothing to soften her rough edges. If anything, the prickly, brittle points of her personality had been honed over time and circumstance to the sharpness of a blade. A lifetime of dealing with fools and incompetents had only served to solidify an inherent tendency toward stubbornness, a certain predilection for harsh judgment. She expected the worst from people; it had been her experience that they usually delivered.

Maggie was born at the end of 1941, just in time for her Navy captain father to kiss her goodbye before he reported for duty in the Pacific, shortly after the bombing of Pearl Harbor. She was four years old before she saw him again, when the war was over and he'd been granted a two-month leave.

Two months, as it turned out, was too long for each member of the family. Jeanine, her mother, had gone to work in a shipyard during the war, helping to build supply ships, trying to meet the endless demands of the war. Maggie and her mother had established a relationship based on mutual respect for space. Maggie was independent from the moment she could sit up, and she stayed to herself, in the yard or the house or the garden, observing all the various forms of life around her.

The addition of husband and father, four years later, especially one who was a captain in the Navy, rocked their boat considerably. Henry

Edwards was accustomed to issuing orders and having them obeyed. The consequence of disregarding one of his orders on board a Navy vessel, particularly in wartime, was court-martial for treason, maybe even death. So he was caught completely off guard when he told his four-year-old daughter to come inside and clean up that mess in the front room. Maggie was squatting on the front walk, examining the slime left by worms. "I can't. I'm watching the worms make trails."

His voice came sharper. "Margaret."

Maggie stood up and put her hands on her hips. "I said I'm busy." She glared at him.

His wife also demonstrated a resistance to taking orders from this man she hadn't seen in so long. Working at the shipyard had given her a sense of power, a sense of control over her own life, a sense of her value as a human being. With her contribution to the war effort, she had come to see herself as far more than a wife and mother and cook and housekeeper. She and Maggie had learned to eat when they were hungry, whatever was handy, and she had long since abandoned the idea of cooking three squares a day, for anyone.

When her husband left for the war, they were newlyweds; Jeanine was still trying to prove she could be a good wife. She kept a spotless house, cooked meals that she thought he would like. Four years later, she didn't seem to care about house or food or even what her husband might think about any of it. When he asked, "What's for dinner?" she turned and looked at him as if he'd just spoken in Greek.

"I don't know. Have you looked in the refrigerator?"

Henry ran his hands through his hair, poured a little more scotch in his glass, and the three of them tried to ignore each other for the remainder of his leave. By the time his next leave was secured, more than a year later, Jeanine had decided that the position of Navy captain's wife might not be as attractive a career as she had first imagined in those heady months before the war. She pulled up stakes, and she and Maggie went to live with Jeanine's uncle George in Copper Cove.

It wasn't that Maggie didn't like men, or more particularly, her own father. But the reality of a father who ordered her about, and told her to eat her peas and make her bed, was strikingly different from the father she had always known—the portrait of Navy captain Henry Edwards that had perched atop the piano. The father in that picture was easy to love—he just sat there looking handsome and regal. He never issued orders, or brought his hand down on the dining room table in anger, making the dishes jump, just because Maggie forgot to say, "Yes, sir."

Uncle George was much easier to navigate. He was in his seventies, crippled with arthritic knees. He moved immediately into the cabin, just up the hill from the big house, telling Maggie and her mother that he wanted to give the girls their space. It was a perfect fit—all three of them profoundly enamored of personal space.

Uncle George often sat on the porch of the cabin, or in the main room when the weather was nasty, using his spyglass to watch ships in the channel or passing whales. Uncle George was the perfect companion. He didn't care about messes; in fact, he didn't even seem to notice them. He didn't require special care and attention; if Jeanine cooked a meal every second or third day, and invited him to join them, he was happy to get it. Sometimes, when the weather was fine and his knees cooperated, he would make bacon and eggs and pancakes for all three of them.

It was Uncle George who told Maggie all about the blackfish—the orcas. He watched them through his spyglass, and let her look.

Maggie watched, as one after another of the big creatures jumped up out of the water, turning sideways before diving back under. "What are they doing?" she asked excitedly.

"It's called breaching. I think they're playing. Jumping up out of the water because they're happy. Because they're having a good time."

Maggie was not familiar with that kind of playing. She was familiar with independence, with scientific inquiry. But jumping and playing just because it felt good? That was not an activity she had ever seen before, and what she watched through that spyglass was infectious. The orcas were obviously having a good time. Maggie quickly grew to love this life by the water, watching everything that went on out there, from the whales to the sea lions to the storms that blew in from the west. And she was growing increasingly fond of Uncle George.

The kids at the small school in Copper Cove were another matter. Most women had returned to the kitchen after the men returned from the war. The girls at school were mostly interested in boys and babies and the matching sofa pillows they would have once they married and had their own homes. Maggie's passion for marine life, for trying to figure out how things worked, was hers and hers alone.

She learned to ignore them. She focused on science and math, and won a scholarship to the University of Washington, where she majored in marine biology, the lone female in that line of study. It was 1959; women who went to college at all majored in liberal arts, a fancy term for husband hunting. Few of them were looking for careers.

Maggie was driven. She had a sense of doing something important, something that would help the world. When she graduated in 1962, she immediately began her postgraduate work. She had just finished her thesis when Uncle George died, in 1965, and she went back to Copper Cove for the funeral. She never left.

Her mother was there, her life focused on gardening and reading and long walks in the rain. But the orcas were there, too, at least part of the year, and Maggie secured a part-time research grant. It didn't pay much, but she didn't need much. She moved into the cabin, up the hill from her mother, who was still in the main house, and Maggie continued her lifelong habit of watching the water at all times of the day or night.

Dr. Donald Carter taught marine science at the University, and he came to the island to do field work the summer of 1968. Ten years older than Maggie, gray was beginning to mark his dark beard. He was gruff and rough and cursed like a sailor, but he knew the waters. She had to admire his knowledge, the way he handled every situation with such surety.

She had studiously avoided all men at the University, if those tadpoles of male students could actually be called men. Their interests seemed to be centered on female anatomy, and they steered clear of anything approaching academics. But Donald Carter was different. He was definitely *not* a tadpole. There was no mistaking his keen intelligence, his dedication to his work.

He kissed her one night, leaning up against the pier when they had finished unloading the boat, and her body responded, something that she was totally unprepared for, her mind having always been able to keep strict control of all systems.

"So the great Maggie Edwards is human after all," he whispered with a smile. And then he kissed her again. Maggie let herself be kissed.

She let herself go much further than kissing.

As the summer progressed, Maggie started to envision the two of them as the next Marie and Pierre Curie—a scientific team dedicated to the study of killer whales and their habitat. A partner seemed totally acceptable to her, if it allowed her to continue her work, and if she was working with someone of equal intellectual stature and mutual interest in marine life.

What she hadn't envisioned was a baby. She was completely bewildered when the local doctor told her that she was four months pregnant. She had never had normal cycles, and had been told as a teenager, by this very same doctor, that with those ovaries, she would never be able to have children.

Dr. Carter thought it was quite entertaining. "A marine biologist who doesn't know the signs that she's pregnant," he laughed.

They went through a quick civil ceremony, one in which Maggie carried no flowers and did not want a ring, which would just get hung up on something when she was working on the boat. No sentiment for Maggie Edwards, not even under the influence of pregnancy hormones.

And she kept her maiden name, preferring to answer to Dr. Edwards than to muddle through the confusion of two Dr. Carters in the same household.

The baby arrived in February of 1969, looking a little like a fish, only with arms and legs. She did the best she could, but her maternal instincts were not as strong as her scientific interests. It wasn't that Maggie didn't love the boy. Her attention was on her work and always had been. She was easily distracted by the sea; there were moments out on the boat when she almost forgot that she had a son. Brian spent his first few years out on the water, learning to sleep and crawl and maneuver to the rocking of the waves and the sounds of marine life.

She was relieved when he became old enough to fend for himself, and she no longer had to remember to feed him or change him. At the age of four, he made his own peanut butter and jelly sandwiches, inventive enough to pull out the lowest drawer of the kitchen cabinets and use that to climb his way up to the countertop, where he had access to the toaster.

She and Donald Carter managed to stay married for ten years, which was more than enough time for Maggie to see that she had married a man who wasn't interested in being a partner. Donald Carter was more like a god, and he wanted everyone, including his wife, to worship at his feet. He had a fondness for scotch and young female interns, both of which were necessary for maintaining the god illusion.

To Maggie's credit, she had recognized a few of his inadequacies even before they tied the knot. He wasn't particularly neat or punctual. His shoes were never shined. He liked more than one glass of scotch in the evenings, sometimes to the point where his eyelids hung at half-mast and his words turned to slush.

But Maggie had seen her father whip his underlings into shape, and she felt certain that she could do the same with Donald Carter. She certainly did make strides; he did neaten up a little. But no matter how much whiskey she poured down the sink, he still managed to make it to the bedroom every night with his body listing to port.

One night, after a hellacious fight in which she clearly enumerated his numerous shortcomings, he packed a bag and moved to his boat, his brain just sober enough to tell her, "Go command some other ship, Maggie. I'm leaving port."

He thought he was so clever.

She was left in command of their son and the house, hers by inheritance after Uncle George, and then her mother, had passed away. She also commanded a string of interns from the University of Washington, normally much younger than that Alexandra Turner. And she'd kept it all afloat, running about as smoothly as any ship could properly expect to.

Maggie turned away from the window and stood in front of the bookshelf, gazing at the pictures of her son. Brian Carter had dark eyes and a chiseled jaw, courtesy of Maggie and her own father. She'd done a fine job of raising him, and he'd turned out well, despite the lack of genetic material from his own father. Although she may have lacked the instinct for showing him love, she had no problem with issuing orders. Maggie had taken what there was in that young boy, and pushed and pulled and pummeled and formed that lump of clay, turning out a fine figure of a man. He lived back east, working in the field of sonar.

Maggie swallowed, one tiny drop of emotion sliding down her throat, coated in the taste of abandonment. She forced it down and sighed, looking away from the photographs of Brian and his two boys, her grandsons, and out the window. It wasn't his fault, really, that he no longer came back to the island for Christmas. His work kept him busy; his family was growing. She'd tried once, several years ago, to spend the holidays with Brian, but his wife didn't appreciate Maggie's efforts to help get their house in shipshape order, everything running smoothly.

That chore list that she had drawn up for the children was only meant to help. Or the way she had tried to organize the hall closet. Maggie had not been invited back.

She wasn't being mean, at least not in her own eyes. She was just direct, forthright. She said what she thought. Some people just couldn't handle that, preferring that polite old adage of "if you can't say something nice, don't say anything at all." In Maggie's book, that was just totally ineffectual, denoting a certain strain of weakness. Really, if a person can't handle the truth, how could they expect to get along in life?

It seemed that her advancing age only served to make her more irritated, more often. As if all the fools of the world were conspiring to make her later years an absolute headache. And she certainly didn't trust this younger generation to take over when she left off with her work. On the downhill slide to eighty, and yet she was still working every day, partly because she didn't see anyone else around who was as dedicated and thorough as she herself had always been. She was hardworking and meticulous and straightforward, with superb attention to detail. Practical. Intelligent.

And Maggie was intelligent enough to have noticed that the facts about Alexandra Turner did not quite add up. The story she concocted about that black eye, for instance. Either a total fabrication or the woman was an absolute klutz. She'd parked that car with the New Mexico plates back in the trees, away from the street, and hadn't started it since. It would be covered with moss by the time she left the island.

And afraid of the water? The girl couldn't swim and moved to an island, in the wettest part of the continental US, to work for a marine biologist? What had she been thinking? Ridiculous. Maggie had noticed the way she jumped at the slightest sound, the way her hands sometimes shook as she worked or when she poured herself a cup of coffee at the stove. So jumpy. With nerves like that, how had the woman been able to hold down a job?

Maggie stood at the window, watching as Alex turned on the kitchen light in the house across the driveway. She took a swig of cold coffee from her cup. *I don't know what you're up to, Alexandra Turner,* she thought. *But I know a liar when I see one.*

THIRTEEN

Emmie's baby was born in early May of 1970, on a perfect spring day when the sun was shining and the rhododendrons were wreaking havoc on the senses, blooms turning the landscape into a Persian carpet. Throughout her labor, she stayed in her own cottage, with Kate Taylor nearby and the doc on alert, should Emmie require transport to a real medical facility. Most of those hours, she focused on the robins outside her window, busy feeding their babies and singing about spring. So when Kate Taylor placed that little dark-haired girl in Emmie's arms, she named her Robin.

Emmie liked to say that the baby saved her. She filled all the holes in Emmie's heart, all the wide-open spaces that had been torn apart with the death of her brother in 1968 and Dusty in 1969. All the yawning chasms of loneliness and isolation were filled by this tiny, dark-haired girl.

Despite becoming a mother at the age of nineteen, Emmie took to the task as if she had been born to it. She was calm and patient, as serene as a much older woman might have been. She loved holding that little girl, every possible moment. Like all new parents, she marveled at the tiny fingers and toes and eyelashes, loved to watch the way the baby stretched her small arms over her head, hands in fists the size of walnuts. Emmie could watch her endlessly, and she was always tuned in to every sound the baby made. She woke in the night, holding her breath, listening for the soft exhalations of that tiny girl in the basket next to the bed, unable to take a breath in her own body until she heard the breaths of her little girl.

With the birth of Robin, Emmie remembered how to smile and laugh; she reveled in the warmth of that small body next to hers. As she nursed, the child watched Emmie intently, one tiny hand reaching to grab the long braid of Emmie's hair.

"You have found your calling" was the way Doc Taylor described it. He and Kate had never had their own children, and they took to the baby as if she were their own granddaughter.

Emmie learned how to match her own heartbeat and breath and rhythms with those of her daughter. And it wasn't long before she was transferring that intense harmonic resonance to every other creature that she came in contact with.

They started arriving shortly after she gave birth to Robin. In the middle of a midnight rainstorm, she heard the mewing of a kitten, so loud and insistent and scared that she got out of bed and pulled on her coat. She went out to find a bedraggled, tabby-colored creature, sitting on the front porch and crying. The kitten looked to be only a few weeks old.

Emmie held out her hands, not saying a word, and the kitten climbed in, as if she'd been on this specific mission, when she set out from God-knew-where in the middle of a storm. As soon as Emmie touched her, she knew: the mother was dead, along with any other littermates. She could not say exactly *how* she knew that—if it had something to do with the touch or if she was tuning in to some other energetic force. Emmie carried the kitten inside and bathed her, fluffing the gray fur with a towel and introducing her to the wonders of warm cow's milk.

The dog showed up a month later, with what appeared to be a broken leg. Another gray and rainy afternoon, and the dog limped up the driveway and stood outside Emmie's house as if he knew just where he was headed.

"I'm on my way to Bellingham," Doc Taylor told her when she went to get him. "I'll have to look at him later."

She watched the doc pull away in his truck, and turned to the dog, his brown fur matted and his eyes swimming in longing. "Don't look at me like that," Emmie murmured. "I have a baby and a kitten, and I can barely support myself as it is." She turned to walk back to her own house, and the dog followed, limping along on three legs. He managed, somehow, to follow her up the four steps to the porch.

Emmie stood at the screen door and let out a long sigh. "I guess if you can make it up the steps, then you might as well come in," she said. "It isn't getting any warmer out here."

When she reached down to touch the dog's shoulder, she felt a buzz of electricity shoot up her arm, and she jumped back, shocked by the intensity of that jolt. She sat down on the rag rug, next to the mangled mutt, and gingerly put her hand on the shoulder once again. She knew immediately. The leg wasn't broken. But this dog had been kicked, several times, over several months. Emmie held her hand over that spot on his shoulder, and very gently began moving her palm in a circle, and then pushing her hand down the leg and out the foot. Over and over, she massaged that spot, feeling the trapped energy of all those kicks as it slowly loosened.

The dog settled himself on the rag rug, lying on his side, and closed his eyes. She repeated that same massage a few times over the next two days. When Doc Taylor pulled up in his truck, exhausted after his trip up north, he did a double take. The dog was trotting along beside Emmie as she moved outside, hanging clean cloth diapers on the clothesline. Emmie smiled and waved.

The doc just shook his head. "She's like Snow White," he murmured. "All the animals want to hang out with her."

Like his wife, Doc Taylor had a mind that was open to possibilities, and he asked Emmie to show him what she had done with the dog. He asked her to explain, as well as she could, what she saw and felt when she was working on an animal. And before long, Emmie was helping out, not on every animal that came in but on a few where the doc thought it might add to the treatments he provided. Emmie never went back to work as a waitress.

One morning in October, the rain was coming down in a steady rhythm. The air was gray green, as if the rain and the cedars had melded together. The Taylors had left for Seattle, one of their rare trips to the University of Washington. Emmie was doing dishes when she heard the car pull up in the driveway, jerking to a halt in front of Doc Taylor's office building. A woman got out of the car and pounded on the door to the office.

"Where's Doc Taylor?" she shouted, her voice frantic with fear when Emmie stepped out on her own porch.

"He's out teaching. Said not to expect him back until late tonight."

The woman took a big breath, fighting to control her emotions. "There's something wrong with my horse." The words whooshed out, as if learning that the doc was not around had just taken every bit of her hope.

"Where?" Emmie dried her hands on a dish towel.

"At my house, just up the road."

Emmie looked at the woman, at the cloud of emotion in her blue eyes. "Let me get my daughter. I'll be right back."

She tied Robin into a baby sling around her body and headed back to the woman and her truck. The tires spun in the mud as the woman backed up and started down the driveway.

"Name's Grace Wheeler," the woman said.

"Emmie Porter. And this is Robin. She's four months old."

"My daughter is four years old," Grace said. She bit her lip. "You work for Doc Taylor? Don't you need a medical bag or something?"

Emmie swallowed. "I'm not exactly a vet tech. But I do help out a little with the animals." She wasn't sure just how much to say about the work she did.

Grace nodded. "I hope you can help with mine. I've had that horse since I was a little girl. My father bought him for me when I was ten."

Emmie glanced at her. Grace had long blonde hair in a braid down her back and lake-blue eyes. Emmie guessed her age to be somewhere in the mid-twenties. Fear radiated from the woman's body; it pulsed inside the cab of the truck.

It took only a few minutes to reach the farm, a neat collection of buildings and barns. The house was yellow with white trim, and was circled by a large front porch that looked down toward town. Flowers filled almost every available space, a messy mix of roses and delphiniums, phlox and heather, most of them starting to show the change of the seasons. Green pastures ran down the gentle slope from the barn to the road, thick trees separating this farm from the next.

"Over here," the woman murmured when they got out of the truck.

The horse was lying on his side, just inside the shelter of the barn. His eyes were closed, and it took a minute or two before Emmie could see that the animal was still breathing.

"Would you mind holding the baby?" Emmie unwrapped her baby sling and handed Robin into Grace's arms.

She made her eyes go soft, a little unfocused, and she knelt beside the animal, running her hands over the head and neck. Stress and fear had stiffened the muscles and made them lock up, as if some kind of sudden jolt had caused the horse to panic. She closed her eyes for a moment, trying to sense whatever it was that had caused the horse to seize. "Did a tree fall around here last night?" She didn't turn to look at Grace but kept her eyes on the animal.

Grace nodded. "Just behind the barn. That windstorm was fierce. When the tree fell, we all jumped, it was so close. Loud enough we thought it was an earthquake for a minute."

Emmie ran her hands down the horse's flank, down the legs. "Feels like he's injured something, back here in the hindquarters. Like he might have jumped when that tree fell." Emmie waited a minute, trying to absorb all the information that was radiating up through her hands and arms and into her being. Trying to figure out if the pain was only in a muscle or if there was some kind of internal damage.

She knelt in the muck of the barn and slowly ran her hands over every inch of the horse's body that she could reach. She concentrated on that pulled muscle, and when the heat began to soften in that area, she moved back to the head. She sat down, taking the horse's head in her lap, and laid her hand on his forehead, gently rubbing.

They could both see that the horse was breathing deeper, long, slow breaths.

Grace stood nearby, Robin balanced in her arms. Tears raced down her cheeks. "I know this is how life is, on a farm. They're born. They die. It's all part of the process." She brushed tears away with the back of her hand. And then she raised her eyes to Emmie. "He's twenty-four years old; it's not like he's a young colt. But I'm not ready to let him go just yet."

Emmie stared into the blue eyes of the woman, and then refocused her attention on the horse. She continued to rub the forehead and jaw and neck. Though she had soothed the torn muscle, Emmie sensed that the horse was still suffering from that feeling of fear, from the adrenaline rush of the life-threatening crash that had started the problem. She kept her hands on the horse's head, rubbing gently. The horse kept his eyes closed. He lay completely still, barely breathing.

"Oh, God." Grace turned away, raised a hand to her mouth, and bit on the side of her finger. With baby Robin still in her arms, Grace sank down on her knees beside the animal.

The horse rolled slightly, raising his head and neck, and pressed his muzzle against Grace's arm. Grace reached to touch him; she watched as he struggled to get his legs beneath him and stand up.

"Easy, boy," Emmie whispered. She continued her massage, even after the horse was standing, working her hands over every part of his body, easing the tension and fear and cramped muscles. Trying to ease the apprehension that had lodged in the horse's mind. Half an hour later, the horse walked over to the hay that Grace had put out earlier that morning and began to eat.

The horse recovered and lived another eight years. And Grace Wheeler became Emmie's best friend.

For Emmie, that was the beginning of earning a living from her skill set. From the moment she first held Robin in her arms, she knew that she could not go back to work at the Drift Inn, that she could not leave this child for hours every day. And so she decided, as if making up her mind was all it took, that she would find a way to make a living that would keep her at home with her baby.

After Grace told a few people about how Emmie managed to help her horse, others showed up. They weren't keen to have that bit of knowledge spread around town, and most of them were even a little embarrassed to have to ask for woo-woo medicine for their dogs and cats and horses and, even once, a chicken. But word spread, and though they called her the "village witch" behind her back, they still showed up when they had an animal in trouble.

Some paid her. Some didn't. Some brought her firewood, or a side of beef, or vegetables from their gardens. Some brought her fleeces from their sheep. Emmie used it all. She cleaned the fleece and carded it, and

Kate Taylor taught her to spin and weave. Emmie may not have had a great deal of cash, but neither did the people who needed her services with their horses or dogs or cats.

The great abundance of wool gave Emmie opportunity for another income stream. After she spun the wool, she used her knitting needles to make scarves and hats and mittens and sweaters for herself and Robin. With the long dark hours of winter, and the excess of wool she traded for, she soon had extras to sell at the Christmas bazaar, held every year at the old Hadley house.

That first day of her first Christmas fair was awful. No one wanted to buy from her. Despite the fact that she knew most of the people in town and had treated animals for a fair share of them, none of them were willing to acknowledge Emmie's role in their lives. They stayed away from her booth, and none of them would dare to look her in the eyes. The idea of wearing something made by the village witch, made by that woman who did all that weird mumbo jumbo with the animals, was far more than any of the townspeople could handle. As if anything Emmie touched might carry some kind of dark magic.

Sales stayed at a slim nothing until Saturday afternoon, when Maggie Edwards walked in the door and moved slowly around all the tables. She stopped at Emmie's booth and picked up a thick sweater, a spectacular cabled Aran cardigan in deep gray wool that Emmie had carded and cleaned and spun herself. Maggie paid her $200, an absolute fortune in 1972.

Maggie put it on immediately, running her hands down the fronts of the cables, and said as loudly as she could, "Witch, my eye. You people, I swear." She turned to look at everyone who stood in the room, meeting each set of eyes until they were forced to look away. After she left, a few brave souls stepped up and bought mittens or a hat, believing that if Maggie Edwards thought it was safe to buy Emmie's knitwear, it might be possible to wear it without incident.

The next year, sales picked up. Maggie had worn her gray sweater all year and hadn't died or become lame, so perhaps Emmie's knitwear wasn't cursed, after all. She never made a fortune at those Christmas sales, but every bit helped in eking out a life for herself and her daughter.

Maggie might have made it acceptable to buy Emmie's knitwear, and even to wear it, but that didn't keep people from casting side-eyes at Emmie when she walked down the street. And nothing would ever keep them from turning to whisper to each other as soon as she had passed. She attracted gossip the way most people attracted lint.

That was over forty years ago. Emmie walked down the road with her old dog Pete, stopping at the edge of the cemetery, as she always did. Maggie may have helped her out, way back then, but they hadn't spoken to each other since 1987. Emmie gazed up the hill, in the direction of Maggie's cabin. The trees were too thick for a direct view, but if she gazed long enough, her eye usually picked up a glimmer of window glass, or sometimes the pale glow of a lamp, always lit in these dark days of winter.

It certainly did not appear that Maggie was ever going to forgive her.

FOURTEEN

Alex stood at the mirror in the front hallway, looking closely at the skin around her eyes. The bruises had faded; a yellow color remained, something like you might expect with a person who had had the flu. She stepped back, searching for the small makeup bag that she carried. It wasn't much—just a tube of concealer and a small bottle of foundation. Just enough to cover the weird colors that sometimes bloomed across her face. She pulled out the tube of concealer and squeezed a drop of white goo on her fingers. She dotted it around the discoloration, blending it in as well as she could, wincing once or twice when she caught an area that was still tender.

She stared at that eye, remembering the eye of the orca when it had rolled under the boat.

The memory came flying back, a sudden specter from the past, as if she were standing in front of that same mirror at work, all those years ago. She'd gone to the ladies' room, taking her time in the stall until the room was empty, and had then stood in front of the mirror, trying to apply the concealer she had bought just a few days before. Alex had never worn makeup; she had bypassed all those girls in high school and college who might have taught her the proper ways to apply it. She had practiced a few times now, but she still managed to make a gooey mess more often than not.

The door to the restroom swung open, and Renee Timothy walked in. Instead of making a beeline for a stall and giving Alex a chance to hide her makeup bag, she went straight to the sink. Alex saw that her hands were covered with ink.

She looked at Alex in the mirror in front of them. "I didn't know you wore makeup, Alex."

Alex swallowed and zipped her bag closed, stowing it in her purse. "I don't really. Not much, anyway." She met Renee's eyes in the glass. "Trying to even out my skin tone a little."

Renee nodded and reached for a paper towel. "Yeah, you do look a little tired." She smiled broadly. "Must be that new husband, eh?" She poked her elbow toward Alex's side. "Keeping you up nights? Did he wrap it in a big red bow for your Christmas present?"

Alex bit her lip and tipped her head, a gesture that could mean absolutely anything.

That wasn't exactly what had happened, but she felt no need to explain. The two women were just back from the Christmas holiday, the library being closed along with the rest of the campus for Christmas and New Year's. If Renee had seen Alex's eye a week ago, there would have been no question about what had caused those dark circles.

They'd been married almost a year at that point. Up until then, most of Daniel's threats had come in the form of a loud voice, or slapping a hand on the table, or grabbing her a bit too forcefully. This was different.

Her mother had been cooking for three days, excited as she always was for Christmas. Frances made the traditional foods that she had grown up with: tamales, *bizcochitos*, pumpkin empanadas, fruit salad. All those years that it had been just Alex and her mother, but Frances had always cooked as if a very large family might appear on their doorstep, making far more food than the two of them could ever eat.

And her mother was always happy to share, if there did happen to be someone at her office who needed a place to spend Christmas. She loved it, every part of the food and lights and Christmas carols. This would be the first Christmas with Daniel in the family, and Frances had gone all out.

"Ready?" Alex asked.

Daniel was sprawled in his favorite chair in their living room, legs spread wide, a beer in hand. The television set was blaring. He looked up at her and waved his hand for her to move. "I'm watching the game."

Alex moved to the side and looked at the clock. "Mom said two, and it's already ten minutes till."

He ignored her, taking a swig of beer, his eyes locked on the television.

She waited for him to respond. "Can't you watch it at Mom's? She's been cooking for three days . . ."

She never had a chance to finish that sentence. Before she saw it coming, he had stood and swung, hitting her squarely in the left eye. She staggered and fell, the pain sending sparks all over her skin and face. She raised her hand and saw that blood was dripping from her nose.

Daniel stood over her for a moment. "Mom this. Mom that. You're *my* wife, goddamn it! We'll go when I'm ready. If I'm ready."

He left the room. She heard him in the kitchen, grabbing another beer and popping it open. She tipped her head back, trying to stop the trickle of blood from her nose, and headed to the bathroom. The eye wasn't black yet, but it was swelling quickly, and there were broken blood vessels. She leaned over the sink, trying to get a good look at the damage, trying not to give in to the tears. She could hear Daniel in the front room, yelling, *"YES!"* as his team scored.

She cleaned up as best she could, balling up her ruined shirt and stuffing it in the trash. And then she headed to the kitchen for ice. Her whole body trembled; she forced herself not to cry. She called her mother fifteen minutes later.

"Mom?" Her voice vibrated with emotion; she could barely breathe, her nose starting to swell along with her eye. She was sick from the pain, sick from the idea that her husband would haul back and hit her right in the face. Sick sick sick that she would not be going to spend Christmas with her mother. Frances would be sitting alone, with all that food. Alex forced herself to swallow, to keep going.

"Mom?" She gulped, another wave of emotion threatening to pull her under. She forced herself to breathe. "I'm not feeling well. I think I might be coming down with the flu." Alex hated the thought of lying to her mother, but she had no idea what else to do. She wanted to run to her, to cry on her shoulder, to curse the man who had just done this to her. But she had watched her mother suffer enough, all those years ago, and she wasn't about to lay anything else on Frances' shoulders. "I don't think there's any way I can make it today." That part, at least, was true.

"Oh, honey!" Her mother waited a fraction of a second, the way she always did when she was trying to compose herself. "Is there anything I can do? Do you want me to come over there? I could pack up some of the food. At least Daniel could have Christmas, and—"

"No, Mom, that's okay." Alex felt tears stinging her eyes. "I don't want you to catch this . . . whatever it is."

A moment passed, and Frances' voice was soft and quiet. "Okay. I hope you feel better. Call me if you need anything."

"I will." Alex fought hard to keep her voice level.

Her mother waited, as if holding on to her daughter. "Merry Christmas, honey."

Alex took a shower, put more ice on her eye, and went to bed. He came in around eleven, the smell of sour beer breath enough to make her feel like she might throw up. When he put his hand on her arm, she jerked away.

"Alex. Alex. Alex. Are you okay?"

She lay completely still, her back to him.

"I didn't mean to do that, Alex. It's just . . . it's just that . . . I love you so much. You have no idea how much." He took a breath. "Sometimes I . . . I can't stand the thought of sharing you with anyone. Not even your mother." He rubbed his hand up and down her arm. "I just want you all to myself."

Tears were leaking from the eye that still opened.

"I can't live without you, Alex. I really can't." He nuzzled his whiskered face against her upper arm and lay down behind her, wrapping his arms around her.

Alex stood in front of the mirror at the house in Copper Cove. She spoke to her reflection, as if speaking to the man who had hit her, who had turned that eye to such an awful color.

"Never again," she murmured. She felt her jaw go hard, her teeth grinding together. "You will never hit me again."

She stood, staring into the mirror. Her musing was broken by a loud *click*, like the sound of a door being unlocked. Alex came slowly back to awareness, staring at her face in the mirror. And that was when she saw it, reflected in the glass right next to her face. The door to the back porch behind her slowly swung open. Cold air rushed in and swirled up around her.

She stared into the glass. No one was there.

Alex turned and went to the back door. She stepped onto the back porch and lifted the shade to look outside, out into the dark curtain of giant cedars. There was no one there. No one outside, no one on the porch. No one that she could see. She closed the door and turned the lock.

She shivered, still wrapped in the embrace of that rush of cold air.

FIFTEEN

By the time the afternoon rolled around, Alex was ready to get out of the house. There was no television, no radio, in this house on the cove, and she was hungry for sound. She headed downhill, not exactly sure where she was going. And then she saw the warm glow of lamplight at the old Hadley house. She hadn't planned on going back, but as soon as she noticed the light, she decided. When she opened the door, the smell of strong coffee and a ring of laughter rose to greet her.

"Alex! You look like hell." It was the first thing out of Caroline's mouth when Alex walked into the parlor.

"Thanks. Nice to see you, too." Alex stood for a moment, looking around the group.

"Ignore her," Grace said, stopping her spinning wheel for a moment. "We are glad you could make it, Alex. I was really hoping you would come."

"I didn't mean anything awful by it. I mean, cripes! She is working for Maggie. And living in a haunted house." Caroline huffed.

Alex looked up; Caroline's eyes were focused on her knitting, a narrow scarf on huge needles.

"Everyone in town lives in a haunted house," Grace quipped. "According to the venerable editor of our local newspaper, anyway."

Grace stopped spinning and indicated the chair next to her. "Alex, come sit here by me. I brought a spinning wheel that I'm going to loan to you. Spinning is the perfect medicine for anything that ails you."

Alex moved to the chair next to her and sank into it, trying to force her body to relax. "I don't know how to spin."

Grace smiled. "You will."

"We're glad you could make it, Alex. I was hoping Caroline hadn't scared you off for good," David said. "We don't often get someone under fifty in this group. Forgive us if we latch on to you like a life preserver."

Alex smiled. "I saw the light on and thought I'd say hello." She felt better already, surrounded by this small group of spinners.

"From the look on your face, it appears that no one has shared the secret of surviving winter in the Pacific Northwest." David's head was tipped back, looking at her down the length of his nose.

"You mean coffee and baked goods?" Alex asked.

David laughed. He shook his head. "No, although that is an important piece of survival strategy. But the other absolute necessity can be found in a bottle." He shook a bottle, held inside his fist. "Hold out your hand. I'm dispensing drugs over here."

Caroline leaned over to examine what he was shaking out into Alex's palm. "Since when does heroin come in gelcaps?"

David turned and gave her a pained look. "Vitamin D. We have a severe shortage out here. Short days, long nights, very little sun this far north. I mean . . . you could stand out in the rain all day, naked as a jaybird, all your skin exposed to whatever light is available, and you still wouldn't absorb enough vitamin D to make a difference. And of course, you'd freeze to death first."

"Is that what you've been doing on your patio?" Caroline leaned back away from him. "Absorbing vitamin D?"

David ignored her. "You've been here what? A week?"

Alex nodded. "Pretty close, yeah."

"Then I saved you just in time. Another three or four days, and you'll be standing on the side of a bridge, thinking your best career path is to jump.

"The more depleted you get, the worse things seem. Tired, sweaty, depressed. The list of troubles from vitamin D deficiency sound like cocaine withdrawal at a Betty Ford clinic. Nasty stuff." He shook his head and made a face, and showed her the bottle in his hand. "You'll want to get a bottle of this as soon as you leave here today. Or maybe a case."

Alex swallowed her gelcaps and nodded. "Thanks, David."

"This will help, too," Grace said, clicking the parts of a small spinning wheel into place. "Spinning is almost as good as meditating. It's my happy place. All my troubles just slide away."

David stopped his own spinning wheel and pulled his glasses down, sending Grace a hard look over the tops. "Don't lie, Grace. It doesn't become you."

"All right, maybe it isn't a happy place right at the beginning."

"Or maybe even the first six months," David added. He turned to look at Alex. "But once you get the hang of it . . . ahhh. Peace is yours. Along with way too much handspun yarn."

"Peace sounds nice," Alex murmured. "I wouldn't know what to do with the yarn, though."

Grace looked at Alex for a moment, searching her face.

"Don't worry," David said, leaning forward and tapping her knee. "We can help with that, too."

Grace went through a whirlwind description of the parts of the spinning wheel. "So this is roving," she began, handing Alex a pile of white fluff, a substance that was cleaner and fluffier than when attached to the sheep, but not quite to the stage of yarn. "You're going to hold this in your left hand, loosely, like you're holding a baby bird."

David was spinning away in the chair on Alex's left side. It sounded almost like music, the rhythm of his feet on the treadles, the soft song of the wheel turning. Alex watched him for a moment. He made it look easy. The sound of the wheel was soothing.

"And with your right hand, you're going to draft—pull a few of the fibers loose from the bunch. You treadle the wheel, let those fibers build up twist, and then you feed them onto the bobbin."

Caroline sat forward. "And all while you are treadling with both feet. It's like patting your head and rubbing your stomach as you dance across the living room. Don't let these old ladies fool you, Alex. Spinning is nothing but an exercise in creative cursing."

David smiled. "Absolutely true, at the beginning. You will spit out curse words that you never knew you had even heard before. But most of us"—he gave Caroline a pointed look—"can graduate from the cussing stage to the 'oh my God, I've got it' stage. And then . . . the wonders of handspun are at your fingertips." He sat back and raised his eyebrows.

Caroline pursed her lips and leaned forward, as if sharing a dark secret. "The only reason David likes spinning is because it gives him an excuse to whack his wool."

Alex felt her lower jaw drop. "Excuse me?"

"Caroline! Must you always be so crude?" Grace looked at Alex and shook her head. "I believe it is Caroline's mission in life to shock people. She feeds on it."

"That's right," David chimed in. He leaned forward slightly in his chair. "And you are nowhere near being ready to whack your wool, just yet."

Grace sighed. "The two of them are like teenagers, aren't they? But whacking the wool is part of the process. First, you spin a bobbin of yarn; that's called a single ply. And then you spin another. Ply them together. Then you'll take that two-ply yarn and soak it in hot water. Take that skein of wool, still slightly wet, and whack it hard several times. Against the floor or a kitchen counter. It helps to strengthen the plies and straighten everything out."

"Oh," Alex breathed, sitting back a little.

"Just be sure to take your glasses off first," Grace added, looking at Alex over the tops of her purple frames. She shuddered, and then continued her spinning.

"Yes, exactly," David continued. "You have to whack it really hard." He sat back and started his own wheel again. "So Grace, where do you whack your wool?"

She looked at him and scowled. After a moment, spinning away on her own wheel, she murmured, "I like the kitchen counter."

David nodded sagely. "I like to whack mine on the patio. But it does tend to be hard on the patio furniture," he continued.

"Man, your patio sees a lot of action, doesn't it?" Caroline said.

Grace said, "Hush, and let her learn. She doesn't have to worry about whacking anything just yet. Here, Alex. Start by using just the foot treadles. See if you can make the wheel stop, and then start turning again, the same direction."

Alex started practicing, moving the treadles with her feet. It was harder than it looked, controlling the direction of the wheel, making it stop and start without going backward, but she could feel, almost immediately, that it was a distraction from her troubles, something that required all her concentration. After fifteen minutes or so, just messing with the foot treadles, Grace gave her a small pile of roving, and Alex tried doing all the maneuvers at the same time. "Damn it!" she spat, within a minute of beginning. "I broke it already."

"Is that the best you can do?" Caroline laughed. "Come on, Alex. Show us what you've got. A couple of *fricking frick frick frick*s are in order when you start to spin. Or a *son of a stinking sailor*." Caroline waited a moment, while Alex tried again to get the fiber to spin and feed onto the bobbin. "Besides, you work for Maggie. You need a whole arsenal of curse words."

Alex started the wheel again. "Ahhh . . . ," she gasped. "I did it, for like three seconds."

Grace touched her hand softly. "No need to put the death grip on that roving, Alex."

David laughed again. "Like learning to water ski, no? You drink a whole lot of lake at first, for those few seconds when you can actually stand up and feel the water beneath you. But . . . the fact that you've managed three seconds of spinning? That puts you way ahead of our little redheaded waitress over here."

Caroline scowled at him.

For a few moments, the only sounds were those of the spinning wheels and the clack of knitting needles in Caroline's hands. Occasional bursts of frustration exploded from Alex's corner. Fifteen minutes later, she stopped, exhausted. "This is harder than it looks—trying to coordinate all those different things at the same time."

"Told you," Caroline quipped. "So how is Mad Maggie the last few days?"

Alex took her feet off the wheel and rested her back against the chair. "She took me out to see orcas this morning."

Grace leaned forward, her mouth in an O. "Wow. You haven't been here a whole week and already you've seen the orcas? In winter?"

Alex nodded. "One swam under the boat, and it turned and looked right at me. It was the most amazing thing I've ever seen. They seem so . . . intelligent. Aware."

"Did Maggie give you her orca speech?" David asked.

"Speech? As in singular?" Caroline interjected. "She's got a Navy sonar speech, and the dangers of salmon farming speech, and an oh my God all the shipping speech. Watch out, Alex. You could get speechified working there."

"Did she tell you they can read minds?" David asked, his spinning stopped, his voice dropped to a murmur.

Alex looked at him and pushed her glasses up on her nose. "She told me about their sonar—about being able to see what's inside things by bouncing sound waves off different objects. Like ultrasound or something."

David shook his head. "No, it goes further than that, although I don't imagine Maggie would be the one to tell you about it. She only values what she considers 'real' science. Anything that's been verified by scientific procedures."

"So what makes you think they can read minds?"

David leaned forward in the chair, looking around as if making sure that there was no one to overhear him. "You know about the captures? All those killer whales that were captured in the late sixties and early seventies? They were taking orcas to all these marine parks around the country—teaching them to do tricks for the audience. Quite a moneymaker.

"Well, there was one orca lady—she lives up in BC now, but she had started studying orcas a few years before that. She would go into these marine parks after hours and record the sounds the captive orcas were making, and take notes about what they were doing when they made the sounds. Trying to figure out which sounds went with which activities. And one day, she's standing there, talking to one of the trainers, and the trainer asks her if she has any other ideas for tricks they could teach the orcas for the shows. Maybe something she had seen orcas do in the wild.

"She told the trainer that she had seen orcas out in these waters kind of roll onto their sides as they're swimming by, and then flap their pectoral fin. Just like they were doing the royal wave." David held his arm close to his chest and demonstrated. "The trainer really liked that idea and said she would start working on how to teach them to do that. And the two women turn around, and there in the tank, right in front of them, the orca turns on its side and swims around the perimeter, waving its pectoral fin."

"Huh. Could the fish have understood what the women were saying? The language?" Alex asked.

"Maybe. Orcas and dolphins have both shown an ability to understand lots of words—even to pick up on subtle changes in sentence structure." David leaned forward again, as if he were talking about something very secretive. "But that seems to me to be more than understanding a few words.

"And there's another story. One of my favorites. I actually wrote about it for the paper. It was in all the papers around here—even the *Seattle Times*."

"Cut to the chase, Mr. Hill. You don't have to start with Genesis," Caroline advised.

"The Suquamish Tribe? They're down close to Bainbridge Island, just west of Seattle. It happened in October 2013. The Seattle Museum had given them back a lot of their ancestral materials, including some rare tribal artifacts. Several of the elders took the Bainbridge ferry over to Seattle, to pick up all this stuff and bring it back to their own museum, on the tribal lands. It was a really big deal to the tribe. Some of those things had been taken from them a hundred years before. So here they are on the ferry, heading back to Bainbridge Island, with this cargo of precious artifacts, and the ferry has to stop, completely stop, right in the middle of the Sound. It was surrounded by a pod of orcas, swimming and breaching and flipping their tails. Like they were happy. Celebrating. That route has two ferries, running every forty-five minutes—one headed toward Seattle, the other headed the other way. Only one ferry that had to stop that whole day, because of the orcas. The one carrying all those tribal artifacts. A ferry sometimes has to stop to let a pod of orcas swim past. But jumping and playing? Explain that to me."

"Wow," Alex said. She sat back in her chair.

David continued, "Come on, Grace, help me out here. You're best friends with the animal energy guru. Are they reading minds or what?"

Grace let out a long sigh, her own spinning abandoned, her hands resting in her lap. "I don't know. And I don't know what Emmie would say about it. But I can tell you that I've seen a lot of animals over the years that know a whole lot more than we think they do.

"And I have another orca story, although you may not believe it. My husband and I were out on our boat, several years ago, and when we came back to the dock, there was a man there, frantic. He'd gone out in his kayak and told his dog to stay on the beach. He'd done this kind of thing before, and the dog usually stayed put. But this time, when he came back, the dog was gone.

"We helped him look. My husband went back out in the boat, looking for the dog out in the water. I helped that man look up and down the beach. Nothing." Grace looked up at the people around her. "And then a small group of orcas came up, and one of them had the dog, riding on his back. They swam as close as they could, and the dog jumped off and swam in to shore."

"You're making that up," Caroline said.

Grace shook her head. "It was like the orcas *knew* that the dog was in trouble. Picked up on it somehow. Even though it was a completely different species. And then they figured out where the dog belonged. As if they could sense all the fear and emotion in the owner."

Grace stared into the fire for a moment. "Did they pick up on some thought? Or some other form of energy? Some emotion?" She shrugged. "I don't know. But they picked up on something." Grace turned and looked at Caroline. "And apparently it has happened more than once. Some of those stories are published."

Grace continued, "There are stories about people in London, in World War II, who could tell by the way their pets were acting if an air strike was coming, even before the air-raid sirens went off. And another story about a herd of water buffalo, grazing near the beach before that tsunami in 2004. They raised their heads, as if they could hear or sense something out in the water, half an hour before anything actually happened. And whatever it was they sensed sent them stampeding up the hill, away from the beach.

"I believe animals are a lot more sensitive, a lot more intelligent, than we have ever imagined." Grace picked up her roving, but she did not start spinning again. "But I think there are *people* who can do that, too. Like Emmie. I don't know how she does what she does. I don't know if she picks up on thoughts from the animal or if she picks up on some other clues. But somehow, she figures out where the animal is hurting.

"I've watched her several times over the years. It makes me think of the way detectives are trained to tell if a person is lying or not. Maybe they can't read the criminal's mind, but they can pick up on those subtle signs in body language. Like looking away, or touching their face, or waiting too long to answer. They say that some women blush when they lie. I would imagine that there is a lot more to this energy sensitivity thing than any of us really understand, at the moment."

Grace looked up.

David raised his eyebrows, as if to say, *I told you so*, and leaned back in his chair. He picked up his roving and started his wheel again, his eyes on the yarn that was spinning from his hand to the wheel. "So that orca looked you right in the eye this morning?"

Alex nodded.

"Well then, watch out, Alexandra. Whatever secrets you thought you were keeping? All the Southern Resident orcas know them by now."

SIXTEEN

Alex sat down at her desk in Maggie's cabin the next morning. She had a cup of coffee next to her, and she turned on the computer, waiting for the antiquated machine to fire up. Outside, the branches of the cedars, heavy with drops of water, caught the sunlight, looking as if they were decked out in their finest jewels. She stared for a moment, caught by the way the light made everything sparkle.

Alex reached inside the box she'd been working through and grabbed another pile of papers and articles. When she lifted it from the box, a small photograph slipped loose and fluttered down to the floor. Alex stooped and picked it up.

It was a picture of Maggie's boat, the same one Alex had been on the day before, and three people, smiling broadly. The woman in the middle had dark hair and glasses, but was much younger than the doctor of marine biology who sat across the room. Alex stood and walked over to Maggie's desk. "Is this you?" she asked, holding the photograph out for Maggie.

The woman peered through her glasses. "Yes, it is. Before my hair went gray. That must have been taken . . . oh, I don't know. Late eighties, maybe."

"Is that your son?" Alex asked, indicating the bright-eyed young man standing at the wheel of the boat. He was tall and muscular and smiling broadly in the photo. Alex glanced at the photographs of a young man that stood on the shelves at the back of the room. There were numerous framed photographs of him.

Maggie nodded. "Yes, that's Brian. He worked with me in the summers during high school and a few of his college breaks."

Alex looked at mother and son in the photograph. They were strikingly similar, with strong jawlines and body height. "And the girl? Is that his girlfriend?"

Maggie glanced at the photo, readjusting her glasses. "Hmm. Some intern, I think. I've had so many, I can't remember all their names."

"She's very pretty," Alex murmured.

Maggie shrugged and turned away. "If you say so." She returned to the papers on her desk.

"Do you want me to scan this?" Alex asked, holding up the photo. "I know it's not related to the science, but there may come a day when someone will want to have archival photos of you at your work."

Maggie looked over the tops of her glasses. "That won't be necessary."

Alex returned to her desk, laid the photo to the side, and began work on the first scientific paper in her stack. She was just starting to find her rhythm, to let her mind get lost in the information, when she was interrupted.

Maggie stood and walked over to her desk, holding a newspaper in front of her. "Have you seen this?" she asked.

Alex swallowed. She felt a flush rising to her face, and she shook her head. "I haven't really been keeping up with the news." Her heart slammed against her rib cage, the sound so loud she thought sure Maggie would notice. Her years with Daniel had made her afraid of everything, always expecting the worst.

Maggie put the paper on the desk. It was the *Seattle Times*. The headline read: "Ninth Orca Baby Born This Year." Alex exhaled and lowered her head to read the story about the scientist farther up the coast, who had spotted a ninth new baby in the Southern Resident Killer Whales. "Wow. This is great news."

Maggie stood at the window, a cup of coffee in her hand. "Yes, it is."

"Is that unusual? To have so many babies in one year?"

Maggie shrugged. "It's happened a few times. I don't remember there ever being *nine* in one year. But considering there were no new babies at all in 2013 and 2014, this is a good sign. Means they have found enough to eat, at least for a while."

Maggie took a swig of her coffee. "In the entire population of Southern Residents, there are only two dozen reproductive females. The window for having babies is pretty narrow, and this population is fragile. *Every* whale is important. And so is every single baby."

The ringing of a bell rose up from the streets of town, and they both turned toward the sound. It was a little like a church bell, only less significant, the note higher-pitched and not as resonant. Alex stood and moved to the window.

"What's that?" she asked.

"Whale bell. Whenever someone sees a whale out in the strait, they yank on that bell, so everyone can run out and take a look." Maggie's face held the closest thing to a smile that Alex had yet seen. "Not necessarily orcas. Could be a gray whale or who knows what. But grab your stuff. Let's go look."

They hopped into Maggie's truck, "just in case we have to keep driving," and Maggie steered it the three blocks downhill to Main Street.

Next to the Strait Up Tavern was a tiny park, with steps that led down to a wooden deck and railing, looking out to sea. A man stood there, ringing the whale bell. People were trickling out of houses and businesses, many of them in pajamas and slippers and coats thrown on over. It was nine in the morning, and moving fast did not seem to be on anyone's agenda.

Maggie pulled the truck to the curb, and they hopped out, moving downhill to stand next to the clusters of people who had gathered in the park and were filling up the observation deck.

"Orcas. It's orcas," the man at the bell called out. "And a baby with them," he bubbled, watching through binoculars.

Everyone strained to see, and those who had binoculars were sharing them with others. Maggie stared out through her own glasses, and Alex stood, trying to get a good view. "Looks like part of Granny's clan," Maggie said, her voice bubbly. "And let's see—a couple of her grandchildren."

Maggie handed the glasses to Alex, so that she could take a look.

"She doesn't have any children that are still living. Granny is believed to be over one hundred years old. I can't see her, yet, but maybe she's out there. After all these years, seeing J Pod—any of the Southern Residents, for that matter—is like seeing family."

"Will this be enough to take them off the endangered list?" Alex asked.

"Oh, God, no! The odds are that half of these babies won't make it through the first year. We don't yet know if any of these calves are females. And then we have to worry about the babies, and their parents, finding enough to eat. There are so many things that can go wrong. Even with all these new babies, there are still less than eighty of the Southern Residents. That's a precariously low number to try and keep a population going. Imagine if there were only seventy-eight humans left in the world."

Her eyes still glued to Maggie's binoculars, Alex stared out to sea, where she could see a group of six or seven orcas. They swam close together, one or two coming up for air, pushing a huge spray of water into the sky. The exhalations caught the light, turning into miracle explosions of color and sparkle. Those blackfish would curve back into the water, and behind them, a few more would rise in graceful arcs, taking in the air.

And there, just between two larger orcas, came the new baby, rising up next to her mother. While the older fish were black and white, the baby's coloring included a faded yellowish brown.

A cheer went up from the people standing in the park. The sight brought smiles and laughter and louder voices to everyone who stood watching, as if that baby orca were spreading a germ of happiness to everyone who witnessed the youngster. Alex felt a surge of energy, an excitement, and she stood on tiptoe, breathing in the magic of the air on that cold December morning. Beside her, Maggie Edwards did the same, a smile lighting her face, crinkling her eyes behind her glasses.

The crowd watched as the orcas swam past, heading farther south.

Maggie turned to Alex. "Let's head down to Lime Kiln Point, see if we can get another look. Maybe they'll stop for breakfast. Might be salmon there."

"Sounds great," Alex said, turning to follow Maggie to the truck.

Emmie Porter stood at the back of the crowd of people, slightly removed from the rest of the group. She had a dog on a leash, milling around the grass at her feet, sniffing. She was staring out to sea, at the group of orcas moving past, the tiny new baby in their midst.

Alex had never actually seen Emmie smile. She was smiling now, her face glowing as she watched those orcas. Her eyes were a deep brown; her features were well spaced, with high cheekbones. Alex had not noticed it before, but as she looked at Emmie smile, there could be no doubt—the woman had once been quite beautiful.

Emmie turned, and their eyes met. She looked at Alex without making any indication that she knew her, without saying hello. Her eyes traveled down the length of Alex's body, stopping at the stomach area. She stared, as if she could see through the coat and layers of clothing that Alex wore. Alex unconsciously brought her arm across her middle. Emmie looked up, meeting her eyes, and the smile drained from her face.

SEVENTEEN

Alex sat at a chair by the front window, the small spinning wheel in front of her on the floor. She started the treadles and began pulling fibers out of the nest of roving in her left hand. It was becoming a habit with her. Almost as soon as she came home from Maggie's every evening, as soon as she had eaten a bowl of soup, she sat down at the wheel. The spinsters were right. The gentle sounds of the wheel turning, the motions of moving her hands and feet, the concentration of trying to make the yarn even, totally absorbed her attention. It was like dropping into a zone of quiet, a place so deep inside that she had not known it existed. This was a place of total peace, a place far removed from all the horrors of her past. After a few minutes of spinning, she stopped, her eyes coming to rest on the window as another long-buried memory floated to the surface.

For someone who was a supposed expert on categorizing and sorting and organizing information into patterns, Alex had completely missed the cycle of abuse that was happening in her life with Daniel. Each incident was handled separately, as a completely unrelated occurrence. Each incident required adjustment, required learning the new limitations imposed on her existence. But she approached each one as if it were an isolated event—just one more thing that she needed to deal with. Adjust. Normalize. Move forward.

She had not begun to see the patterns, repeating again and again and again, until now—now that she was two thousand miles away. Now, after eleven years of abuse had already happened. Now, when it was too late to change anything, when it was too late to enjoy her mother's company.

Her mother had seen those patterns. As quiet as Frances Turner could be, as much as she worked to keep her opinions to herself, they were evident in the look in her eyes. Almost like looking into the eye of that orca a few days ago, the memory curling up from the depths of her psyche like the mist that was rising from the graves of the dead in the cemetery outside. Her mother had had that same look in her eye—as if she saw everything. As if she understood everything.

They had been married six years when it happened. Alex opened her eyes to unfamiliar surroundings. There was an IV dripping into her arm; she was lying in a hospital bed with the railings up. She could hear the noises of nurses talking, people moving around, the sounds of televisions in other rooms. Alex turned her head, intense waves of pain flooding over her, and found her mother sitting in the chair next to the bed.

She looked in her mother's eyes, and Frances let out a sigh of relief, dropping her rosary into her lap. Snippets of memory from the night before came rising to the surface. Alex remembered being in an ambulance, blood pooling on her legs and thighs and stomach. She had a flashback of the look on the face of the EMT who was monitoring her blood pressure on the way to the ER. She vaguely remembered the lights in the ER, too bright, almost painful to look at, and she had closed her eyes. She could hear Daniel, his voice full of concern and fear, telling the doctor that Alex had fallen on the stairs in their condo, trying to carry a box from upstairs.

"All the way to the bottom," she remembered him saying.

Alex remained mute, shut off behind her closed eyes and the need to turn it all off—the lights, the noises, the voices of the doctors and nurses as they clustered around her. She remembered the oxygen mask; she remembered the doctor telling Daniel he would have to wait outside.

When she woke, with no idea how many hours had passed, she was in a hospital bed, in a semiprivate room. Her mother sat in a chair, the sun from the window behind her gilding Frances' hair to bright silver, like a Christmas angel. Daniel was nowhere to be seen.

Alex met her mother's eyes. Every inch of her body ached. She swallowed, her throat painful and scratchy. "My baby?" she whispered.

Her mother looked at her for a moment, her eyes full of pain, and then shook her head.

Alex turned her head away, tears flowing into the pillow.

They released her four days later. Her body was a mass of bruises; she could manage walking to the bathroom, but not much farther. Daniel was there, playing the concerned husband, pushing her wheelchair down the hall and into the elevator, to the front doors of the hospital. Her mother walked alongside, carrying the flowers sent by Alex's colleagues at the University library.

They had all agreed that Alex would stay with her mother for a week or two, until she could get her strength back. The stairs to the bedroom in the house that she shared with Daniel were out of the question, and Alex was secretly relieved that she did not have to go home with him.

He wheeled her to the passenger door of Frances' Subaru and helped Alex maneuver into the front seat of the car. And then he knelt down, squatting on the pavement beside her, and took her hands in his. "I have that job in Las Cruces, so I'll be gone a few days. But if you need anything . . ."

Alex nodded. She wanted, more than anything, to jerk her hands away from him. She could not bear his touch; she could not stomach the smell of the hair cream that he used to tame his thick curls. She looked at the top of his thick brown hair as he bent to kiss her hand, and all she could think of was grabbing that hair and yanking hard. She wanted to kick him, to watch the surprise blossom on his face when he fell backward onto the sidewalk. Instead, she took a deep breath and swallowed her feelings. Swallowed the hatred. Swallowed the anger. And nodded once again.

She moved into the bedroom that she had had since the fifth grade, sleeping under the quilt that her grandmother Edna had made when she was little. She ate chicken tortilla soup and pumpkin bread—at least she made an attempt to eat, since her mother was trying so hard to provide all of Alex's favorite foods. But mostly, she lay curled in a ball, in the fetal position, staring straight ahead, seeing nothing.

She'd been five months into the pregnancy, and for the first time in a long time, Alex had felt excited, hopeful even. The baby was the answer, and she could feel it in every fiber of her being. Daniel would ease his grip on her life, once he had a child to look after. And she would have something to call her own, someone who needed her and loved her and wouldn't dress that love in jabs and punches and sarcastic comments that cut to the bone.

Now her hope was gone. Her excitement for the future had drained away, just as the blood of their child had drained onto the floor of their home. The doctors had told her there was little hope that she could conceive again with all her internal injuries.

Her respite lasted ten days. She was starting to move again; she and her mother were spending time on the little patio in the backyard that Frances had filled with geraniums and pansies and petunias. Her appetite had returned, and she was eating more than just a few bites.

And that's when he showed up again. As if he had a radar for the exact moment when she might be finding her strength. As if he had a radar for the exact moment she was secretly pulling away, preparing herself to leave. There he was, knocking on the door of her mother's small house, bearing a huge bouquet of yellow roses.

"You're looking better," he said.

Alex nodded, just barely. "I've been resting a lot. And my mother has been cooking." She did not want to see him, did not want to talk to him. All she really wanted was for him to go away, to leave her alone, to let her find a little peace.

Daniel looked up at Frances, who took the flowers from his hand. "That's good. I know how you love her cooking."

Alex looked at him, wondering what he was up to. She knew him well enough, or maybe she was just cynical enough, to believe that compliments always had something attached; they were always a part of some scheme, an attempt to oil the machine as he marched ahead with his own agenda.

He nodded at Alex. "But I imagine Frances is getting a little tired of all the work, don't you?"

Frances came into the living room, bearing the vase of yellow roses. "Never. I like cooking. And it's so much nicer to have Alex to cook for. Somehow it never tastes the same when I'm cooking for myself."

He looked at Frances. Her words were pleasant; her face was calm and composed. A flicker of anger flashed in Daniel's eyes as he watched her. He nodded. "Good, good. I'm glad. But everyone needs a day off now and then. What do you say, Alex?" He bent down on one knee, just in front of her chair. She shifted her knees to avoid him. "How about lunch at Rio Seco? Give your mother the afternoon off?"

It was a show, a part he was playing. Alex didn't buy it anymore, and she was certain that her mother didn't either. Daniel was the only one of the three of them that still believed his acting was real.

"I know how you love the chicken mole enchiladas. Maybe some flan for dessert?"

Alex stared at him, a flicker of interest flashing briefly in her resolve. It was her favorite restaurant, her favorite meal. She loved sitting by the fireplace, looking out the windows at the town of Albuquerque below them. And other than going out on the patio, she had not been out of the house since the accident. Alex looked at her mother. Frances said nothing; she gave no movement or sign about how she felt. But there was a look in her eyes, a plea. Alex turned away from it.

"We have a lot to talk about," Daniel continued. "The two of us." He pressed on, as if he could sense her willpower dissolving, like a boxer who senses his opponent may be tiring.

It was just one lunch—just an hour, no more. They did have things to talk about. And she fell into the trap that had caught her so many times in the past. Some part of her wanted to believe that he would change, that he would do the right thing. Some part of her wanted to believe that he truly was sorry. When he was like this, it was hard for her to ignore. Despite the war going on in her own head, she still wanted to believe that it would all turn out well.

"All right," she murmured. "But just for lunch."

Behind Daniel's shoulder, she watched her mother's face fall.

They never made it to the restaurant.

Instead of turning left, heading back into town and the lunch that Alex had agreed to, he turned his work truck right, at the end of her mother's block. There was a nature preserve down this way, a five-mile path that wound through reeds and cottonwoods and junipers, a favorite spot for birders.

Alex sat up straighter in the seat. "Where are we going?" She turned to look at him.

Daniel's jaw was hard as rock, clenched as if he were fighting the urge to punch a wall. He pulled into the small dirt parking lot of the preserve. There was one other car parked there on this Wednesday at lunchtime, the occupant somewhere along the five miles of trails that began here.

Daniel cut the engine. He turned and looked at her, wrapping his hand around hers, rubbing his thumb over the top. "Oh, Alex. I know it's been tough lately. I know this has been . . . hard. But I need you, Alex. I really do. You believe me, don't you?"

Alex said nothing; she did not pull her hand away from his.

"Don't you think it's about time for you to come home?"

She turned away from him, staring out the windshield. Words deserted her, just as they always had in his presence. She did not want to go home with him, that part she knew absolutely.

She and her mother had been talking about it, in the quiet afternoons on the patio. They had talked about the social workers who came to visit Alex in the hospital and had left a stack of papers about domestic violence. Alex had not wanted to read those papers, not in detail, but she had glanced at them, had absorbed pieces from the lists of warning signs. They had talked about finding an attorney, getting a restraining order. Alex would move back in with her mother, at least for the time being. But as she sat there in the truck with him, Alex could not begin to think how to tell him this. She was petrified to tell him this.

He watched her for a moment, staring straight ahead, not looking at him. He let out a long sigh, and leaned forward slightly, reaching under his seat. When he sat back again, he had a small cloth bag on his lap.

Alex turned her head and watched as he took a pistol from inside the bag. Her stomach dropped. Her mouth went dry; her heart slammed against her rib cage.

Daniel sighed heavily and took a rag from the console between their seats. He began to rub the stock of the gun, small circles that polished the metal until it gleamed.

"I guess I just wondered when you were going to come home," he said quietly. "Seems like you're feeling better now. Eating better.

Walking better. I'd say you've spent long enough at your mother's house. Don't you think, Alex?"

She sat, dumbfounded. "Where did you get that?"

"This?" He held it up slightly, the end tipped vaguely toward her head.

She flinched.

"I've had it for years. I'm out in the field a lot, you know. A man can run into all kinds of trouble out in the wild—snakes, coyotes. Once I surprised a mountain lion, taking a drink at a creek on a windy afternoon." He held the gun up in front of him, pretending to site into the trees. "Comes in handy."

They sat for a few moments, neither of them saying a word. Another car pulled up into the lot, and two women got out. Daniel shifted the gun lower in his lap. They watched the two women in windbreakers, one a rusty orange and the other a bright green, colors that flashed loudly against the winter landscape of gray and brown and gold.

He turned toward her again. "Your mother walks down here, doesn't she? Since the path is so close to her house?"

Alex went completely rigid.

"I could swear I've heard her talk about it. All the birds she sees out here. She usually wears those little binoculars, right? The ones you gave her a few years ago."

Alex felt as if she had been kicked in the stomach; she could not take a breath.

"Flickers. Pileated woodpeckers. Red-tailed hawks." He examined the sky outside the windshield. "I have been listening, Alex. I have been paying attention. She walks here every day. Through those reeds." He raised his nose toward the bank of reeds that obscured the path ahead, the reeds that had swallowed the two women in bright jackets. "I've noticed a whole lot more than you think I have."

Daniel held the gun up in front of his face and blew lightly on the barrel. "Looks good." He smiled. He wrapped it in cloth and put the gun underneath his seat, flipped open the console and returned the rag to its original location.

He turned his attention to his own window, looking out the side, away from Alex. "You're my wife, Alex. Things have been rough, I know. But you're my wife. And it's time for you to come home now."

For years, she had not let herself think about those things, had even managed to bury them so deeply that she could pretend that none of it had ever happened. Now here they were, coming back to haunt her. Coming back to invade her thoughts and her dreams like weeds in a garden.

Alex heard a sound at the front window, and it pulled her out of that awful memory. The sound was like fingernails on glass, a scratching, squeaking sort of sound. She stood and walked to the front window. It was dark outside; the cemetery a few yards away only visible in tiny snippets.

There it was again, the squeak of something on the windowpane. A branch moved back and forth in the breeze. It was a rosebush, not quite completely devoid of leaves. The wind pushed the branch; the thorns scratched at the glass. One drop of moisture hit the windowpane, sliding down slowly. Alex shivered. In the darkness, it almost looked like blood.

Cold air brushed against her arms, and Alex ran her hands up and down. She turned back to the room, back to her wheel. It wasn't until she was sitting down, about to start spinning again, that it hit her.

She could smell roses. On a dark December night, in the dead of winter, it almost smelled like she was in a rose garden.

EIGHTEEN

"Mama? There's a man outside with his dog." Four-year-old Robin stood inside the screen door of the cottage, looking out into the day.

Emmie stood at the kitchen counter, kneading a loaf of bread dough. She wiped her hands on her apron and moved out to the front porch. The man was wearing a hat, pulled low on his head, and had just finished knocking on the Taylors' front door. He turned and headed back to his truck.

"Can I help you?" Emmie called out.

He looked up at her, his eyes shadowed under the hat, and walked over to the bottom of her porch steps. "Do you know when the Taylors will be back?" he asked.

"They went for supplies. Couple hours, probably." Emmie looked at the man's truck. A dog sat in the front seat, looking for all the world like it was ready to drive off as soon as its master returned. "Did you want me to take a look at your dog?"

The man shrugged and murmured, "You can if you want to, I guess." He opened the door of the truck, and the dog bounded out, heading straight for Emmie, who still stood on the porch. The dog stopped at the top of the steps, just next to her feet, and sat down, looking at her expectantly. His tail swished back and forth.

Emmie looked carefully at the dog, letting her eyes take in everything about him. She bent down and put a hand on the dog's head. She could see nothing amiss. "What's wrong with him?" She raised her eyes to the man standing at the foot of her steps.

He took a breath. "Well, he gets a bit surly if I try to take a bone away from him. Only listens to orders when they're in agreement with his own plans." He looked up at Emmie again, his dark eyes dancing. "And he's a terror for passing gas in the evening. Sometimes gets so bad even *he* has to relocate."

Emmie laughed. "That's it? You're not here so that I can fix your dog?"

The man smiled. "If you can fix that passing-gas thing, I'd be grateful. But no. I'm here to see my Aunt Kate." He stepped forward and offered his hand. "Name's Finch."

"Emmie."

They stared at each other for a moment. Emmie felt her face flush.

Robin had come out on the porch and she patted the dog, which promptly cleared her face of any remaining breakfast odors. She stood up and stared at the pickup truck in the driveway, a canoe perched on top. The girl folded herself in half, hanging her head upside down to get a better view. Her dark curls fell around her face like a messy curtain as she righted herself. "Is that your orca boat?" she asked, indicating the carved and painted orcas on the front and back of the canoe, currently upside down on top of the truck.

"It is," Finch replied.

"Can I go for a ride?" The child turned to look at her mother. "Mama, can I go for a ride in the orca boat?"

"Robin, this man isn't here . . ." Emmie could not finish her sentence.

"It appears that I do have a little time on my hands. Since my Aunt Kate isn't home." He raised his eyes and met Emmie's again. "I guess we would have to check with your mom and dad."

Robin looked up at him. "My daddy died."

Finch dropped to his knee, and addressed the child in front of him. "I'm sorry to hear that." He touched Robin's curly dark hair, rubbing it between two fingers. "That's some pretty hair you got there."

Robin sucked in her bottom lip. "Yep. I know."

Emmie put her hand on the girl's shoulder. "Say 'thank you,' Robin."

"Thank you, Robin," the girl murmured.

Finch smiled. "I would love to take you out on the orca boat. But only if it's okay with your mom." He stood and met Emmie's eyes again. "And only if your mom comes, too. I don't think we can handle that canoe, just the two of us."

Robin took Emmie's hand and started jumping up and down. "Can we, Mama? Can we? I wanna go in the orca boat."

The canoe sliced through the water in almost perfect silence. Morning mist, the color of a pearl, hung low over the water and kissed their faces with dew. Emmie sat in front, facing backward, so that she could watch the waters behind this man with the dark eyes. Finch sat in the stern, rowing rhythmically, using the excuse of navigation to cast several long looks at Emmie. Robin sat in the middle, wearing a bright yellow life vest, the dog sitting right next to her. She and Jack had already become best friends.

It was as if they were inside a magic spell, gliding over the water effortlessly, the soft lap of the waves the only sound. Mist curled and twisted like smoke, sometimes revealing tall pines along the shoreline.

They cut through the waters of Haro Strait, staying close to shore. The canoe was cedar, not more than twenty feet long, and the carvings on the front and back were of orcas, coming up out of the wood as if they were coming up out of the water.

"This is a beautiful canoe," Emmie said, rubbing her hand along the smooth finish of the wood. "Where did you find it?"

He looked at her from under his canvas hat. "I made it."

Emmie sat back. "You made it?"

He watched the water around them, focusing on the steady rhythm of moving them through the mist. "I'm a fisheries biologist. Went to work for the Samish Tribe, as soon as I graduated from U Dub. They've been making canoes like this for . . . forever, I guess. And I was lucky enough to get to watch. When I mentioned that I wanted to try it myself, they smiled and nodded. Watched me make just about every mistake known to man. And then they stepped up and taught me how to do it right."

He moved them along the edge of the island, and Emmie felt the peacefulness of the sea on a still morning, the water around them like beautiful antique glass.

"The Samish—most of the tribes around here—make some huge canoes, a hundred feet long or more. Use them for racing, for fishing. Beautiful handwork. And some of their canoes have been in the families for years—a hundred years or more. This baby," Finch said, indicating the orca boat, "is four years old."

"The same as me," Robin bubbled.

"Do you race in this?" Emmie asked him.

Finch shook his head. "I fish. For salmon."

"Isn't this a little . . . I don't know . . . unsteady? For fishing?"

The corners of his mouth lifted, just barely. "Can be. Depends on what you hook." He stopped paddling and let the boat drift slowly in the calm waters. He looked directly at Emmie, and she blushed under his gaze.

"It's quiet. No engine noise, no oil and smoke. No messing with a motor when you're cold and wet and ready to go home. I'm not dumping any chemicals in the water. And it's peaceful. Most peaceful place I've found. I can almost feel like I'm part of the water. Part of all the life out here."

His words hung in the air like poetry, like some magic spell. Emmie had to force herself to look at something besides Finch's dark eyes.

"When I was growing up, all my friends and I would try to find boats that made the most noise, the fastest speed across the water. We weren't listening to anything; all we wanted was to beat everyone else. And we didn't care if what we were doing might be hurting the life in the water. Didn't care if we were polluting the water. We didn't think about anything . . . except our own fun.

"And then I went to work for the tribe. I saw them doing things in a different way. Slower. Quieter. They respect all life, not just their own. Not just human life. They think about the consequences of every action they take. About how it will affect everything around them, now and in the future."

His eyes were mostly hidden under his hat, and Emmie felt a small shiver on her spine. It *was* quiet. They heard the call of an eagle, and Emmie and Finch both looked up, catching the bird circling over their heads.

"Sometimes, I come out here in the quiet and fish for salmon. Same as the orcas," he added, looking at Robin. "Except that I don't need as many as they do. One or two will last me for quite a while."

"Have you seen the orcas?" Robin had a hard time sitting still in the bottom of the canoe. The dog put a paw on her leg, as if trying to hold her down.

"A few times. We like to fish the same spots."

"Can I see an orca? Can you make them come up?" she asked.

He smiled again. "I wish I knew the secret, but I don't. They'll come and see us if they want to."

"I bet I know how to make them come up," Robin said, leaning to one side and dipping her hand in the water. She started singing, a boisterous version of "Raindrops Keep Falling on My Head," a song she had heard on the radio for months now. She had made it her own and sang it every time she was outside in the rain, an almost daily occurrence. She finished one verse and started another.

And suddenly, not thirty feet from the canoe, one orca popped up in a spy-hop, holding his head above the water to examine the origin of the sounds.

"There he is! Look! Look! There's an orca!" Robin was so excited she bounced, rocking the boat as she leaned and pointed, and Finch put his oar in the water in an effort to counterbalance her motions.

That orca went back down, but around them now there was a group of about ten, making their rhythmic dance to the surface, blowing out the old air into the morning mist, and grabbing more before submerging again.

"Ooh, they have stinky breath," Robin said, wrinkling her nose.

Finch smiled. "Fish breath, huh?"

They could hear the clicks and pops and screeches, the way the orcas talked to each other and checked out their surroundings. And right in front of their eyes, they watched one large male catch a salmon and share it with a smaller, younger orca.

They all stared into the water as the orcas continued to fish for salmon not thirty yards away. "They share their meals. None of that 'what's mine is mine' stuff with these blackfish. They always try to make sure that everyone in the family gets to eat."

The three people in the boat kept their eyes on the orcas moving around them.

"We could learn a lot from them, if we were actually listening," Finch said quietly. "They take care of each other. Travel in families. Stay together their whole lives, at least until the mother dies. Brothers and sisters, sometimes aunts and uncles and cousins around to help take care of the young ones. Pretty solid support system."

"I want to be an orca, Mama," Robin whispered. "I want an orca family."

Finch smiled. "There is a story in the tribe about a young maiden, walking by the shore, gathering kelp. She was singing. And an orca popped up out of the water, just like that one did, so that he could see who it was that was making that beautiful sound."

Robin smiled.

"He fell in love with the woman with the beautiful voice. And eventually, the maiden went to live with him in the sea. He married her."

Robin exhaled. "I like that story. I like the orca families."

They sat quietly, the water sloshing against the side of the boat, and watched as the orcas moved away, out into the deeper waters of the strait.

"Those orcas have been around for a very long time. A lot longer than humans. The tribal people say that man is the youngest of all the creatures on the earth. And that we have the most to learn."

For the first time in her life, Emmie felt as if she were in the presence of someone who was as different as she was. Someone in love with the quiet, in love with nature. As if Finch were someone she had known for a very long time. Her breath grew steady and quiet, tuning in to this man at the other end of the boat.

He rowed them back to shore. Robin leaned over the side of the boat, trailing her hand in the water. They could hear the songs of birds in the trees. When they reached the shallow water on the beach, Finch hopped over the side. He settled the boat in the water and reached in to lift Robin out. Jack jumped out beside the girl and started shaking furiously, making Robin laugh.

Finch turned and held his hand out to Emmie. She slipped her hand into his and stood, the boat rocking slightly, as she stepped onto the beach. She could not meet his eyes, but with that one touch, Emmie knew her life would never be the same.

NINETEEN

Alex went back to him. She went back to the house she shared with Daniel. She slept in the same bed with him, just as she had for the past six years. Every morning, she came down the stairs and walked right over the spot where she had lain on her side, her blood and the blood of their child leaking out onto the floor.

She had put all her hopes into that baby, as if that child held all the answers to everything that was wrong in Alex's life. Everything that was wrong in her marriage to Daniel. She had let herself believe that the baby would solve everything, would magically change Daniel into the kind of husband that she wanted. The baby would give her life meaning, would give her somewhere to focus.

Now all she wanted to do was pull the covers over her head and lie in bed. She wished there was a way to just stop breathing, to just stop. To just send a message to her brain—*that's enough, no more. I can't take anymore.* She wished that somehow the brain would listen and would do as instructed, just shut down all those other systems—stop the heart from beating, stop the blood from flowing, stop the involuntary process of taking in air. Shut down. Shut off. She spent hours staring at a random spot in their bedroom. Everything blended together, melted into a pool of dirty snow water, all brown and slick and opaque with unbearable pain.

If he had threatened her own life that day in the car, she might have said, "Go for it. Take your best shot." By that point, she no longer cared if *she* lived or died; she had had enough of his rants and his angers and his threats and his insults. She had had enough of the punches. Enough of the blood.

But Daniel had almost a sixth sense when it came to reading Alex. He knew better than to threaten *her*; he didn't say that it was *she* who would suffer. A threat to her mother was worse than anything else she could imagine. She could not manage another loss in her life. Her mother was the only person she had left, the only person who loved her without any kind of agenda attached.

There was no way she would leave him now, no way that she would take the chance that he might actually carry through on that horrible threat of shooting her mother while she was out walking. Alex lay on her side, feeling as if she had been sentenced to life in prison—the prison of marriage to Daniel Frazier.

For weeks after that incident, she lay in bed beside him, not sleeping, staring into the dark corners of the room, unable to see anything but the endless universe of pain that was hers to endure.

One night, she rolled onto her back. She could hear him beside her, his breathing deep and slow and regular. There was one brief interlude when his breath stopped. It lost its regular rhythm, arrested for just a few seconds before it continued again, a slight snore the only sign that anything had changed. She listened more carefully, her ears tuned to the rhythm of his breathing. For several moments, it was regular and deep, and then, once again, there was that pause, right before a raspy snore.

He rolled onto his side, and his arm curved over the top of her pillow, his hand lying beside her face. She stared at that hand, the fingers white in the dim light. *Like the hand of a dead man*, she thought.

It hit her, like a shooting star in this constellation of despair. Someday, Daniel would die. It would happen; death came to everyone. There was a woman at work, a coworker, whose husband had dropped dead of a heart attack at the age of forty-six. He'd never been sick; he ran every day. And just like that—gone. Things like that did happen.

This was the first time she actually let her mind go into that space of thinking about Daniel being dead and *gone*, unable to inflict any more harm. Unable to haul back and punch her in the eye or kick her in the stomach, kicking her over and over again as Alex lay coiled, trying to protect their baby, and finally losing consciousness.

She did not lie there in bed and think of trying to kill him; it was nothing like that. It would never occur to Alex to *kill* him, no matter how much she despised him. But something in her grabbed on to the idea that someday he would be dead, that someday, she might have a life without him.

It was the first ray of hope that she had felt since losing the baby, since coming back to live with him. Someday, Daniel *would die*. He might have a heart attack. Or an accident at one of the drilling sites. Or perhaps his car would slide off a road one night, coming home from work.

Someday, Daniel would be gone, and she could have her life back again. She could claim control of her own paycheck; she could make her own decisions about what to buy. She could have a space to herself, someplace where she would not have to hear him or smell him or submit to his many demands. Someplace where she would not have to listen for his car in the driveway, feeling her stomach clench in fear. Someplace where she would not have to wonder what horrors the night would bring.

That was exactly the moment when Alex's health began to improve. She got out of bed and took a shower and went back to work. She came home and cooked his meals, even managed to remember all his demands for her cooking (no onions, no pepper, no casseroles, for God's sake—that's just slop). She cleaned the house. She gave in to his demands in the bedroom.

And after he went to sleep, she let herself slip into that wonderful world that would be hers after he was gone. Sometimes she imagined traveling to Europe, she and her mother visiting museums and art galleries in Paris. Or sitting at a coffee shop in Vienna, some incredible pastry placed in front of them. She imagined the little home she would have. She imagined going out to dinner and ordering what she wanted to eat, not whatever was cheapest on the menu just to preserve the peace.

Someday. Like a prisoner of war, she managed to keep going with her dreams of someday.

She'd been back at work about a month when Rachel Medina, now the head librarian, strode into Alex's office back by the museum safe and closed the door behind her. She leaned against Alex's desk and put one piece of paper on the desk in front of her.

Alex looked down at it. It was the number and information for a domestic violence hotline. All her air rushed out like a waterfall.

"Alex, you have to do something. How can you stay with that man, after what he's done to you?"

Alex moved her chair and reached into the file drawer on the right side of her desk. She pulled out a file, over an inch thick, of papers she had been accumulating, and opened it. "How can I stay with him? You want to know how I can stay with him? Have you seen these statistics? From the National Coalition Against Domestic Violence?"

Rachel looked her in the eye and shook her head.

"The most dangerous time for anyone in a domestic violence situation is when they try to leave. Read this. It boggles the mind." Alex leaned back against her chair and met Rachel's dark eyes.

Rachel picked up the paper and scanned some of the statistics:

- *Domestic violence accounts for 15% of all violent crime in the United States.*

- *On average, twenty people per minute are physically abused by an intimate partner in the United States.*

- *50% of female murder victims are killed by intimate partners.*

- *44% of mass shootings between 2008 and 2013 involved intimate partners.*

- *Having a gun in the home increases the risk of intimate partner homicide by 500%. In households with a history of domestic violence, the risk increases 2000%.*

- *Women in the United States are eleven times more likely to be murdered with a gun than in other high-income nations.*

Rachel leaned against the desk, her shoulders sagging. "Does he own a gun?"

Alex nodded.

Rachel shook her head. "But . . . you could call the police. Get a restraining order. Go to a shelter."

Alex pushed her chair back and stood, walking to the one window in this back office. She stared out at the campus. "Call the police?" She turned and looked at Rachel. "Exactly when should I call the police? In the middle of the assault? Should I put up my hands in a time-out signal and say, 'Excuse me, I need to make a phone call'?" Alex took a breath. "Or maybe I should call them when the assault is over. When I'm either unconscious or barely conscious? When any small whimper could set him off and start the whole nightmare all over again?"

Alex took one quick step and tapped the papers on her desk. "Or maybe I should call the police *before* the assault. Like Nicole Brown Simpson. Do you know how often she called the police, with O.J. outside her house, pounding on the door and trying to break in?

"Over and over and over again, *before* he was inside the house. And even with the cops on the way, he still managed to beat the snot out of her. We all know how that ended."

They stood silently; Alex's breathing punctuated the air with small explosions.

She shook her head. "The people on the outside, who have never had to live like this? They think it's so easy. Why don't you leave him? Why don't you get a restraining order?"

Her words flew like punches, shooting into the air. "A restraining order didn't save this woman," Alex spat, flipping a paper over in the file. "She and her attorney were shot and killed on the steps of the courthouse. It's all right here, in these papers." Alex jabbed the list of statistics. "One study found that one-fifth of homicide victims with temporary restraining orders are murdered within two days of getting that protective order. One-third are murdered within the first month."

Alex raised her eyes to Rachel's and forced herself to slow her breathing. "A restraining order is only a piece of paper. You can't hold it up like armor if he decides to come after you. There is nothing magical about a restraining order."

Rachel was completely quiet.

Alex sat down, frustration making her breath ragged. "They came to see me in the hospital, you know. The social services workers. They brought all this information—the hotline numbers, the list of warning signs. The number for the shelter. I've read it all." She raised her eyes to Rachel again. "Suppose I do check in to a shelter. He can't find me that night or the next night. But what about when I come to work? Do you want him to come in here, looking for me? With a gun in his hands? Blazing angry, because I left?"

Tears welled in her eyes. "And even if I didn't come to work. Even if I stayed in the shelter and gave up my job—he knows where my mother lives. He knows where you live, Rachel. Do you really think he wouldn't try to find me?"

Alex leaned forward and shuffled through the papers in her file. "Did you know that twenty percent of the murders related to domestic violence are not the victims themselves, but a relative or a neighbor? A cop, or someone who tried to intervene?" She pulled out a copy of a newspaper article from the *Chicago Tribune*, October 2008. "Jennifer Hudson lost her brother, her mother, and her nephew. Murdered by the man who had been married to her sister."

Rachel reached for a chair and sank into it.

"I'm not stupid, Rachel. But no one—no cop, no restraining order, no shelter, can keep an eye on Daniel every minute. And I'll be damned if I'm going to let anyone else get hurt."

Their eyes met, both pairs blurred by tears.

"This was my mistake, getting hooked up with him. No one else should have to pay for that."

"But . . . what are you going to do? You can't just stay with him. You can't just wait until he kills you."

Alex exhaled. "I don't know. But I'm working on it. I'm trying to figure out a way to do this so that no one else gets hurt."

They both sat, still and quiet, for a full minute.

Rachel leaned forward and put her hand on Alex's shoulder. "Alex, I'm sorry. I had no idea about all this. If there's anything I can do to help . . . anything at all . . . you'll tell me, won't you?"

Alex nodded. They never talked about it again.

It wasn't long afterward that she started to lie to him. It wasn't planned. She had no design, no grand scheme in mind when it started. But there she was, standing at the checkout of the grocery store, buying the groceries for the week. She ran the debit card through the machine, and that question popped up, as it always did—would you like cash back?

She stared at it. Never, in all these years since she lost her own account, had she considered that question. She pushed the button for yes, unable to stop herself from looking side to side as she did, almost as if she were robbing a bank. She pushed the button for ten dollars. He had never, in her experience, asked to see the actual receipt for groceries. He checked their account online, watching where she shopped and the total amount. Maybe, just maybe, if she was very careful and did not take too much, he wouldn't notice.

She took the bill that the clerk handed her and realized that her first deception would now require another. Where would she put it? How could she hide it? None of the zippered pockets in her purse seemed safe enough. She stuffed the bill in the pocket of her pants and took her groceries to the car. And there she sat, pondering the possibilities.

She tried to conjure all the possible hiding places in their home— maybe her dresser or a coat or somewhere in the kitchen. Somehow, the idea of leaving it in the house, the chance that he might find it when she wasn't home, seemed too big a risk.

She looked at her purse again, and it was then she noticed the cardboard bottom, covered with the fabric that lined the inside of the bag. It slipped out easily, and she laid the bill flat, underneath it. She did not think about the long term; she had no vision in mind. But just the small comfort of having that ten-dollar bill made her feel better. It gave her a sense of power, a sense of control over her own destiny that had been missing for years. If she wanted to, she could go buy a coffee or a scone or a magazine.

She did not want any of those things. She wanted this feeling, this sensation of hope, this small glimmer of personal power. She wanted her own money. She wanted her own life.

And then she waited. It was harder than she had ever anticipated, to act normally, to act as if nothing in the world were any different than it had ever been. She was lying. She was hiding money from him. Waiting for him to check their account, almost holding her breath from the suspense. It gave her a small taste of what criminals must feel after committing a crime. No immediate fallout, no immediate detection, but how to go on living as if none of it had happened? How to go on living, knowing the truth?

It was a full three days before he sat down at the computer and checked the bank statement. Alex sat huddled in a corner of the couch in the living room, ten feet away from his desk, a library book in front of her. She could not even see the words of the story, much less perceive the meaning. Her palms grew clammy, and she wiped one on the leg of her pants.

Daniel clicked through the recent charges to the account. He turned off the computer and sprawled on the couch beside her, flicking on the television and flipping through the channels. He put his left hand on her knee, his eyes locked on the television screen. Alex forced herself to breathe, to flip a page of her book as if everything were exactly normal.

He stopped his channel surfing and leaned back into the cushions. "Have you seen this show, Alex?"

"What show?"

His eyes never left the television. "It's called *Dexter*."

She looked at the television and shook her head. "I don't think so."

His left hand stroked her thigh. "Pretty fascinating stuff. This guy— Dexter—is a serial killer. But not the regular kind that just snatches random people. This guy is very methodical. He only kills people who really need to be killed." He turned and looked at her. "Only the people who have done something awful. The ones who deserve it."

For a moment, she could not breathe, her eyes locked on his. Then she forced herself to swallow, to take a breath, to lower her gaze to her book. "Huh. Sounds interesting."

That night, when he rolled on top of her, she pretended to enjoy it. She pretended that nothing awful had ever happened between them, pretended that she loved him just as much as she had on the day they married, six years before. Her body, her breath, were those of a woman in love.

Another lie. When Daniel rolled off of her, she turned her back, facing away from him. She remembered the scene in the movie *When Harry Met Sally*, the now famous deli scene.

Move over, Meg Ryan, she thought. Faking an orgasm was the least of her lies.

TWENTY

"Where have you been? It's almost five." David stopped spinning to address Caroline, just coming in the door of the old Hadley house armed with two plastic bags.

Alex, sitting in the corner with her borrowed spinning wheel, was happy to see her. Without Aditi or Emmie or Caroline, the room had been too quiet.

"Jeez, what are you, my mother?" Caroline dropped her bags on a footstool in the middle of the circle and plopped into a chair. "I went shopping. Hey, Alex."

"In Copper Cove, that would not make you almost an hour late to the spinsters."

"I didn't shop in Copper Cove. I went across the pond. To the dark side." She raised her eyebrows.

David leaned back in his chair, away from her. "You went to the mainland to go *shopping*?"

Caroline nodded and tipped her lips toward the bags. "Target. They were having a sale."

David sat still, a look of stunned incredulity on his face. "You took a one-hour ferry, and drove another . . . I don't know what . . . to go to Target?"

"And Trader Joe's."

David sat back in his chair and shook his head back and forth. "What exactly was on sale that would make it worth the price of a ferry over and back? And almost a full day of your time?"

Caroline took out her knitting, which had been conveniently left behind, stuffed into the back of the seat cushion of the chair she always sat in. "You know. Stuff. Sparkling water. Butter. Ho Hos."

David starting laughing. "Ho Hos?"

Caroline looked stern. "Chocolate. Anyone want a chocolate Ho Ho?" She took a big bite. "Alex? Grace?"

Grace shook her head. Alex smiled and murmured, "What's a Ho Ho?"

Caroline held up the cellophane-wrapped package. "Hostess cupcakes."

Alex smiled. "Ah. I think I'll pass, thanks."

"Caroline, do you have any idea how many preservatives are in those? They probably baked those cakes in 1950."

Caroline smiled, a crumb of chocolate frosting on the side of her mouth. "Yep. Better living through chemistry."

David tipped his head to the side. "You mean better dying through chemistry. With the preservatives in that cupcake, science will be able to dig up your body one hundred years from now and still see everything you have ever put through that stomach." He leaned forward and poked through the two bags. "Vegan cookie dough? And butter? Tell me how that makes sense?"

"Have you tried the vegan cookie dough at Target? It's delicious." Caroline picked up her knitting again, still staring at it as if she couldn't quite remember what was supposed to happen next.

"It's a knit stitch, Caroline. Just knit it." He lifted his hand from the bag, and his mouth dropped open just a little. "Ah. Now I see."

Caroline leaned forward and snatched at his hand, which he pulled back away from her.

"Now we have the real reason." He held a box in his hand, shaking it back and forth. "You can't buy condoms at the general store?"

Caroline exhaled. "Not the large size box. No one in town has sex that often, apparently. Besides, if you buy condoms at the general store, then everyone knows about it." She snatched the box away from David and replaced it in the bag.

Grace chuckled. "Far better to bring them to the spinsters and show them to the editor of the newspaper." She shook her head. "Makes perfect sense to me."

David put a hand on his wheel and leaned forward, his voice dropping to almost a whisper. "Don't worry. It won't make the paper unless there's a crime involved."

Alex glanced at David, trying to read his expression.

"Which reminds me. Have you ladies heard the scuttlebutt?" he continued.

"Is there a rumor you haven't yet printed in the paper?" Grace asked, continuing to spin and not the slightest bit bothered by talking at the same time.

"Shows what you know." David sat back. "I always make sure that any rumors that go into print are corroborated by at least two sources."

"A bartender," Caroline supplied, raising her right hand to point at her own head, "and a waitress," she continued, pointing with her left index finger. She turned to David. "Would it be three corroborating sources if we include the fact that I'm also a potter?"

David scowled. "You think you're so clever."

"Well, they are the people in the know." Caroline picked up her knitting needles again, still studying the stitches for clues.

David leaned forward, his voice dropping a notch. "I don't need a corroborating witness. I saw the whole thing with my own eyes. Heard it with my own ears."

All spinning and knitting stopped, waiting for him to continue.

"Ryan Collins and his wife had a hell bender of a fight this morning, about five a.m. She threw all his clothes out in the yard, right in the middle of the rain. Said she had it on good authority that he was a lying, cheating, no-good scum bastard of a man." He sat back for a moment and shook his head. "The words that woman used. You'd almost think she was learning to spin."

Caroline's face flamed with color. Her arms dropped to her lap, her knitting now a pile of sticks and string. She made a sound, something similar to a balloon with a slow leak.

David looked at her. "You're looking a little flushed there, Caroline. Caffeine-induced hot flash?"

Her voice continued to make tiny squeaking sounds, but she did not speak.

"Alcohol-induced hot flash?" David's shoulders dropped. "Oh . . . oh, Caroline. No. Oh, Caroline." He shook his head several times. "When are you going to learn to leave the married ones alone?"

Caroline shook her head back and forth and slumped forward, dropping her forehead into her hand. "But there aren't any single ones. I never expected them to break up. It's not like I'm in the market for a *husband* or something. I just wanted a little fun, you know?" She leaned back in the chair and took a deep breath. "I hadn't had a date with anyone but Bob for almost a year."

"Bob?" Grace asked, her hand on her stopped wheel.

David turned to look at Grace, lowering his glasses and looking over the top, as if considering whether or not she could handle this information. "Battery operated boy," he murmured.

Grace stared at him.

"Required equipment for single ladies. Kind of like a blow dryer."

Grace sat back, slightly stunned. "Oh." Her face turned coral-colored with the dawn of understanding.

David sat back in his chair and let out a long sigh. "Oh, you heterosexuals. I swear." He picked up his spinning and then shot

171

Caroline another look. "Well, if it's any consolation, I did hear her say that he could just go live with that 'Becky with the Good Hair.'" David lowered his glasses and examined Caroline's messy bun. "Clearly, she doesn't know it's you."

All eyes turned to look at Caroline, sporting that same Pebbles Flintstone messy bun on top of her head.

David leaned toward her. "What is that in your hair today, Caroline? A chicken bone?"

Caroline slumped back against her chair. "Turkey. The wishbone. From Christmas. Completely washed and dried, I'll have you know. Aren't wishbones supposed to bring you good luck or something?"

"You're supposed to break the wishbone, Caroline. Not wear it," Grace chided.

"Hmm." David pursed his lips. "Is that your perfume of choice, then? Dead animal? Eau d'ewww."

Caroline gave him a dirty look.

David laughed until tears ran from his eyes. "Next time, why don't you try sheep carcass. We could call it eau d'ewe. Perfect for a spinster, don't you think?"

Caroline scowled. "Very funny. Don't knock it. Seems to be working."

David exploded with laughter. "Yes, I can see that. If you're in the market for a vulture. Or Ryan Collins, who needs instruction from YouTube to tie his shoes. And comes with a *WIFE*."

"He doesn't need any instruction in the things that really matter." Caroline sighed. She shook her head. "Now what am I going to do? I sure as hell don't want to *live* with him."

David sat back. "Well, that would definitely put an end to the sex. You will have wasted all that money." He picked up the large box of condoms and shook it back and forth.

Caroline leaned forward and grabbed it.

"Don't worry." David picked up his spinning and waited, enjoying the drama. "That Collins woman has a hell of a temper. They've had some knock-down, drag-out fights. Once she figures out who it is— which shouldn't be too difficult, if her olfactory senses are working at all—you may not have to live with him for very long."

Caroline's eyes went wide. "What do you mean by that?"

"Lovers shot by jealous wife," David continued. "Good headline, don't you think?"

"That's a little harsh, even for you," Caroline responded.

"David, that's not funny," Grace whispered.

Alex stopped her wheel. She rested her hands in her lap, unable to breathe.

"I'm not trying to be funny," David responded, his eyes on his spinning. He looked up and met her eyes. "I've known that Collins woman since way before she married Ryan. And if I were you, Caroline, I think I'd sleep with one eye open."

TWENTY-ONE

They stood outside the old Hadley house, spinning wheels and knitting bags in tow. David locked the door, and he and Caroline said their goodbyes and headed north on Main Street.

"I'm going to go have dinner with my daughter," Grace said. "Can you manage getting that wheel up the hill?"

"I think I'll be fine."

"Good night, then," Grace called. "And Alex? Your spinning is looking pretty good. I'm glad you're sticking with it. It's so nice to have you in the group."

"Good night." Alex turned to head up the hill to the house. It was only six in the evening, but the dark was solid. As she moved away from downtown, the streetlights were spaced farther apart, creating only small pools of light, surrounded by dark shadows. Near the gate to the cemetery, there was the amber glow of one lone streetlight, the last before the hill plunged into total darkness. Alex stopped there for a moment to catch her breath. It still surprised her, the difference that walking two blocks could make. The noise of town almost disappeared and the quiet descended, thick and heavy.

Somewhere near the back of the cemetery, back in the trees, she could hear the sound of voices. A woman was talking; she heard the ebb and flow of a conversation. Sometimes the voice went quiet, but

Alex could not hear anyone answer. She listened for a moment, hearing only the sound of one voice, rising and falling. She turned and noticed Emmie Porter.

The woman stood in a corner of the cemetery, closer to the water and the trees. Her white hair glowed in the semidarkness. She wore her long coat, no hat, and a big thick scarf wrapped around her neck. Her voice carried in the air, but Alex could see no one else out there.

Alex watched her for a moment, wondering what creature she was talking to, wondering if a deer lay wounded in the trees.

Emmie turned and looked right at her. "Can you hear that?"

Alex looked behind her in the street, and turned slowly back to Emmie. She shook her head.

"Come over here," Emmie said, and turned her gaze back out to sea.

Alex left the spinning wheel by the cemetery gate and walked carefully through the stones, watchful not to hit one in the dark. She reached the corner where Emmie stood, and stopped a few feet away from the woman.

"Listen," Emmie whispered, tipping her head to one side.

Alex waited, half expecting to hear another voice somewhere in the trees.

Emmie looked at her. "There."

Alex heard it then, that *kwoosh* sound of an orca coming up for air. She met Emmie's eyes and nodded.

"Orcas," Emmie mumbled. She turned and scanned the horizon. Overhead, the sky was paler. Dusk had painted the water a murky navy gray. "There."

Alex moved closer to Emmie, and she saw it, too. The gentle arc of an orca, coming up for air, the spume of expelled breath. It was followed almost immediately by another orca, another breath. As she watched, a line of orcas, about seven in all, rose to the surface, one after another, expelling spent air, taking in fresh.

"They're sleeping." Emmie's voice was hushed.

Alex stood close to her now, and they both watched quietly as the line of orcas moved past Copper Cove, heading farther south.

"They don't sleep, not the way we do. They have to keep half of their brain awake all the time. If they ever go completely to sleep, they would die."

Alex glanced sideways, trying to get a look at Emmie in the darkness.

"Every breath they take is a conscious decision. They have to remember to come up and take another lungful of air." Emmie turned and looked at Alex. "Not like us. We can be knocked unconscious or put under anesthetic, and our bodies will keep breathing on their own. We don't have to think about it."

Emmie's voice stayed low and quiet. "Not the orcas. They have to keep part of their brain awake all the time, to remind them to come up for air."

They stood, listening to the rhythmic *whoosh, whoosh* of each orca coming up for air. The exhalations went all the way down the line of blackfish, and then the first one came up again, starting the queue all over again, like dominoes, one after the other.

"They have a system—sleeping like that, so close to one another. In a line, one following the next. It's a way to stay close enough to keep an eye on everyone else in the clan. A way to keep track, to make sure that everyone takes another breath. Always watching out for one another."

The two women listened. The breaths were a rhythm, a soft, melodious song that rose from the depths of the dark water. It sounded almost like music—the music of the deep.

"Do they ever decide not to breathe? Not to come back up?"

Emmie took a long, slow breath. "There's no way to know what they're thinking. But yes, there have been instances where an orca goes down and does not come back up."

Their eyes met in the dark. "Suicide?" Alex whispered.

"I wouldn't call it that. They might be sick, or hungry, or just too weak to keep going. It's more like they know that they're at the end. That it's their time now."

The two women stood completely still. The sound of the orcas grew fainter as they moved farther south in the water.

"There have always been people who knew when it was their time to die. Not that they were causing it to happen—only that they were aware it was coming. Going off to die, when the time is right. Dogs will do that, you know. Slip off somewhere, in a bush, to die quietly."

Alex nodded, and for no reason she could name, felt tears snaking slowly down her cheeks. She looked out at the water, away from Emmie. She could no longer see the line of blackfish; the sounds of the water completely obliterated the sounds of the orcas.

"Your mother knew it was her time."

Alex inhaled; her shoulders twitched. It took a minute before she could find her breath. "How did you know? About my mother?"

Emmie turned and looked at her. "It's written all over you." She stared at Alex for a full minute, their eyes locked on one another. "The color of death is swirling all through your body."

For a moment, Alex met the woman's gaze. Then she pulled her eyes away, remembering what Caroline had told her about Emmie, about her ability to read minds. She wanted to run, to get away. She was standing too close to this woman who felt energy, who could see energy in other beings. Despite the cool night air, she felt sweat pop out on her lip.

"I'd better go," she whispered, without meeting Emmie's eyes. "Good night." She turned and headed back to the gate. She reached for the case with the spinning wheel and looked back into the trees in the corner.

Emmie stood quietly, not talking. Her eyes were still focused on Alex.

TWENTY-TWO

From that first day that Finch took them out in the canoe, both females fell head over heels in love. Emmie could not stop thinking about that man with the dark hair and dark eyes, the one who loved the quiet and the sounds of nature as much as she herself did. Though she told herself it was silly, that he lived with the tribe, more than a two-hour commute away, she could not seem to stop herself from watching for his truck in the driveway. He had not been to visit his Aunt Kate during the first five years that Emmie lived there, but that didn't stop her from hoping he would make an appearance again soon.

Robin fell head over heels in love with the orcas. As soon as they returned from the canoe trip, she started to imitate the orcas. She jumped on Emmie's bed, trying to twist her body the way she had seen the orcas doing when they breached. She moved across the living room floor, arcing up and down, exhaling, inhaling, and diving back under the imaginary water. She sat at the table and shared her dinner with her "orca family," a ragtag collection of stuffed animals that had begun their lives as other creatures—dog, cat, teddy bear—but had been pressed into service as orcas, magically transformed into the aunts and uncles and cousins and grandparents that Robin wanted.

She pretended to talk to them in a series of clicks and whistles and sudden screeches.

"Robin, do you want more mashed potatoes?"

"Shh, Mama. I'm talking to my daddy." She continued a series of clicks and pops and squeaks.

Emmie leaned back in her chair and sighed. How precarious life must be for a little girl and her family of one. Even with Kate and Doc Taylor nearby, even with the occasional visits from Emmie's mother, she realized that living alone—just the two of them—was not an adequate security net for a four-year-old. And for the first time since Dusty died, Emmie felt it, too—that need for connection. That need for someone else in her life.

When Finch returned, three weeks after that first visit, both Emmie and her daughter were ready. He drove up in the yard, canoe on top of his truck, Jack riding in the passenger seat. When Finch stepped out of the truck, he threw one glance at his Aunt Kate's house and headed straight for the door of Emmie's cottage.

He had barely made it to the top of the steps before Robin came flying out the screen door, yelling, "Finch!" and throwing her arms around his legs. For a moment, he was unable to move. He reached down with his left hand and cradled the back of Robin's head.

"Hey there, Miss Robin," he muttered. Jack followed him to the top of the porch, and Robin threw her arms around the dog, releasing Finch.

Emmie stood in the doorway, watching.

Finch brought his right hand from behind his back. In it, he held a bouquet of wildflowers, thick with the scent of violets. He held them out to the woman with the dark hair. "For you," he murmured. "I picked them myself."

Emmie felt a hum, rising from her toes to the top of her head.

The three of them fell into a rhythm, a pattern of being together, that was completely natural. They took quiet walks along the beach or into the forest, Robin always running nearby, happy to scoop up a shell or a frond of cedar, aged until it looked like a copper feather. Finch showed Robin how to watch the crabs scuttling along the sand. He taught both of them how to dig for clams. Sometimes they found a spot to lie down on the ground and watch the clouds and the birds. Finch had stories about everything, from the flickers, with their bright orange feathers, to the tiny Anna's hummingbird. The three of them supported each other in all the right ways, almost like Robin's imaginary orca family.

Finch loved his job with the tribe. Every time he came to the cottage, he had stories that he shared with his girls. Emmie liked her own life, too, even though it meant never being fully accepted by the people of Copper Cove. But she knew she was needed, knew that the work she did was valuable and necessary. She and Finch learned to share their lives in bits and pieces. He came to the Cove as often as he could. She and Robin went to visit him on the reservation whenever there was a ceremony or potlatch or just for an occasional break from Copper Cove.

The arrangement worked well for both of them. Emmie and Finch were two quiet souls who loved nature and animals and had grown comfortable with long spells of solitude. The fact that they could share their lives with one another, even on a limited basis, was enough. Neither one of them ever asked for more.

Once again, though, Emmie managed to inflame the gossips of Copper Cove. She didn't care. Her life was full; they could talk all they wanted. They would anyway; she knew that. And so she learned to live with it.

For Robin, that was not as easily done.

As a little girl, Robin was as bright and outgoing and bubbly as a girl could possibly be, always singing and dancing her way through the day. She begged Emmie to let her listen to the radio, and on those rare days when she could be outside, she made up dances to go with her latest song craze. For a while, it was Stevie Nicks and "Landslide," followed by "Dancing Queen" and "American Pie." She knew the words to them all and sang with her whole heart.

It wasn't long after her first encounter with the orcas that she started to display another type of gift. Finch and Emmie were in bed asleep when Robin came to the door of their bedroom, deep in the middle of the night. "Mama? I had a bad dream."

Emmie propped herself on her elbows and looked at her little girl, standing in the doorway, a stuffed orca cradled in her arms. Her nightgown was like a pale blue pearl in the dim light. Emmie patted the bed next to her, and Robin crawled up between Emmie and Finch. The two adults lay on their sides, looking at each other as Robin settled in between them.

"Tell me about it," Emmie whispered.

Robin took a disheveled breath, still soaked with tears. "I was swimming with my family. My orca family. We went everywhere, looking for something to eat. But we couldn't find anything. My sister found one fish, and she shared it with us. But it wasn't enough. I was hungry." Robin wiped a tear from her face. "And I was getting cold."

Emmie met Finch's eyes over the body of her little girl. It had crossed her mind a few times, wondering if Robin would have the same sensitive nature that Emmie did.

Finch took Robin's hand in his, gently rubbing his thumb over her palm. "You know what, Robin? That's pretty darn special—to be able to feel what an animal is feeling. Not very many people can do that."

"But I was scared. I was hungry and cold. And I was getting tired."

Finch nodded. "Sometimes it is scary, to feel what another creature is feeling. I think that's what your mom does, too. It can't be easy, to feel another's pain."

Emmie nodded in the dark, her arms wrapped around her little girl. "Sometimes, when I was a little girl, I would feel the pain of the horses or the cows. It made me cry."

"Where I work, with the Samish people? Dreams are important. Sometimes dreams are sent to guide you," Finch whispered. "To tell you something you need to know. You know the best thing you can do? With these feelings? These dreams?"

Robin shook her head. "What?"

"Use it. Use it to help, any way you can, any creature you can. Maybe since you love the orcas so much, you will grow up to be a great orca scientist. Do research, like that Maggie Edwards. Study the orcas. Help them. Figure out why they can't find enough food. Figure out ways to help them get more."

Robin got very quiet and still.

"When I was a little boy, my dad used to take me to fish for salmon," Finch murmured. "I remember that first one I caught. So beautiful. The pink color of the flesh, the silver scales. I think I fell in love with the salmon." He put her hand down and took a deep breath. "When something touches you like that, then use it. Follow it. That's how you find your way in this world."

Robin's tears had stopped. And just like that, her path in life was set.

Up until school started, Robin had never even considered the idea that she and her mother were different from everyone else. The fact that Emmie walked through town, talking to almost every creature she met—dogs in yards, cats in windows, birds in the trees, sometimes even the trees themselves—had always just seemed normal.

The confrontations began as soon as she started school. Robin got a firsthand look at just how cruel children could be. Classes were small in the Cove, and there were only fifteen students in the first grade. All of them had heard their parents talk about Robin's mother; all of them were well acquainted with the word *witch*. And now she heard the other students using that word to describe her mother, and herself.

Three weeks into first grade, she was in the cafeteria at lunch when she happened to hear Brian Carter, in the second grade, whisper the word *witch* as she walked past him. She stopped right next to his table and turned to look at him. "What did you say?" She said it loudly enough that everyone at the table heard it.

Brian smirked, but he didn't repeat it.

She waited for him outside, after lunch. As soon as he walked out the door of the cafeteria, starting to run toward the slide, she charged him from behind. His own momentum, combined with the surprise attack, sent him sprawling on the rocks, his face in the gravel. Robin had thrown herself on top of his back. "Don't you ever call me or my mother names," she whispered into his ear. "I know magic that will make your penis fall off."

She stood up, brushed herself off, and walked away. That was the first indication that she would not handle things the same way that her mother always had.

Where Emmie was always quiet and circumspect, and let the gossip of town roll off her, her daughter could not. Robin displayed none of the qualities of patience and forbearance and calm that had kept her mother going all those years. They were like yin and yang, night and day, black and white, in the way they approached life—total opposites.

Robin always forced the issue. She pushed, she challenged, she refused to back down. And somehow, she made it work. What started in the first grade as fear and ostracizing gradually turned to grudging tolerance. The boys, at least, started to look at her as someone who was tough and hard and able to hold her own with any one of them. The students learned to give her a wide berth, managed to keep most of their gossip and insults to themselves. If they didn't, cuts and bruises always ensued, Robin often going home with fewer than anyone else.

Emmie told her repeatedly to let it go. "Let it roll off. Who are these people, anyway? Their opinions don't matter."

Finch told her it was important to pick her battles, to save her strength for the ones that really mattered.

All that advice swept away in the breeze, none of their wisdom sticking in her head when confronted with the latest bit of insult from the catty girls in school. Robin had to scratch and claw and fight her way through school. She was never the type who would sit at the back of the room like some shy church mouse and watch while the others made fun of her.

She filled her hours at school doing two main things: sketching and singing.

Song tracks looped through her head, and she came to class late, singing, dancing her way down the aisle. Stephanie Spencer rolled her eyes and leaned to whisper to a friend, and Robin stopped right in front of her. "Too bad you don't know how to dance," Robin said, loud enough for the class to hear.

When she wasn't doing actual classwork, she spent every moment in the classroom sketching. Trees, flowers, orcas, all flowed from the tips of her colored pencils and gave her somewhere to focus her energy. Occasionally, she would draw a sketch of one of those catty girls, her face contorted into that of a sea monster.

Though they would never have admitted it, the boys liked her. She was cute and funny and played tag football as well as any of them. Secretly, they all hoped that Robin would tackle them, a real tackle that would "accidentally" bring her body down on top of theirs.

After school was a little easier to navigate. Schools in Copper Cove weren't large enough to have swim teams, but if they had, Robin would have been a champion. During the summer months, and into the fall, she spent many mornings down at the sea wall park, just below the main street of town, where she could dip into the waters of the Sound and swim along the shore. It was fairly shallow there; she could stand up if she got tired, and it provided her with a physical release for all the frustration of not belonging. The only time when she wouldn't go in the water was the dead of winter—November, December, January. February was always iffy—but there were occasional days when she went ahead, wearing a wet suit given to her by Maggie, after an intern had left it behind. It was swimming that brought Robin a small level of peace. She loved the feel of her hands cutting into the water, loved the way the water shimmered silver off her arms and shoulders as she moved. For those fifty minutes that she was in the water, she could erase all the ugly comments and rude looks from the girls at school.

And so she survived her adolescence in Copper Cove, swimming and sketching, and all of it accompanied by the endless soundtracks that ran through her head. Billy Joel, Michael Jackson, Queen, Prince—she knew them all. Stevie Nicks remained one of her favorites, even when she wasn't singing with Fleetwood Mac. Robin thought the woman was brilliant. She knew the words to every song, and she also knew how to harmonize, letting her own voice weave with Stevie's into a blend she was sure even Ms. Nicks would approve. Stevie Nicks seemed to be the one person who wasn't intimidated by the idea of witches and their offspring.

Her plan worked pretty well for most of her elementary and middle school years. She turned sixteen at the end of tenth grade, and when she came back to school that fall of her junior year, everything was different.

TWENTY-THREE

Daniel loved surprises. Not the kind of surprises that included boxes of candy and bouquets of flowers, not the kinds of surprises that might elicit a smile. The kind of surprise that really intrigued Daniel was the one that would make Alex afraid.

He would sneak up on her while she was cooking or doing laundry, touching her shoulder ever so lightly, and watch as she shrieked and jumped. He liked to have her in the car beside him, one hand on her thigh, the other on the steering wheel, as he sped up, headed straight for a group of trees. He loved the look of terror that came over her face, the way her fingers dug into the upholstery of the car seat. He'd hit the brakes at the last minute, laughing as the car screeched to a stop, sometimes even fishtailing.

"Just kidding, Alex. Why do you always get so worked up about things? Don't be silly." And then he'd lean across the car, his hand traveling up her thigh, and press his face into her neck.

Her terror seemed to be the one thing that always turned him on. It did not have the same effect on her.

She was always a little afraid of him, afraid of those surprises, even before they turned physical. And that was before she had started lying to him, hiding bits of cash. Now there was a wariness in her that went well beyond those adrenaline rushes of fear. She had that secret knowledge, and the weight of carrying all those lies was beginning to take its toll.

It was another ordinary evening, ordinary for the life of Alex and Daniel, at any rate. Daniel had not come home for dinner, despite the fact that he was working in town and was not out on some remote job location. He did not call to say that he would be late, or when he would be home, or what he was doing. And Alex had learned, years ago, that life was more peaceful for her if she did not ask.

She could still remember the first dinner that she had had to toss out, ruined after sitting for three hours, waiting for Daniel. She asked him where he had been and why he was so late. He spun around, grabbing a fistful of her shirt and lifting her off the ground. "If there's something you need to know, then by God, I'll tell you. You sound like a jealous wife."

Alex felt her jaw working, trying to find the words. "It's not that. It's just that I made dinner, and now it's ruined."

He set her on the floor, but his eyes were blazing. "Dinner ruined? That's what you're worried about?"

She said nothing else, her eyes locked on the anger that flamed in his face.

He turned to walk away from her, running his hand through his hair. He stopped, and her heart stopped at the same time. "I'll give you something to worry about," he whispered. He picked up one of the plates on the counter and turned quickly, hurling it at her head, food and all. She ducked. It hit the wall behind her, spaghetti sliding down the wall and onto the floor.

She learned to quit asking where he had been.

So on this particular evening, the third one this week in which he had not come home for dinner, she simply stood up from the table and carried his plate to the kitchen. She stood over the trash can, the fork in one hand. It took only a moment to decide: instead of scraping food into the trash, she tossed in everything—plate, silverware, meatloaf, all clattering into the bin. And then she went to bed, not bothering to change out of her sweatpants and sweatshirt. She lay down and pulled the covers up around her.

Lying in bed, she seethed. It was not jealousy that churned her anger, not the idea that he was once again out with another woman. For a few years, at least, she had fantasized that he *would* fall in love with someone else, that he would leave her for another. It was just another version of the "someday Daniel will be gone" game that had kept her afloat, that gave her a reason to keep going.

What really galled her was that she had never liked to cook. She hated coming home from work, tired and wanting a few moments to herself, and having to start her second job—the job of Daniel's wife. He expected a meal on the table when he got home. If he came home. And she never had any way of knowing ahead of time whether he would show up or not. She had just wasted another evening, standing in the kitchen, preparing a meal that *he* liked, for no good reason. Another evening, gone. Her whole life was wasting away in these little dribbles of resentment, in these endless efforts to try and keep the peace.

She said nothing when he came into the bedroom three hours later, dinner forgotten as he climbed in bed beside her. Many nights, when he came in late like this, he reached for her, ready for sex. As if the woman who permeated the atmosphere around them with Chanel No.5, who had already bathed him in the scent of sex, was simply the first course in a multicourse meal. As if his manhood was proven, beyond a shadow of a doubt, if he could have sex with more than one woman per evening.

That night, though, instead of crawling in beside her, he grabbed her shoulder and turned her toward him. His movements were rough, his voice clipped and lethal.

"You little slut." He slapped her across the face.

"What?" Alex raised a hand to her cheek, still shaking off the fogginess of coming up from a deep sleep. "What are you talking about?" Even as the words left her mouth, she could feel the truth flushing her face with color. She was lying to him. She had amassed more than $600 in the past several months.

"You're lying to me, Alex. I always know when you're lying."

He grabbed her arms, pulling her up from the bed. His breath smelled of whiskey. "Don't play innocent with me. I'm not some dumb high school kid. I've been down this road before. I know a lie when I smell one." He half-pulled, half-dragged her from the bed and pushed her, stumbling and barefoot, into the living room.

Alex willed herself not to look at her purse, sitting on the table by the front door.

He pushed her hard, and she fell in a puddle on the carpet.

He got down on one knee and leaned close to her face, his breath hot and sour. "I can see it, Alex. I can see it written all over you."

She opened her mouth, but no sound came out. Her fear had ratcheted from zero to deathly afraid, in the space of only a few moments.

"Who have you been fucking on this carpet? Who have you been fucking while I was at work?"

The words left her stupefied. She looked at his eyes, bloodshot, his head reeling slightly from drink. "What are you talking about?"

"I can see it, Alex. I can see where you've been fucking your little friend. It's written all over your face. It's written all over my house."

He slapped her, and then pulled her to her feet and slapped her again. She fell on her side, and he was on top of her in an instant, turning her head and grinding her face into the fibers of the carpet. "Smell that, Alex? I can. Two filthy bodies, fucking, on my living room rug."

Alex went completely still, shocked, yet again, at the level of his anger, at the craziness of his ideas. She said nothing; she did not look at him directly. He stood, wiping his hand over his face. And then he turned and kicked her, as hard as he could. She curled into a tighter ball.

He stood over her, swaying slightly, as if he couldn't quite remember where he was or what he was doing. And then he stumbled off to bed.

"Ahh!" Alex shot awake, her heart racing. The memories assaulted her, jumping at her from every angle. Haunting her, plaguing her sleep, creeping up to surprise her when her mind was elsewhere. Like a soldier returned from war, every little thing set her off, sent her right back to those moments when she crouched in terror. It didn't take much: the smell of Giorgio Armani aftershave, a glimpse of a tall man with dark wavy hair, the sight of a black Volvo driving down the road.

Alex took a deep breath and leaned back against the wall. She knew what it felt like to sleep with one eye open, to sleep with only half her brain, like the orcas. She'd been doing it for years. Listening for the sound of his car in the driveway. Listening for the sound of his steps on the porch, his key turning in the lock.

Her stomach clenched even now, with the memory of hearing him come home. The thought of wondering if this would be the night when he actually killed her. Despite the fact that she was two thousand miles away, that he could not hurt her anymore, she still woke with the taste of terror in her mouth, the adrenaline rush of fear.

Alex threw back the covers and headed to the kitchen for a drink of water. She stood at the sink, her eyes closed as she drank deeply, trying to find her way out of the talons of fear that still gripped her. She lowered the glass and took a deep breath. And then she heard it, just behind her, at the door that led to the back porch. She turned to look.

The doorknob twisted. The latch released with a soft *click*. The door creaked open, like a slow-motion horror film. She could hear footsteps on the floor in the kitchen, not far from where she stood. A rush of cold air brushed past her.

No one was there. The back door stood open; cold air swirled into the room. But no one was there. Before she could even think about moving to close it, before she could begin to process what she had just witnessed, the door slammed shut, the dead bolt turned in the lock.

"Ah!" she gasped. With her hand at her throat, Alex tiptoed over to the back door and peered out into the night. There was no one outside, no one on the back porch, no car in the driveway, other than her own. Nothing that she could see. She moved back into the house and checked the dead bolt, making sure it was locked in place.

And then she felt it, moisture seeping through the bottom of her socks. Alex turned to look at the floor. There were footprints across the wood, starting at the back door. Wet footprints, as if someone had entered with wet shoes. She knelt and touched the floor with her fingertips. They, too, came away wet.

Alex ran a hand through the tangles of her hair. *I must be losing my mind. This can't be happening. This can't be real.*

It didn't seem to matter that she was two thousand miles away. All the horrors of her past had followed her here, seeping into the woodwork, twisting into the very structure of this old house in Copper Cove. As if the house itself were forcing her to look backward, to pay attention, to *remember*. As if every scratch at the window, every turn of the lock, every wet footprint, was scraping at the layers of fog in her brain. Whispering in her ear. *You cannot escape.*

She sat in the chair the rest of the night, wrapped in a blanket, her eyes glued to the handle of that back door. Watching. Waiting.

TWENTY-FOUR

Alex was out the door the next morning before the sun was up, heading downtown to the café. She needed food, she needed coffee, she needed to be out of that house. She needed to find somewhere she could feel safe, at least for a short time.

The bell on the back of the door at the Drift Inn tinkled her arrival. The aromas of home-cooked food rose to greet her: homemade bread, bacon frying, coffee brewing, pancakes on the griddle. She stood for a minute, her nose in the air like a dog, savoring the breakfast bouquet, listening to the sounds of real people around her. Real people going about their ordinary, everyday business. She hung her jacket on the hooks by the door and turned to the main part of the restaurant.

"Alexandra! This is perfect. Now we have a foursome." David stood and held out his hand. "Would you like to join us?"

Alex walked over to the table by the window. "Good morning," she murmured, her voice hoarse. She was enormously grateful to see David, as if he was the perfect antidote to her dreadful night.

"This is my partner, Jeff."

Alex shook hands with a man with brown hair and glasses, his face warmed by a neatly trimmed beard, just beginning to gray at the edges, his smile lighting his face.

"Happy to meet you, Alex."

Caroline turned slightly and let out an enthusiastic greeting of, "Hey, Alex."

"Do they let you sit down for breakfast?" Alex asked, sliding into the vacant chair and looking around the restaurant, too early to be truly busy on this winter morning. Seeing Caroline made her breathe just a little easier. At least she had a couple of friends now, people who seemed just as happy to see her as she was to see them. Alex felt a little of her tension slide away.

"I'm not working. Sherry is back from her holiday, so I'm back to my other job. Trying to sell pottery to the one tourist who comes up here in January."

"Ah." Alex turned to a woman who had come to take her order.

"Coffee?"

"That would be great," Alex said, and took the menu from her hands. Before she could get it open, David interjected.

"She needs a maple bacon scone," he said to the waitress before turning his attention back to Alex. "You're not gluten intolerant, are you? Vegan? Vegetarian?"

Alex shook her head.

Jeff leaned forward. "Even the vegans and vegetarians eat bacon. Everyone eats bacon."

David slid back into his own chair. "The pesto-pistachio omelet is out of this world," he continued. "Parmesan, pesto, pistachios—it's p-p-p-perfection."

Alex nodded. "That sounds great. I'm starving."

The waitress left, and Alex turned to meet Caroline's gaze.

"You don't look so good, Alex. Is it Maggie?" Caroline asked.

Alex looked at her, so exhausted her brain wouldn't function properly. It was deep in her nature to stay isolated, to keep her thoughts and fears and problems to herself. How well did she know Caroline? Or any of that group of spinsters? She had met them less than two weeks ago. She liked these people; she was glad to have them around her. For one moment, she thought about the release of telling her awful story. But she couldn't, she wouldn't, allow herself the freedom of unburdening, no matter how attractive it might seem.

Alex shook her head and let out a sigh. "I don't know. I'm just not sleeping that well, I guess."

Caroline leaned forward and put a hand on Alex's forearm. "Don't let the bastards get you down. Or bastardess, as the case may be. Maggie has always been hard on people."

She leaned back and continued, "All of Maggie's interns end up leaving rather suddenly, have you ever noticed that? And I can tell you, as someone who works in this restaurant quite a bit in the summertime, almost all of them look like hell when they come in here. Like they haven't slept. Just like Alex."

Their plates arrived. David sat back, waiting for the waitress to leave, before he dived into his food.

"It's not Maggie," Alex whispered.

"The ghost?" Caroline asked, leaning forward, her eyes eager.

Alex shrugged. "I don't know if I believe in ghosts. I never used to, anyway."

Jeff met her eyes. "Have you seen something?"

She shook her head. "I haven't actually *seen* anything. No."

"But?" Caroline asked.

Alex sighed. "I'm not sleeping very well. I wake up, and . . . I hear things." She turned her head toward the window and looked out at the choppy gray water in Haro Strait. "I'm never quite certain if it's real or if I dreamt it."

"What kinds of things?" Jeff's voice was soft and kind.

She shrugged. "Branches against the window. Footsteps on the floor. Sometimes that back door comes open, all on its own. I feel cold air."

"Is the lock broken?" David asked. "Do you want me to take a look at it?"

She shook her head. "I don't think so. Maybe."

"So it's the classic ghost story kinds of things."

"I don't know about ghosts," said Alex. "All that research I've done, almost twenty years of pulling together available information, and I've never even considered the idea of ghosts. Have any of you? Seen a ghost, that is? Or heard one, or . . . whatever."

David looked at Jeff, and his mouth curled. "This is embarrassing, coming from the person who leads the ghost tours. But no, I've never actually *seen* a ghost. Never heard one, either."

"Then . . . how did you get started . . . What made you get into the ghost tours business?" Alex asked.

David grinned sheepishly. "I started that newspaper in what?" He looked at Jeff. "Nineteen ninety-five, maybe?"

Jeff nodded.

"And sometimes, there just wasn't all that much news. Small town. At certain times of the year, it can get . . . boring. I was losing my patience for 'so-and-so's daughter was here for the weekend.' I once wrote a front-page cover story on the explosion of the bunny population." He shook his head. "I was getting tired of trying to dream up new things to write about. And so I started hanging out at the tavern, asking some of the old-timers about these old buildings."

Caroline leaned down and whispered, "Most folks who see a ghost need a drink shortly thereafter."

"Or had several shortly before," Jeff added.

"I did hear a few things, from the bartender and from some of the old-timers who hang out in the tavern. Have you ever been on a ghost tour, Alex?" David asked.

Alex shook her head.

"They aren't usually heavily into fact, if you know what I mean. It's usually just a collection of stories, anecdotes, urban legends, that have been told about a place. Things like footsteps on the stairs or that cat at the bookstore. Not necessarily a lot of history."

David sat still for a moment. "I think most of the folks who take those ghost tours are looking for a good scare. A chill. They want a Stephen King kind of moment."

He took a bite of his own breakfast and closed his eyes. "Ahh. Rodrigo is quite the cook, isn't he?" He pointed at his food with his fork and said, "Next time you come in, try the salmon benedict with pesto hollandaise. Mmm." He shook his head back and forth, and then kissed the tips of the fingers on his right hand.

"The truth is, there isn't some central registry that keeps track of everything that ever happened in a house over the years. Sometimes, if there's some grisly murder or something, that would make it into the newspapers. Everyday life and death, though? That pretty much goes unreported. Mostly what you hear about these old places is just anecdotal, just stories people tell. Maybe they heard something when they were a kid. Or maybe they thought they saw something on the way home one night. I just started gathering all the little stories. Like that cat, down at the bookshop."

Alex nodded.

"And the stairs, at the little store. Just stories. That's all."

"Did you ever hear anything about the captain's house?"

"No, not much. Some of those old-timers talked about seeing the captain in one of the windows. Nothing very specific. I never go up to the captain's house on the ghost tours. There is quite enough to fill a two-hour walk just on the two blocks of Main Street. Besides, most tourists don't want to walk uphill, and there's no restroom up that way. But I do point to the house, up there next to the cemetery, and tell them that many people have reported seeing the captain."

Jeff spoke up. "The paranormal researchers have wanted to go in there for a long time. To set up electromagnetic meters and tape recorders and such."

"But of course Maggie won't allow that. The paranormal is not science, in her estimation," David added, he and his partner adept at finishing each other's sentences. "I think that house has been in her family for a while. She inherited from an uncle or something."

Alex met his eyes. "Is there a library? Someplace where I can look things up?"

David pointed to a small, darkened alcove, just behind the front door of the restaurant. "Library is over there. It's on the honor system. Take a book, bring it back. Put it away yourself." He leaned forward and whispered, "If you're looking for something specific, it might take a while. Not everyone in this town knows the alphabet."

"Anything on local history, maybe?"

"Hmm. I don't remember seeing anything in there." He looked at Jeff.

"There's a local history museum attached to the back of the general store," David continued. "They have some of the records for property owners, that kind of thing. They even have a few records for some of the people who are buried in that cemetery. Where they came from, what they did for a living. And a few antiques and memorabilia that were found in some of the houses, way back in the Dark Ages."

Alex nodded.

"There is a newspaper out of Sea Rose Harbor, called the *Saratoga Sentinel*. Covers the whole island. But again, it would have to be something pretty sensational to get into the news. Most of the living and dying in this community—in any community—over the past hundred and fifty years goes unremarked. You might chance upon an obituary that will say something like, 'So-and-so died peacefully at home.' But most of it? A child who died of typhoid? Or a woman in childbirth? Somebody injured at the sawmill? Most of that never makes it into any written record.

"Have you ever looked through the stones in that cemetery?" David asked, taking a bite of his homemade sourdough toast.

"A little."

"Lots of people who died young. Children, of course. That's normal for that time period, no matter where you are. No antibiotics. Almost anything could take them—flu, strep throat, typhoid, scarlet fever. But even a lot of the adults didn't live long. You'll see several graves of people in their twenties and thirties."

Alex felt a shiver crawl down her spine. "Is that unusual?"

David shrugged. "Probably not."

Jeff tipped his head toward the white-haired woman walking past on the other side of the street. "I've heard Emmie say that everything has energy. Trees, rocks, wood. And in some weird way, she's right. If you think about everything being made of atoms, and that those atoms have energy, then technically, she's correct. But she also says that emotions have energy. Anger, fear. She says the energy of those emotions can get trapped. That's what happens with animals. That's what causes some of their health problems. And it happens with people. Maybe it even happens with houses."

"Do you believe that?" Alex asked.

Jeff shrugged. "I'm not sure what I believe. But once, when I was in college? I went on a trip through Colorado. And one of my stops was the site of the Sand Creek Massacre."

Jeff looked out the window again. "Happened in 1864. Huge force of US cavalry massacred Cheyenne and Arapaho Indians. They were camped there, supposedly under US protection, waiting to be moved to reservation lands. The Indians were flying US flags, and white flags, at that camp. But none of that mattered. Here comes this preacher, John Chivington, and he attacked the encampment, right at dawn. Horrific, if you read the eyewitness accounts. All kinds of ghoulish things. And two-thirds of those killed were women and children. Including a baby, torn from its mother's womb. The two bodies, lying side by side." Jeff shivered.

Alex raised her hand to her mouth.

He looked up and met the eyes of the people at the table. "I could feel *something* there. Maybe not ghosts. Maybe not spirits. But something." He took a breath. "Almost as if all that pain, all that suffering, was still hanging in the air."

David was quiet for a moment. "People say the same thing at some of the Civil War battle sites. Or the Little Bighorn, in Wyoming. Like the energy of all that trauma hasn't gone away."

They all sat quietly for a moment, absorbing the idea.

David rested his fork on his plate, his eyes watching the other side of the street. "You know, there is one other possibility."

"Oh?" Alex leaned forward just a little.

"For all the noises and such, at the captain's house. Maybe it isn't the captain."

Three pairs of eyes riveted on David's face. "Most of the ghost stories are about a ghost or a spirit that stays in one place, one house. Either because they like it, like that cat at the bookstore, or because there was some trauma, some emotional wreckage, that they haven't been able to deal with." David sat forward and leaned his elbow on the table.

"But there are also stories of ghosts, spirits, whatever you want to call them—that don't stay in one place."

Alex felt her throat tighten.

"There are stories about ghosts that get attached to certain objects—like a piece of furniture or maybe a piece of jewelry that had sentimental value. And then there are stories about ghosts who follow people. Like a relative or something. All kinds of ghost stories about people who see their mother or father, or husband or wife, or some other relative, nowhere near the place where the person lived or died. As if the ghost is attached to the living person and not a specific place."

David looked at Alex. "Did someone in your family die recently, Alex?"

Alex froze, unable to breathe. She nodded slowly. "My mother," she whispered, her voice hoarse.

"Maybe that's it. Maybe it's your mother." David looked at her, his eyes kind. "I'm sorry for your loss, Alex. That has to be tough. Were you close?"

Alex nodded, and her eyes dropped to her plate.

Caroline leaned forward and lowered her voice. "Don't turn and look. I don't want this to be obvious. But there's a man at a table over there." She tipped her head toward a table behind David's shoulder. "And he's been staring at us, for way too long.

"Alex, you need to get a look at him—see if it's someone you know. David, could you knock your napkin on the floor? Between you and Alex?"

David smiled. "You are quite the little con artist, aren't you, Caroline?" Using his elbow, he brushed his napkin onto the floor.

Alex reached to pick it up and looked at the man sitting at the table across the room. Nothing about him looked familiar to her.

"Do you know him?" Caroline whispered.

Alex shook her head. "I don't think so."

"Hmm. Maybe he's trying to flirt with me and just has vision issues or something," Caroline said.

David laughed. "Yes, Caroline, I'm sure that must be it. Is he wearing a wedding ring? Because that would definitely be your cup of tea."

She stuck her tongue out at David, and then leaned closer to Alex. "No. Not my type at all. He's got a definite cop kind of vibe to him. Law enforcement."

Alex went rigid, the way she always did if she saw a cop on the road, an automatic fear response, an automatic lifting of her foot from the accelerator, even though she rarely drove over the speed limit.

"And you are familiar with this law enforcement vibe for what reason, Caroline?" David asked.

She looked him in the eye. "Marijuana wasn't always legal, you know." Caroline pushed her chair back and stood, donning her jacket and scarf. "Well, folks. I'm going to go play in the mud."

She waited, her hand on the back of her chair. "Hey, Alex? You've seen my place. It isn't very big. But if you need somewhere to stay, let me know. We can come up with a bedroll or something. If you need to get out of that house."

Alex swallowed and nodded. "Thanks, Caroline. I appreciate it."

TWENTY-FIVE

Alex sat at her table across the room from Maggie, both of them reading and working at their computers. Both heads shot up at the sounds coming through the hydrophone, the pops and clicks and squeaks that could only mean orcas in the area.

Maggie grabbed her binoculars and stood at the window; Alex joined her. "They've been awfully quiet lately," Maggie said, her voice soft. "Lots of reports that they aren't finding enough to eat. They spread out when that happens, travel in smaller groups."

"Does that put them in more danger? Traveling in smaller groups?"

Maggie sighed heavily. "Not danger from other animals. The only animal that preys on the orca is man. But when they travel in small groups like that, it usually means they are not finding enough food."

Maggie moved her glasses to continue watching the blackfish. "We've messed with every river in the West. Building dams, straightening channels, you name it. And every time we do that, we mess with the salmon."

They stood silently, listening to the sounds of the orcas out in the strait, echolocating in their search for salmon.

"When is your divorce final?" Maggie asked, her eyes still glued to her binoculars.

Alex startled. The question was so out of the blue. For one moment, Alex debated lying about it. And then she heard Daniel's voice in her head. *Don't lie to me, Alex. I can always tell.*

"I haven't actually filed yet."

"No? I thought you had mentioned that you were getting divorced."

Alex swallowed. "I am. I just haven't gotten around to it yet."

"So you're not going back?"

Alex met Maggie's eyes. Did she mean going back to Daniel? Or going back to Albuquerque? Alex shook her head. "No. I'm not going back."

Maggie turned back to the water. "That's something I've never been able to understand. If a man hits you, why would you stay?"

Alex said nothing. She did not ask how Maggie knew; she did not disagree.

Maggie turned and shrugged. "Maybe it's easier just to disappear, wouldn't you say?"

Alex met her eyes.

"To take a car, not registered in your name." Maggie looked at the car parked next to the guesthouse, with the New Mexico plates. "No stopping at hotels, since they require a driver's license, a license plate number."

Alex forced herself to take regular breaths, to stay as even and centered as she possibly could. *Don't panic. Don't panic.*

"Applying for a job, an internship, perhaps. In a letter, written on a typewriter. No phone number, no e-mail address. The only contact information a post office box. To use only cash, no bank accounts. Cash your paycheck at the general store."

Maggie turned and looked Alex in the eye.

"When I got your letter, back in November, I thought it was quaint. Old-fashioned. But now I wonder."

Alex felt her hands begin to tremble. They were slick with sweat.

"It could be someone running away from an abusive husband. Or it could be someone who has something to hide. Running away from something else. The law, perhaps."

Maggie turned and walked back to her desk. She sat down and looked up at Alex once more, straightening her glasses. "I am aware just how much you love research. But sometimes it's better to let sleeping dogs lie. Don't you agree, Alexandra?"

TWENTY-SIX

Like a prisoner of war, she managed to endure another five years as Daniel Frazier's wife. Whenever he hit her, whenever he pushed on top of her, she let her mind go somewhere else entirely, as if none of this were happening to her. She let her mind go blank. And then she lay beside him, after he had gone to sleep, dreaming of the day when Daniel would be gone and her life would be her own again. It wasn't a plan—but it was the only survival strategy she had. The only way she could keep getting up in the morning, putting one foot in front of the other.

During those five years, she managed to amass the sum of $1,500 in cash—just by taking a ten at the grocery store, not every week, but two or three times a month. When she had too many tens, she exchanged them for a larger bill, careful not to allow too much bulk to accumulate in the false bottom of her purse. Fifteen hundred dollars wasn't enough; it would never pay a deposit and first month's rent on a new place, but she was comforted by the thought that she could, at least, buy gas and food and maybe even a few nights in a motel, if absolutely necessary. She still had no real plan; like a prisoner, her salvation was based on waiting for Daniel to die, waiting for the torture to be over. But she had developed a strategy for survival and now had a little money, waiting for the day she found freedom.

And then everything fell apart. Her mother got sick. Alex lost track of everything else in her life—she thought of nothing but her mother in those few weeks after Frances' diagnosis. She was swamped by the overwhelming regret she felt. All the mistakes she had made, all the time she had lost. If she had listened to her mother at the very beginning, all those years ago, perhaps the two of them would have been traveling together in Europe instead of living two miles away from one another, paralyzed by the jealousy and control of Daniel Frazier.

Even through that final illness, Daniel remained self-centered and demanding. "Again, Alex? You were just at your mother's last night. You have a husband to take care of, you know. I haven't had a decent meal in a week."

She stared at him, anger flaming in every cell of her body. She forced herself to breathe, her anger piling up inside her. "I'll make it up to you this weekend," she promised, standing on tiptoes to kiss him on the cheek. He turned away, his jaw hard. "She has a different nurse every few hours. I just want to make sure that they take good care of her. She's in so much pain."

"That's why they have those call buttons," he snapped. "She can still press a call button, can't she?"

Alex took a breath, as close as she had ever been to losing her temper with him. It took every ounce of will she possessed not to start screaming. "She's in so much pain, Daniel. Sometimes I think she doesn't even know where she is or that there is a call button."

He jerked away from her. Fumes of anger swept her body in waves, like a heat mirage in the desert, as she drove to her mother's house and the cadre of nurses and hospice volunteers. She forced herself to let the anger go, to leave it behind in the car. Her mother certainly didn't need this.

She sat in the chair next to her mother's bed, her hand on her mother's arm, her forehead pressed to the blanket. The anger was gone; despair was back.

Her mother lifted a hand and brushed at the hair on Alex's forehead. "Is there any ice?"

Alex sat up, and wiped her tears, and reached for the cup of ice, feeding her mother one slender chip.

"You can leave him now, you know."

Alex turned to her.

"You won't have to worry about me anymore. You are free to leave."

Alex looked into her mother's eyes, into the depths of pain and understanding that pooled there. Her first instinct was to deny. But she realized, sitting next to the mother who wouldn't be here much longer, that she was sick of lies. Sick of trying to hide the truth of her life. She'd been lying for so long, to so many people. Lies about the bruises, lies about why she couldn't attend a coworker's baby shower. Everywhere, she was surrounded by lies.

"How did you know?" Alex whispered.

Her mother took a deep breath, wincing with the pain. "I knew it had to be something like that, or you would never have gone back to him after the . . . accident with the baby."

Alex pressed her lips together and looked away for a moment. "That was no accident."

Her mother smiled slightly and touched Alex's hand. "I knew that, too. I was being kind. I know a lot more than you think I do."

Neither of them spoke. They could hear the sound of the nurse, watching television in the front room. They could hear the beeping of the heart monitor, the slow drip of the IV that fed Frances a steady stream of morphine.

"Promise me?" Her mother's voice had dropped to a murmur, hoarse and dry from all the talking.

Alex looked at her, at the gray eyes heavy with weariness, heavy with the strain of leaving her daughter behind.

"Promise me that you'll leave him now. Before it's too late. Before he does something really crazy."

A week later, Alex stood at the cemetery next to the shell of her mother's body. Even as the horrible grief of losing her mother threatened to pull her under, hatred for Daniel seethed in her bloodstream. It kept her from buckling under the weight of the heartache. It kept her from giving in to the desire to fall on the ground and sob like a child.

She *hated* him. And that hatred had force to it, a power that she had never before experienced. Hatred made her stand a little straighter; anger gave her energy that her body could never have found, after the past month of watching her mother waste away.

She watched him, talking on his phone at the edge of the cemetery. *Smiling.* Was it Chanel No.5? Or Lolita Lempicka? Maybe White Shoulders. Far too many women, with far too many perfumes, the vague scents filling her bloodstream with hatred. Hatred. Hatred. HATRED.

There had never been a time in their relationship when Alex's feelings or desires or needs were more important than his, and the night after the funeral was no exception. He pushed on top of her, despite the fact that they had just returned from burying her mother. Despite the fact that she was physically and emotionally exhausted, drained from the stress of the past few weeks. Despite the fact that he hadn't had one word to say to her for the past several hours—not through the funeral or the graveside service or on the drive home. Despite the fact that tears flowed from her eyes even as he took what he wanted.

When he moved off her, Alex rolled onto her side, away from him, the tears still steady and relentless, as if she had developed a leak. But that night, when she turned away, sucked under a tidal wave of grief, was different. For five years after they lost the baby, she had stayed with him. For five years, she endured the pain and humiliation, the constant assaults on her sanity. For five years, she dreamt of the day when Daniel would be dead and she could have her life back.

Now it was all flipped upside down. At least part of her dream was gone, vanished into the ethers along with the spirit of Frances Turner. She would not be able to spend any time traveling with her mother. All those visions of Paris and Vienna were gone, a puff of dust in a windy day.

She no longer had a reason to stay. She no longer needed to protect her mother's life by continuing to live with this monster. She was finished. She would leave him, no matter what it took.

Alex put her grief aside, placed it on the highest shelf in her heart, knowing that someday, she would take it down and look at it, really allow herself to feel it. But not now. Now, right now, in the next few days and weeks, she would come up with a plan and make her escape.

She took a silent vow as she lay in the bed beside him the night they buried her mother. She was finished. She was done with his abuse. She would find a way out, even if it killed her. He would never hurt her again.

The list began to form in her mind. She would not be able to take her cell phone or computer. No e-mail or Facebook or Instagram. No bank account or credit card. Nothing that he could use to have her traced. She would use only cash. She would need to get rid of her car and find something else, something that would not be tied to her name.

And that was exactly when her mother stepped in and helped her out.

The call came while she was at work, on a university phone line.

"Alexandra Frazier? The former Alexandra Turner?" a male voice inquired.

"Yes. This is she."

"My name is Forrest Rogers. I'm an attorney. I represent . . . I work for your mother."

Alexandra went completely still.

"First, I'd like to extend my sympathies. She was a wonderful woman. I've known her for . . . thirty years, I guess. Since the divorce from your father."

Alex leaned her elbows on her desk, completely pulled into the idea of someone her mother had known for so long and never mentioned.

"Your mother specifically requested that I not call you at home or on your cell phone. I hope this is suitable? Calling you at work?"

Alex looked around nervously, as if Daniel might be hiding in a corner. "Yes. Yes, it is."

"I need to talk to you about your mother's estate. Everything is yours, of course. But she left specific instructions about how it was to be handled."

Alex nodded.

"Could we meet? If you are not comfortable coming to my office, I would be happy to meet you somewhere for coffee. You choose the time and the place, and I will make it work somehow. Your mother explained the difficulties involved. I will do my best to be most discreet. I'll be wearing a blue scarf."

That afternoon she had coffee at a Starbucks not far from the University. She left her cell phone and her purse at work, locked inside a desk drawer, knowing that Daniel had long ago downloaded an app that made it possible for him to track her whereabouts. She ordered a coffee, offering up one of her precious ten dollar bills, and then stood at the bar area. A man moved next to her with his own coffee, not too close, absorbed in his cell phone. He was wearing a dark blue cashmere scarf.

Alex looked at a magazine in front of her, one she had grabbed on her way out of the door of her office. The attorney kept his gaze on his cell phone.

"Alex?" he murmured.

She nodded, just barely, as if nodding at something she was reading.

In a very low voice, he told her that she should clean out her mother's home, take whatever she wanted. He had been instructed to put the house on the market and to deposit the proceeds of the sale in a bank account that was held in the names of Frances and Alexandra Turner.

"Joint tenancy," he muttered. "That means you can use that money like it's your own account. No probate necessary. No forms. All arranged years ago."

Alex felt her eyes go wide, but she kept them on the magazine in front of her. She could focus on none of the words, but she did notice the pictures of orcas.

"Her car is the same. Both names. Yours to take at any moment. If you need protection, I can work on getting a restraining order against him."

Alex shook her head. "No. No. A restraining order would never stop him. I want to leave. I want to go somewhere where he can't find me." Her voice was barely a whisper.

"Okay. If necessary, you can get to wherever you are going, and I can wire you money. Just let me know what I can do to help."

He moved away from her, taking his coffee and his cell phone. He put on sunglasses and headed out into the November sunshine.

She turned a page in her magazine, and that's when she really noticed the article. Dr. Margaret Edwards and the forty-year study of orcas. Alex began to scan the article, her eyes skimming over the words *Saratoga Island, state of Washington, Copper Cove*. She stared at the pictures of the orcas, traveling in groups. One line in particular jumped out at her, blazing in her brain. *They stay with their mothers for as long as the mother lives.* Without thinking, Alex took a knife from the counter and carefully removed the pages from the magazine, folding them into quarters and putting them in her pocket.

She picked up the magazine and her coffee, and headed back to the office. It wasn't until several hours later that she realized that the magazine belonged to the University, and that she had just defaced and stolen University property.

❖

Over the next two weeks, Alex moved as if in a fog, completely lost in the tasks that needed to be done, completely absorbed by the need for secrecy. She took more time off from the University to clean out her mother's house. It was not an easy task, sending furniture and bedding and most of Frances' clothes to the Goodwill. Every object she picked up throbbed with memory, beat with the heart of her mother and of the years they had lived together in that house. As much as she wanted to hang on, to take her time, to keep at least some of the things, she knew she couldn't. Not if she planned on leaving.

She managed, in a solid week of working at the house every day, to give away most of the evidence of Frances' too-short life. There were times when it felt like tearing her own heart out, picking up her mother's reading glasses or her favorite earrings. Alex held those favorites, for just a few minutes, absorbing whatever cells of Frances Turner were still left in those objects. And then she wrapped them and put them in a box, marked for Goodwill.

There was one exception, only one small box of items that she allowed herself to keep. She had not known of its existence. Alex was cleaning the top shelf of her mother's closet and stumbled across a small box. When she pulled off the lid, her hand rose to her mouth, her breath forgotten as she stared at the pictures inside.

Shortly after Alex's father had left, shortly after they had moved to this tiny two-bedroom house, her mother had started to draw. She had loved art, way back in her youth, and had left it all behind to become wife and mother. But she brought it back after the divorce, the antidote to a broken marriage and crushed ideals.

Alex remembered coming home from school and seeing her mother sitting in a chair on the patio, drawing wispy representations of petunias, and phlox, and baby's breath. Eventually, she even tried drawing people. There were several small portraits of Alex inside that box: Alex at ten, with her first pair of glasses. Alex flopped on the couch, her nose in a book. There was a portrait of a kitten that her mother had given her, the year her father left.

It was as if every memory of her childhood were tucked inside that box. Alex held the paper to her nose, sniffing, searching for some scent of her mother buried in those drawings, some trace of her mother's cells. She sat there for over an hour, looking at each drawing, letting each small slip of paper take her back.

This box she would keep. This box she would protect. This box would go with her, wherever she ended up going. She took it home with her that afternoon and tucked it into her closet. Waiting for the moment of her escape.

A week later, she finished cleaning out all of her mother's things. She had talked to that woman on Saratoga Island, and now Alex knew she had at least part-time work, starting after Christmas. Her plans were in place. Daniel had a job at a remote location in the southern part of New Mexico starting the day after Christmas, and he would be gone for three days. And that was when she would make her escape.

She took one last look around her mother's house, running her hands along the counter in the kitchen, now completely empty of everything. Every dish, every plant, every piece of art that used to radiate her mother's taste, her mother's personality, was gone. And before long, she would be, too. Alex locked her mother's house and headed home, with no idea that it was all about to fall to pieces.

TWENTY-SEVEN

Maggie was watching her. Alex could feel it, every moment of every day, as she sat at her table, directly across the room from Maggie's desk. She could feel the woman's eyes, burning into her scalp every time she had her head lowered to look at a report. She could feel the woman's glare, boring into her back when she got up to get a cup of coffee.

She wasn't sleeping. Her nights were plagued with dreams, plagued with vague memories fighting to come to the surface, fighting for her attention. And then there was that moment, in the middle of the night, when she would wake and hear the back door, hear the click of the lock, the doorknob turning, the door swinging slowly open. Some vague, nameless ghost that would not leave her alone.

Alex was falling apart. Inside and out, she felt as if her mind and body were crumbling, no longer able to handle the day-to-day requirements of existence. Her stomach was tied in a hard, tight knot. She couldn't stop shaking. Her hands seemed to have a life of their own, one that was not tied to the rest of her body. They shook almost constantly, from the moment she entered Maggie's cabin in the morning until she left in the afternoon.

They shook now, as she poured herself another cup of coffee from the enamel pot on top of the potbellied stove. She turned, trying to use her body to shield the sight of her hands, vibrating back and forth, making the coffee slosh from one side of the cup to the other. Carefully, she retraced her steps to her own table.

"Hm-mm-mm." Maggie cleared her throat, her eyes on her work.

Alex jerked. The coffee cup jumped from her hand and crashed on the floor. Pieces of broken pottery lay scattered; a brown stain spread across the floorboards and dripped off the edge of the table. "Oh," Alex gasped. She ran to the kitchen for a towel, started sopping up the liquid on the table before it could reach the stacks of paper.

Maggie jumped up, too, grabbing files before the coffee could works its way over to them. When Alex finished mopping up the mess, Maggie gave her a hard look. "Is there something wrong with you?"

Alex swallowed. "I . . . I caught my foot on the edge of the rug, and . . ."

Maggie's mouth was a thin, firm line. "Why don't we call it a day?"

Alex nodded slowly. "Okay. See you tomorrow." She grabbed her fleece jacket and headed out. The wind was blowing, and she flipped up the hood of her jacket, feeling the chill seep into her bones. But instead of crossing the driveway, back to her own dark and quiet quarters, back to the ghosts of that house, Alex headed to the end of the driveway and turned right, away from town, down a dirt road that ran past the driveway of Maggie Edwards and curved into the trees. The forest here was tall and thick and dark; the branches of the cedars were draped with silver threads of mist.

She stood there, breathing in the scent of rain and trees. Just breathe. That's all she had to do. Just breathe.

The sound of voices carried through the mist, a rise and fall of sound, murmurs too indistinct to decipher actual words. Alex listened, trying to figure out where the voices were coming from. She could hear the rain, droplets landing on the leaves of bushes and trees with a soft *tick tick tick*.

"Watch out!"

Alex jumped, as if the words had been meant for her. It took her a moment to realize that it was one of the voices she'd been hearing, and that they were not speaking to her. She rounded a bend in the road, and there they stood, one small woman with a red raincoat, her face lost inside the hood, and the other tall and slender. The white hair of Emmie Porter glowed beneath her canvas rain hat, a dark brown cross between cowgirl and world traveler. The two women stood next to a horse that was neighing, moving nervously, trying to pull the bridle out of the hands of the smaller woman. When the horse saw Alex, it stomped a foot on the ground.

A gust of wind swept out of the trees, down across the open space where the women stood. Emmie's hat lifted and wheeled away, making a drunken dash across the grass and right into Alex's path. She grabbed it before it was gone forever, and it was at that moment that the two women noticed her.

Alex walked slowly toward them, hat in hand. The horse pulled back, neighing and moving her head up and down.

"Whoa, Cocoa, settle down." Underneath the hood of the red raincoat, Grace Wheeler spoke softly to the horse. She held fast to the bridle, trying to calm the animal.

Emmie stood in front of the horse, watching her carefully. "Something sure has her upset."

"Is it me?" Alex whispered, standing back behind the two women. They did not turn to look at her.

"I don't know," Emmie murmured. All three women watched as the horse's ears went back flat against her head, her eyes large and nervous. She stepped backward, pulling against Grace again.

Emmie's voice was quiet and low. "They're prey animals, you know. Have to be keenly aware of all the dangers around them. Rattlesnakes, mountain lions, coyotes. Something is happening out here somewhere that she doesn't like. Something that we haven't picked up on yet."

Emmie was quiet for a long moment, studying the horse. "Or maybe it isn't something that is happening right now. Maybe something out here has triggered a memory. She's had some trauma in her life, and she's got PTSD—post-traumatic stress disorder."

"I just bought this horse a few months ago," Grace said quietly. "Got a good deal on her. But that's because she has issues. She belonged to a man who thought you had to *break* the animal to make it work for you. He broke her, all right. Broke her spirit. Made her afraid . . . more afraid than normal, that is. She'd been kicked and yelled at. Tied up where she couldn't even move her head up and down."

Emmie still stood quietly, watching. She made no move to touch the horse. "I saw it so many times when I was growing up. Men who tried to control the animal through fear. Through physical pain. Intimidation. It backfires, every single time. Kick a horse a few times, and you end up creating a monster. Hard to catch, hard to bridle, hard to get a saddle on, because they're afraid of what's coming next. They know what's coming. And they'll do almost anything to avoid it.

"If you do it enough—hit them, kick them, abuse them—one of two things will happen. The horse might just give up, refuse to do anything. Or it might turn on you. Try to bite you or throw you or kick you. Either way, you no longer have a horse that you can work with. I saw a horse take a hunk out of a man's head once, when I was growing up. They had to put her down. Too dangerous to keep around. You can hardly blame the horse, though. Not after everything it had been through. Seemed like a normal reaction to me. When an animal has been abused that much.

"It's like when a soldier comes back from war, or someone who's been in a bad car accident—any kind of really traumatic event. They cope any way they can. But sometimes that means that the brain buries the actual memory. Allows them to forget, at least for a little while."

Emmie turned and looked at Alex. "And then some weird random event will trigger all that buried trauma. Hearing a loud noise, or somebody yelling, or the smell of fire, anything like that—can cause the brain to go right back to the moment it happened. Living the event all over again. And that's when things can get dangerous. I once saw a horse nearly trample a woman, just because she rattled her cup of ice."

Alex could not look at her, and turned away to stare into the trees.

"That's what a lot of Eastern medicine is all about. Reiki, massage, acupuncture, yoga. It's all about moving those places where the trauma, the negative energy, is stuck. Working it out. Getting it moving again. That's what I do with the animals."

Alex spoke softly. "Do you ever work on people?"

Emmie stood in front of Cocoa, her eyes still on the little mare. "No." She took a deep breath. "Horses, dogs . . . they're completely honest. Horses sense if the rider is afraid or not paying attention. If they don't like you, they let you know. If they don't trust you, they let you know. You don't have to worry that they're hiding something."

She turned and looked Alex directly in the eye. "Which is usually not the case with most people."

Alex took a step backward. She swallowed and dropped her eyes to the muddy ground in front of her.

"When I was eighteen, I met this blue-eyed cowboy who showed me that there was another way," Emmie continued. "That the best way to work with an animal is to learn how to cooperate, how to work together. You have to try to understand what the horse is thinking, what the horse might be feeling. What the horse is afraid of. And when you can do that—when you can feel what it feels—then you can make some progress. Then you can work together. Then the horse will do just about anything you ask it to."

Emmie took a long, slow breath. "I don't know what has upset her, Grace, but I don't think you should ride her today." Emmie touched Cocoa gently on the forehead.

Grace led the horse inside the barn stall, and then stepped back out, locking the stall door in place. "You two want to come in for a cup of tea?" she asked.

Alex shook her head. "I better not." After dropping her cup at Maggie's, Alex was certain that she could not handle a teacup, not with Emmie nearby.

Emmie watched the younger woman for a moment, and said, "Thanks, Grace, but I have to pass."

Grace said her goodbyes and headed into the house. "See you at the spinsters, Alex?"

Alex nodded.

Emmie turned to Alex and took the hat from her hands. She dusted it against her leg and put it back on her head.

They started ambling down the driveway, back to the main road. Emmie's voice, when she spoke, was barely audible. "You can't run, you know."

Alex slowed her steps, but she watched the ground in front of her and did not look at the woman who could read energy.

"It never works—trying to outrun the pain. It gets lodged in the body, in the subconscious, and there's no running away from that. Nowhere on earth to escape what we carry in here." Emmie held her hand to her heart.

Alex did not speak. Tears leaked, but she made no move to wipe them away.

The two women continued down the dirt road, curving out of deep woods and back to the top of the hill where Maggie had her house and cabin.

Emmie stopped in the road, directly in front of Maggie's driveway. "Well, this is me," she said. She raised her hand to indicate the small home set back in the trees, almost directly across from Maggie's driveway.

"You live right there?" Alex asked.

Emmie nodded. "For years and years."

"That explains why I see you out walking your dogs so often."

"Yeah. I have to go by Maggie's every time I want to leave the house." She stopped and turned to Alex again. "But I quit asking permission years ago."

Alex watched as a small twitch of a smile lifted the corners of Emmie's mouth. She turned down her own driveway, raising her hand in goodbye.

TWENTY-EIGHT

Alex shoved her hands in the pockets of her coat and turned her back on Emmie, walking down the driveway to the captain's house. The rain had started, yet again, and was coming down hard.

She glanced up at the house, her hood and the mist on her glasses obscuring her vision. It was as if the house itself were watching her, keeping an eye on her comings and goings. The windows stared down at her, like the eyes of an animal. Like everyone and everything was watching her—Maggie, Emmie, the ghost in this house.

It did not feel like home, this house with its own secrets. She had no home, and she hadn't had one in years, not if home meant a place that was supposed to feel safe, to feel like a refuge from the problems in the world. She had run from Albuquerque, run away from that awful marriage and all its deep, dark secrets, but she had not escaped. The ghosts of the past were sifting up from the layers of her mind, refusing to stay silent. And now this house, with ghosts of its own, was twisting and wrapping around her own muddled past, as if the secrets of the house were invading her dreams, invading her thoughts. Conspiring to make her remember.

A movement to her left caught her attention, and she turned slightly to see Maggie, standing in the window of the front room of her cabin. Maggie tipped her head toward Alex, and moved away.

She ran the last few steps to the house and up the porch. She unlocked the door and stepped inside, shaking water from her coat before she locked the door behind her.

It was bad enough that she had her own demons to worry about. She did not want to think about what might have happened here, at this house above the cemetery.

Alex moved to the window, looking out at the graves, staring into the dusk, lost in the gray-green-blue light of hard rain and coming night. Focused on the stones outside, on the movement of the trees, she almost missed it. Something had moved, in the house behind her, reflected in the window. Out of the corner of her eye, she had seen a flutter, just a shadow that registered in her vision. Alex stared at her reflection in the window, stared at the reflection of the area just over her shoulder, barely able to discern the darkness of the house behind her, barely able to see the staircase that twisted up to the second floor. She stood still, listening, watching.

The wood on the stairs groaned, a faint noise that might have been nothing more than the house adjusting to wind and damp. There was a creaking noise, like hinges on a door.

Alex turned and walked over to the front hall, to that weird staircase that wound up to the door. She eased up the steps, watching above her, and put her hand on the door. It was locked, just as she had imagined. She dropped her hand to her side and stood still for a moment. Once again she heard that creaking noise. The doorknob in front of her twisted, she heard the click of a lock, and the door opened. Alex moved, inch-by-inch, step-by-step, keeping her back pressed against the wall as she edged up the remaining two steps and crept through the door.

The upstairs was much like the floor below it. Four-inch thick mahogany trim ran along the bottoms and tops of each wall; it framed every door and window. Three doors opened onto the hallway. She inched along, the shadows thick with the dusk and the rain. To her left was a bathroom, a relic from the fifties, with old pink tile work. To her right was a large bedroom, furnished with antiques. This room was directly over the dining room, and boasted an exact replica of the bay window below. Alex moved there now. The view from this room was spectacular, or at least it would be when the rain and clouds and dark were not clamped down so tight. She could make out the lights of town below, the outlines of the cemetery, the deep black of the water out in Haro Strait. She wondered if this was the place where the captain used to stand.

She turned and went back to the hallway, headed to the last door, at the back of the house. The door appeared to be closed, but when she raised her hand to the doorknob, it swung open easily. The room was cold, much colder than the other two rooms upstairs. Alex shivered and ran her hands up and down her arms.

The room held a bed, covered with a quilt made of patches from old blue jeans. She turned to see a stack of shelves. There were a few books: *Lord of the Flies*, *Heart of Darkness*, *The Best of Edgar Allen Poe*. The owner's taste certainly ran toward the darker titles in literature. Trophies lined the shelves: basketball, football, baseball, mostly from Copper Cove High School. Most valuable player, 1987. Division champions, 1986.

This room must have belonged to Maggie's son, when he was still at home. Alex turned and moved to the dresser against another wall. There were a couple of photographs sitting on it. She picked up the first: a boy, about eight, standing with Maggie and what must have been his father, Maggie's husband. The man had a thick beard, shot through with gray.

She picked up another, and there was Brian as a teenager, dressed in a tux for some school prom or dance. He smiled at the camera, all white teeth and dark hair. He was posed with a young woman who had long dark curls. She was wearing a lacy black gown, smiling just as he was. They made a striking couple. Another photo showed Maggie's son, dressed in his high school cap and gown, that same beautiful girl standing next to him, smiling.

Alex put the photograph down and looked around the room. There were no secrets jumping out at her. No strange noises or whispered clues about what had happened in this house on the hill. She took a deep breath and started back down the hall. She was almost to the top of the stairway when she finally registered the one thing that was not quite right, the one thing that could not be true for rooms that had been locked up for a long time. She could smell roses. Just like this was a June morning in a beautiful garden, the scent of roses wrapped around her. Alex stopped, scanning the darkened corners. She exhaled and started down the stairs, careful to close the door at the top so that no one would ever know she had been up there, snooping.

It wasn't until much later, when she was lying in bed, tossing and turning, that the face in that photograph came back to her. She had seen that young woman somewhere before, she felt certain of it.

She lay on her side, staring out the window. And then it came to her. That photograph in Maggie's box of papers, the one with Maggie and her son and the young woman, all standing on Maggie's boat and smiling at the camera. The girl in the photographs upstairs had to be the same one. She had the same long dark curls, the same striking beauty.

What was it Maggie had said? Some intern? Something about having so many that she couldn't remember all their names. But surely she would remember the name of a girl her son had dated, wouldn't she? Surely she would remember a girl who was that beautiful?

Had the great Maggie Edwards lied?

TWENTY-NINE

Alex sat for several moments, frozen, staring into space. And then she reached for the spinning wheel, pulling it closer to her chair, right square in front of her. She slipped her shoes off, placed her stocking feet on the treadles, and took roving in her left hand. Just a week ago, she had not known how to do this—how to take a handful of roving and turn it into yarn. But now she understood what the spinsters had said the first day she went down to the old Hadley house. Spinning was a place of calm, a place deep inside her where she could lose her conscious awareness. Where she could shake off all the fears, all the odds and ends and bits and pieces of foreboding that hung around her like the heavy clouds of a storm.

Alex swallowed and started the wheel, one hand holding the roving gently, the other pulling a few fibers at a time, letting them build up twist. Every few seconds, she moved her hand forward to feed the twisted yarn onto the bobbin. It didn't take long before she forgot to be afraid, forgot to feed the monster of worry that hung over her shoulder. She felt her body calming, felt her breath changing to an even, deeper vibration. She spun, lost in the rhythm, lost in the quiet song of the wheel, until the clock in the living room struck ten.

She tied off the roving, moved the wheel back a few feet, and stood and stretched. Maybe now she could sleep. Maybe now all the monsters were asleep, as well. She went to the fireplace and added one more log to the coals inside, tamping all of it down with the fireplace poker.

She hung the tool on the hook next to the fire and headed for bed, dropping almost immediately into an exhausted sleep.

Alex had pulled her car into the driveway, grateful to see that Daniel was not home yet. She sat there for a moment, arms over the top of the steering wheel, thinking about the fact that in just less than a week, she would be leaving this car behind. Not that it mattered—she had long since passed the point where she had felt like anything was really *hers*. They had long passed the point where her desires, her likes, had any effect on decisions.

They had sold her Honda several years ago, not long after they married. She now drove the Volvo that Daniel had chosen. It had leather seats, not because he was spoiling his wife with a nice car, but because he often took this car when he needed to make an impression on a new job prospect.

It was five-thirty on a December evening. The sky was black; the house was dark. Alex let herself in and hung her coat by the door. She walked through the kitchen and heaved a sigh. Standing at the counter, she realized that she would have to come up with something for dinner. The last few weeks, she had been so absorbed in cleaning out her mother's effects, the last thing that had crossed her mind was figuring out what to cook for dinner.

She rounded the corner to the living room and gasped. "Ahh!" Her hand rose up to her throat. "You scared me," she said. "I didn't know you were home."

Daniel sat by the fireplace, the one they rarely used, in front of a crackling fire. There were no lights on in the house, and his face was lit only by the glow from the fire. He ran his hands over his face, dark and coarse with beard stubble, and looked up at her, his eyes dark as the night.

"Who is he, Alex?"

She swallowed. "What are you talking about?" She tried to make her heart slow down, tried to keep her body and face relaxed. *Look normal. Act normal. Don't give anything away.*

"The man you've been seeing." He watched her intently. She continued to stand just inside the entryway to the living room.

Alex was stupefied. A man? She had a million secrets, at this point, a whole case of lies and plans that he knew nothing about. But a man? "That's crazy. I'm not seeing anyone."

He was up and on her before she had time to blink, his hand gripping the front of her shirt as he lifted her slightly from the floor. "You're calling me crazy?"

"No. No, I would never . . ."

He slapped her, dropping the wad of shirt that he held in his hand. She stumbled sideways, against the side of the sofa, but did not drop.

He turned, went back to the fire, and sat down in the chair. He ran his hands through his hair, once again, and then leaned forward, feeding the flames. "I know all about it, Alex. Don't bother to try and cover it up with lies."

She moved forward, to his side. "Daniel, I would never cheat on you."

He turned and looked at her. "Oh, really? Well, isn't that interesting. Because Kevin? The kid who runs errands for me? He saw you with a man at Starbucks."

Alex felt the wind go out of her. She stood as still as a fence post, her mind racing. "No, Daniel. It's not what you think."

"You know what I think? I think it might be time for you to learn your lesson."

She looked at him, wondering what horror he had in mind for her tonight. Her gaze dropped from his face to his hands, and that was when she saw the papers that he was feeding into the fire. Drawings. Pencil, colored pencil, charcoal. The artwork that her mother had created over the past forty years, the only box of things that Alex had allowed herself to keep. She looked at the box, sitting next to his side. It was already half gone, and she watched in shock as he fed another drawing into the fire.

He turned and looked at her, a smile lifting the corners of his mouth. "You can't fool me, Alex. I always find out, in the end. I can always tell when you're lying. You think you're so smart. But I always know." He glared at her. "Maybe this will teach you to tell me the truth."

She had heard the expression *seeing red*, a literary reference that she had stumbled across several times in all those years of losing herself in books. And suddenly she knew exactly what that meant. Her anger surged, swelling through every part of her five-foot-one-inch frame, flaming in her blood vessels so that all she could see was the color red. Red walls, red carpet, red sofa. She saw everything he had ever done to her, every time he had hit her or humiliated her, all of it, burning in her mind like a bright red ball of fire.

She flew at him, her hands and feet flailing, pulling his hair, screaming in a way she had never done in her whole life, a bloodcurdling scream that came up from somewhere deep in her soul, somewhere that had been crushed under the weight of too much oppression, too much abuse, for far too long.

He flung her off and stood, his fist coming back and landing squarely on her left eye.

And just like every other time that he had hit her, her mind went blank. A numb black slate that would not allow any of the pain, any of the realization of what was really happening, to penetrate the layers of her foggy brain. It was gone, all of it, every moment of that evening, lost in the will to survive, in the body's need to shut out the horror.

When she woke, she lay on the floor of their living room, curled on her side, every bit of her body screaming with pain. She sat up, looking around the room. Daniel lay nearby, as if he had grown tired of beating her and had lain down for a nap. It seemed odd, off, somehow. Between them, lying on the floor, was the poker from the fireplace. Alex pushed herself up and hurried to get out of there, before Daniel could wake and come after her again.

The next thing she could remember was driving. It was dark; she was on a highway. The lights of Albuquerque appeared only as a vague glow in her rearview mirror. She had no real idea where she was, or what highway she was on. She could not remember leaving. She did not remember getting rid of the Volvo, but she must have done that at some point, because she was now driving her mother's car, an older Subaru Forester.

That was when the pain started to return. She glanced in the rearview mirror: one eye was swollen shut; her side ached and throbbed, although she could not remember exactly what had happened. Her nose hurt, her cheeks hurt, every inch of her body hurt.

She took a deep breath. The only thing she knew, with certainty, was that she was out. Driving away from Albuquerque. Away from Daniel and eleven years of hell. She glanced at the passenger seat and was glad to see her purse and a jacket. On the floor, she could see the straps of her travel bag.

She didn't notice her hands, not until she lifted one to touch her swollen eye. In the dim light, it was difficult to tell what was on her palm, but it felt sticky. It wasn't until she stopped for gas, three hours later, and went to the restroom inside that she could see what it was. Her palm was covered in blood.

Alex bolted up in her bed in Copper Cove, her breath coming in short, ragged gasps. She was breathing too fast, about to hyperventilate. Her hands cramped. In one swift bombardment, all the ghosts that had been buried deep in her subconscious mind rushed back, jumping out at her from all sides. Alex sat, looking at her palm, remembering the blood. Remembering the fireplace poker, lying on the floor of the living room, between the two of them. Remembering Daniel, slumped on the floor. She shook her head. No. No. It couldn't be. She would never actually *hurt* someone. Would she? She didn't remember actually *hitting* him.

Just outside the window of the bedroom, she heard the sound of scratching. The rosebushes sounded almost like fingernails, scraping against the wood of the window frame, occasionally scraping against the glass. Alex stood and pulled back the curtain.

It had snowed during the night. An inch of soft white covered every surface, every branch of every tree. It rested on the fence around the cemetery, dusted the tops of all the gravestones. The snow reflected the light, turned the entire landscape soft and silent and glowing.

Wind sifted through the branches of the rosebush, just outside. The branches were long; a few stubborn leaves clung to the vine. She watched as the wind whipped them once again, watched as they scratched against her window.

She forced herself to take a breath. It was only that rosebush, after all. She started to turn away when something else caught her eye, vaguely visible in the dim light. Alex raised the window, letting the cool air rush in around her. On the ledge, just beneath the window, there were scratch marks in the wood. They looked nothing like the slim marks that would be left by the thorns on the rosebush. These scratches were deep, more like fingernails, reaching for the window, trying to get in. They looked as if someone, not tall enough to actually reach the window from outside, had been trying to pull themselves up, fingernails scratching the wood trim, unable to get in.

Alex looked at the bush below, at the ground around it. There were footprints in the fresh snow, the footprints of one person, someone who had walked right up to the window of this room where she had slept. One set of footprints, walking right up to the window where she now stood, leaning out the window and shivering from the cold.

But there were no footprints the other direction. Whatever had walked up to this window, whatever had tried to scratch its way inside, could not be human. Whatever had come up here in the night had left no trace in the fresh powder of having walked away.

She raised a hand to her heart, trying to stop the rising sense of panic. *No. Oh, please, no. Leave me alone. Just leave me alone.*

THIRTY

Alex drank three cups of coffee before she headed to work at Maggie's, a desperate attempt to counteract the fact that she had not been able to go back to sleep. All day she sat at her table, trying to focus on the words of the reports, trying to focus on what she needed to do. Her hands shook. She could not look Maggie in the eye. She did her best to seem totally absorbed in her work.

And all day long, words ran through her head in a chorus, like the lyrics of a song that gets stuck and won't let go. *I didn't mean to do it. I didn't mean to do it.*

At three, Maggie leaned back in her own chair across the room, removed her glasses, and rubbed her eyes. "Alex, it's New Year's Eve, and you've been at it all day. Why don't we go ahead and knock off for the evening?"

Alex glanced up and gave a deep sigh. "Okay. That sounds good." She turned off the computer and straightened her stack of papers. She pushed in her chair, walked over to the hooks by the door, and with every movement she told herself, *Act normal. Look normal.*

Maggie stood and went to the big window, looking out at the sky. "Storm coming. Do you have plans tonight, Alex?"

Alex stood by the door, pulling on her jacket. "Not really. I might go down to the spinsters for a bit, do a little spinning. Nothing earth-shattering." She winced at her use of the word *earth-shattering*, as if anything she said might give her away, might somehow flash the truth of her situation like the neon signs in town. "What about you, Maggie? Any plans?"

Maggie continued to stare out to sea. She shook her head. "No. I'm not really into the holidays."

Alex paused at the door. "Happy New Year, Maggie."

Maggie nodded. "Yeah. You, too."

Alex showed up at the Hadley house right at four. The storm had started; wind whipped the branches of the trees, and rain pelted them, coming in at a slant as David unlocked the door. They stepped inside the house, shaking off their drops of moisture and stomping their feet on the mat. The house behind them was cold and dark.

Caroline showed up a minute later, running, and she, too, came in shaking and dripping. "It's going to be a humdinger out there. Watch out for flying lawn furniture." She shook for a minute. "But at least the rain melted all the snow."

David bent and started a fire in the fireplace, and Caroline and Alex stood nearby, their hands stuffed up under their arms in an attempt to stay warm. The kindling took, and David stood, shivering.

"No Grace tonight?" Alex asked. "No Emmie?"

David shook his head. "She and Emmie always spend New Year's Eve together, at home. I don't think they like all the crazies that come out on the last night of the year."

David sat down and pulled out his bag of knitting. Caroline stood in front of the fire, warming her backside. Alex slipped into the chair that she had come to think of as hers. She pulled the spinning wheel from her bag and started to lock the pieces into place, but even here, with David and Caroline, her hands continued to shake. She dropped a bobbin on the floor, and it rolled over to David's feet.

He bent and retrieved it, holding it out to Alex.

She reached for it, her hands almost vibrating, and sat down again. She felt sweat pop out on her lip.

"Alex, are you all right?" David asked. "You look a little . . . I don't know. Kind of peaked, is that the right word?"

Alex swallowed. "I'm all right. Just not enough sleep, that's all."

Caroline turned away from the fire. "It's that house, isn't it? Something is going on in that house."

Alex shrugged. She tried to start her spinning, but the fiber broke before she had managed two turns of the wheel.

"Actually," David began, "I did a little checking. Since the other morning, when we talked. Spoke to a few friends."

Alex did not look up. She could not breathe.

"You have friends?" Caroline quipped.

"Why don't you go annoy a heterosexual?"

Caroline crossed her arms over her chest. "That's the plan. Later this evening, in fact."

David looked at Alex. "I know a few people. Because of the newspaper. A few friends at the county records office. One or two at the sheriff's office."

Alex's hands were shaking so hard she did not want to even attempt spinning, and she held them in her lap.

David kept his eyes on his knitting. "My friend from the sheriff's office is on vacation this week, so I couldn't get anything there."

Alex exhaled.

"But I went back to the tavern yesterday evening, to talk to one of my favorite old-timers. He's the one that supplied most of the material on my ghost tours." David waited one moment, counting his stitches, ". . . eight, nine, ten."

He looked at Alex. "Seems there was an intern working for Maggie, many years ago. Late eighties, I think he said. She disappeared."

Caroline sat down in a chair. "What do you mean, 'disappeared'?"

"Just . . . disappeared. No sign of her anywhere. No body. No blood. No indication of foul play. Just nothing. She's never been seen or heard from again. Not that he was aware of, anyway."

"She worked for Maggie?" Caroline asked.

David nodded. "And she was staying in that house. The house you're in right now, Alex."

Alex didn't move. Swallowing took enormous effort. "Did she take her clothes? Like she was . . . fleeing? Running away?" She was almost afraid to say those words out loud, afraid that David and Caroline would be able to read her own history in the questions she asked.

"I don't know the answer to that," David said. "He said they found her purse, still in the house. The funny thing is, I think he mentioned this to me before, all those years ago, when I was gathering info for the ghost tours. But I didn't really think about it. Maggie's interns all seem to leave rather suddenly. I guess I just lumped this story together with all the other interns."

Alex looked up and met Caroline's gaze.

Caroline shivered. "That's creepy. Seems like if you were running away, you would at least want your purse."

David nodded. "I thought it was interesting. That was what? Almost thirty years ago? But still . . ." He was quiet for a moment. "Might be something you need to know, Alex. Since you're living there."

David waited a few moments. "Hey, Alex? Jeff and I are making all kinds of food tonight. Why don't you come spend the New Year with us?"

Alex looked at him, as if she couldn't quite remember who he was. She did not want to go back to that house on the hill, alone. But she also knew there was no way she could handle the strain of trying to act normal, of trying to hide all the memories that had been flying back at her, of trying to look as if she were innocent of any wrongdoing. She shook her head slowly. "Thanks for asking, David. I'm not sure I want to go out tonight."

"Well, not with two gay guys—no. What kind of fun could that be? Your chances of finding any action would be a big fat zilch," Caroline joked.

David sighed and shook his head.

"I'm not really looking for action," Alex murmured.

Caroline looked at her, her head tipped to one side, as if she were trying to figure something out. She leaned forward and put her hand on Alex's forearm. "Are you sure you're okay?"

Alex stared at the fiber in her lap, her eyes burning. She did not look up; she blinked rapidly, trying to chase away the tears. Her head moved in a slow nod. "I'm okay."

Caroline continued to watch her for a moment.

"Well, a little action never hurt a soul, as far as I know," she said, her eyebrows arching up. "Anybody want to join me? A few drinks at the Strait Up?"

"Caroline, haven't you destroyed enough marriages for one year?" David asked.

"It was just the one. And besides, the New Year starts in a few hours. Might as well get a jump on it." She cocked her head to the side. "Actually, it already *is* the New Year in most parts of the world."

David shook his head and waved a hand in her direction. "Go carouse to your heart's content. But they're saying this storm is going to be a doozy. Winds up to sixty miles per hour. Three inches of rain. Branches breaking. Trees falling. Might lose power. No lights, no electricity. You might be in the middle of that vacation crowd, in the dark." He leaned forward dramatically. "Who knows what kind of trouble you could get into?"

Caroline raised her shoulders in a dramatic shiver. "Sounds like fun. Bumping into men in the dark. Maybe a little groping going on."

"Is that your idea of fun? Being groped by perfect strangers in a dark bar?" David grimaced.

"Of course not. I want to be the one doing the groping." Caroline's eyebrows arched.

"You're a sick woman. No wonder Alex doesn't want to hang out with you."

Caroline got quiet a moment. "Hey, Alex? Can I ask you something?"

Alex looked up at her.

"Are you in some kind of trouble?"

Alex sat frozen; she could not speak.

"It's just that . . . this is a small town, you know. We don't have a lot to keep us occupied. And some of the people are talking."

Alex could not breathe properly.

"I'm not trying to be nosy or anything. It's just that . . . well, you showed up here, with that black eye." Caroline's voice went down a little. "And now . . ."

"Now what?" David asked.

"All the regulars at the bar are talking about it." Caroline looked at Alex. "About what, exactly, you are running away from."

David let out a long exasperated breath. "Caroline." He shook his head. "As much as I normally love someone who speaks her mind, it now appears that you no longer have one."

David leaned forward in his chair and put his hand on Alex's knee. "Ignore her. But, Alex? If you need help, all you have to do is ask. You know that, right?"

Alex looked into David's blue eyes. Kindness radiated from him. For a moment, it was on the tip of her tongue, to tell them what had happened. To tell them that she had never meant to kill Daniel, that it was all a tragic mistake. For a moment, she met David's eyes, lost in the need to confess, lost in the need for refuge, for understanding.

At that moment, a huge gust of wind swooped down on the town. The rafters over their heads moaned, and all three of them looked up at the ceiling. They heard a branch hit the roof.

"I need to go," Alex whispered. She stood and grabbed her coat, pulling it on as she walked toward the door. Her spinning wheel and fiber lay abandoned behind her.

She opened the door; wind gusted into the room. Outside, the storm screeched and thundered.

They all heard it, the sound of a large tree going down, somewhere north of town. It hit the ground with a crash, and the earth shook. And then they heard the sputter and fizz of the power lines. Main Street, with all the streetlamps and all the many strings of Christmas lights, buzzed for just one second before it blinked out. The entire town of Copper Cove went dark.

Alex turned and rushed up the hill, away from the Hadley house, away from David and Caroline, her head ducked slightly to try to avoid the rain, lashing at the sides of her face. It was coming in almost sideways with the wind. Her face, her glasses, even her eyelashes were soaking wet; she could barely see where she was going. She ran up the hill, into the darkness.

THIRTY-ONE

When Robin walked through the door, that first day of school in her junior year, she was wearing a black dress, a la Stevie Nicks, and singing "Rhiannon," her absolute favorite Nicks song, since it was about a witch. Almost immediately, all sounds in the hallway went quiet; all eyes turned to watch her. Over the summer, she had changed completely. Gone was the little tomboy, rail thin and wearing jeans and T-shirts, replaced by a dark-haired beauty whose curves had shifted, like the sands after the tide. When Robin walked in the door, everyone, even the seniors who had never noticed her before, took note.

She shimmied down the hallway, swirling her skirts and singing her song, feeling a surge of power that she had never known before, one she immediately recognized as being related to the development of breasts.

Brian Carter, by then a senior and the captain of the football team, was standing next to Stephanie Spencer, both of them in front of Stephanie's locker. Stephanie glared at Robin, but the look in Brian's eyes was something completely different.

Robin stopped in front of them and looked directly at Brian. "Are you finished?" she asked, loudly enough to be heard.

He smiled. "Finished what?"

Robin reached a hand inside her own dress, between her breasts, and brought it back out, closed in a fist. "Here. Put your eyeballs back in your head." She turned to Stephanie and asked, "What's wrong, Steph? Never seen breasts before?" She flounced her dress and danced away, the chorus of "Rhiannon" filling the air behind her.

At lunchtime a few days later, she walked into the cafeteria to hear a group of girls, all clustered around Stephanie Spencer, singing "Ro-ah-bin" to the tune of "Rhiannon." She stopped, walked right over to the table of girls, and leaned in to look at Stephanie. "Didn't your mama ever tell you not to mess with the village witch?" Robin stood straighter and put a finger to her lips. "Let's see. Shall I curse you with pimples? Or small boobs?" She glanced down at Stephanie. "Oh, wait. I see I'm too late. Someone has already done that."

Some of the boys at a nearby table snickered, and Robin blew them a kiss and waltzed away.

The night of the homecoming dance, Robin came in on the arm of Jim Butler, one of her pals from art class. He wasn't much of a dancer and had always been considered something of a geek, but the fact that he was out on the floor with the dark-haired beauty was drawing a fair amount of attention. Apparently, Robin was good at more than just sketching and singing and swimming—her list of talents included moving across the dance floor as if she were destined to do backup for Madonna. There were a few of the boys on the football team who wanted to stand a little closer to that action, and they took turns cutting in. Jim spent more than his fair share of time at the side of the gym, drinking sugary punch from a plastic cup.

When Brian showed up and held his arms out for a slow dance, Robin met his gaze. "Does your bodyguard know where you are?"

Brian laughed. "She's not my bodyguard. I dance with whomever I please."

"Is that right?" Robin smiled. "Are you sure you're willing to take the risk? I might put a spell on you."

He pulled her closer. "I'll take my chances." He held her hand and inhaled the scent of her hair, a mixture of scents that all spoke of nature, like cedar and rosewater, a concoction that was twisting into his gut and swirling through his bloodstream. She *was* working a spell on him. He moved slowly from side to side and let his hand start to drift down her backside.

Robin stopped dancing, took a step backward, and slapped his face. "Watch your hands, Carter. I'm not a football." She turned and flounced away, and he looked up to see Stephanie standing at the edge of the dance floor, glaring at him.

No one had ever talked to him like that. He could still feel the imprint of her hand against his cheek, and for a moment, that mark flamed red.

Brian had always been the star, at the top of everything he touched, the guy everyone looked up to. He was used to getting his way, having grown up in a home where his mother let him do pretty much as he pleased. She was busy with her work, and as long as he checked in at least once a day, she did not concern herself overmuch with his comings and goings. His father had stayed largely out of the picture since the boy was ten, coming to see his son once or twice a year. When he did come to visit, his father was usually accompanied by a younger female from the University, quite often much younger than the venerable Dr. Carter. Brian tried not to take it personally, but he resented the fact that his father never had time for *just* his son, as if he couldn't make it through a weekend without the adoration of a girlfriend to keep him occupied.

His parents may not have given him an excess of attention, but on the other hand, they almost never told him no. He managed to get his own way, growing up, simply because they were too busy to bother. He learned the art of attracting attention from wherever he could get it: teachers, girls, the boys in sports.

Brian was the star athlete, excelling in every sport: quarterback of the football team, center on the basketball team, ace pitcher on the baseball team at Copper Cove High School. He loved being the center of attention. He relished being the guy they all relied on to pull them out of a hole, the guy who had all the answers. And he thoroughly enjoyed the female attention that came with that role. Stephanie Spencer was a cheerleader, always at every game, always right there, rooting for him.

Not one of his friends, not the boys on the team, or any of the girls, and certainly not Stephanie Spencer, ever said what they really thought. Being at the top had made everyone around him, male and female, into some kind of groupie, more interested in Brian's approval, of being seen with him, than in any kind of real connection.

Robin was the first person he had ever encountered who said exactly what she thought, and to hell with the consequences. She didn't need his approval. She didn't need to be seen with him. Having survived her first sixteen years as the social outcast, she had learned to navigate her own waters, without help from the likes of him.

It drove him absolutely crazy.

Spring break came in March, and Robin went to work for Brian's mother. She traded her Stevie Nicks dresses for coveralls and flannel and wool, and was out on the boat every time Maggie wanted to go, taking pictures, recording sounds on the new hydrophone, keeping records about where the orcas were spotted and when. Keeping records about the number of salmon in the streams, helping Maggie take water samples and record the results.

The girl was a hard worker, and won Maggie's approval because of it. Maggie didn't seem to mind at all that Robin was often singing as she worked, almost absentmindedly, as if she had a music track running in her head, a backdrop to the work she was focused on. She provided her own radio accompaniment.

Maggie had offered to help her find grant funding so that she could attend UW after she graduated from high school. There was no way Emmie could afford college for her daughter, and Maggie was willing to help, since Robin seemed so eager and capable when it came to watching the orcas.

Brian did not share his mother's love of the orcas; he really did not want to spend any of his free time with his *mother*. But his attitude changed completely that spring of his senior year, when Robin Porter was showing up every morning to go out on the boat all day. Suddenly, he was more than happy to help. He was especially fascinated when Robin dropped into the water one day to retrieve a piece of equipment that had become stuck in brush. When she pulled herself back onto the boat, water dripping from her body and her clothes plastered to her frame, he nearly fell over backward.

He did what he had always done with the other females at Copper Cove High School. When they were pulling up an underwater camera, he managed to push up against her, his arms brushing against her breasts. But unlike Stephanie Spencer, Robin did not giggle.

Her voice was loud enough that even Maggie turned around. "Watch it, Mr. Hands."

Brian held his arms out to his sides, putting on that innocent smile that never failed with teachers and certainly never failed him with females. "What? I didn't do anything."

"Like hell you didn't. I say who gets to touch these babies and when," she spat, looking right in his eyes but cupping her breasts in her hands. "Not you."

His mother gave him a hard look through her sunglasses and returned to her work. Brian went to the front of the boat, back to the job of taking photos of their surroundings. But he had a hard time concentrating. He was absolutely smitten with Robin, with the way she looked, with the way she smelled, with the way she challenged and pushed. He couldn't stop thinking about her.

When spring vacation was at an end, and they were docking and cleaning up equipment, Brian waited until his mother had started up the hill to the house. He sat down on the edge of the boat and reached for Robin's hand.

She turned quickly, pulling her hand away.

"Robin." He swallowed hard. "I can't stop thinking about you. I dream about you all the time."

Robin leaned back against the other side of the boat. "Stephanie know about this?"

He looked her right in the eye. "Steph and I broke up."

"Oh, really? Since when? Does she know?"

It wasn't exactly the truth, but Brian knew that he *would* break up with her, just as soon as he had the chance. Just as soon as he had Robin securely in his grasp. He reached for Robin's hand again and rubbed his thumb along the top. "Can I take you out for a burger?"

She pulled her hand away and gazed at him, as if through looking she could see inside his mind and figure out what was going on. "Can you keep your hands to yourself?"

He smiled. "Of course." He held his hands out in front of him. "Knife and fork, that's it." He took her to dinner at the Drift Inn, knowing that word would get back to Stephanie. Knowing that he was playing with fire. He wanted Robin, and he was determined to have her. Stephanie could wait.

On Monday morning, back at school, Brian was standing at his own locker, ten feet away from Robin's, when Stephanie marched down the hall and stopped in front of him, her eyes red and bloodshot. "Go to hell, Brian Carter." She threw his letterman jacket and his class ring on the floor at his feet and pounded off.

He looked up and met Robin's eyes, held his hands out in his trademark stance.

Robin closed her locker and walked over to him. "I thought you said that you two broke up."

He held up his jacket. "We did."

She leaned in close to his face, her words hissed into the air. "If you lie to me again, Brian Carter, you will live to regret it." She turned and headed to her first class.

Brian followed her, skipping up behind her and tapping her on the shoulder. "Will you go to prom with me?"

When they took to the dance floor, there was no question that Robin was getting lots of admiring glances from the males in the room. It made Brian feel even bigger, even more important. They all wanted this beauty, and now she was his. They may have *looked* like a fairy tale, Brian tall and athletic, Robin short and beautiful. But from the moment that Brian and Robin stepped out on the dance floor, trouble fanned out behind them, like the wake from a boat.

It started shortly after that first dance. Brian made his way to the punch bowl, leaving Robin standing at the edge of the room. Stephanie Spencer sidled up next to him, pouring herself a glass of punch and leaning against the table as Brian poured two cups.

"I see the witchy woman has worked a spell on you," she whispered, her eyes on the dance floor behind him. "I guess I thought you were smarter than that."

"I'm the one working the magic, Stephanie," he said. "I seem to remember it worked pretty well with you." He smiled.

Stephanie smiled back. "Hmm. Well, be careful. Because your magic seems to wear off very quickly." She flicked her nose toward the dance floor, and Brian turned around, two cups of punch in his hands, to find Robin gyrating across the floor with the Thomas kid, the voice of Madonna belting out "Like a Virgin" through the speakers.

Brian's jaw clenched. He turned and put the punch on the table, then leaned closer to Stephanie. "That's our song, isn't it? Like the very first time?" He slipped her punch cup out of her hands, and they swung out onto the floor. Brian made sure to move the two of them as close to Robin as he could, just to make sure that she noticed. He elbowed the Thomas kid, and the two of them switched partners. With Robin back in his arms, Brian smiled and whispered, "That's more like it. You're mine now, you know."

For once, Robin didn't argue. Instead, she let herself relax into his arms. The outcast, the daughter of the witch, in the arms of the most popular boy in school.

Prom happened the first weekend in May. Robin turned seventeen right after that, and for the next few months, she and Brian were together almost constantly. She stood at his side for all the graduation hoopla at the end of May. They both worked on the boat with Maggie throughout the summer months. Maggie moved into the cabin, intent on closing up the big house as soon as Brian left for college.

It was mid-August; Brian would be leaving for Seattle over the weekend. They pulled up to the dock and began to stow equipment; Maggie headed up the hill to the cabin. Brian waited until his mother was out of sight, and then he stood behind Robin and wrapped his arms around her, his nose in her hair. "I love you, Robin. You know that, don't you?"

She turned and lifted her face to his. Later that evening, she called Emmie and told her not to wait up. And then she and Brian climbed the stairs to his room, and she lay down with the young man she had grown to love. The next day, he left for Seattle and the University of Washington. And she didn't hear from him for four months.

When he came home, at Christmas break, nothing was quite the same. He'd been home for two days before he showed up at the cottage Robin shared with her mother, knocking on the door. Robin opened it and leaned against the doorjamb.

"Hey," he said.

"You must be lost. Your house is over there"—she tipped her nose toward the trees—"on the other side of the road."

A smile flashed on his face. "I missed you, Robin."

"Yes, I can tell. By the way you came right over to see me. By all the phone calls that I didn't get while you were gone."

He reached for her wrist, and she jerked it away. "I live in a dorm, Robin. There aren't any phones."

She laughed. "No pay phones anywhere in Seattle? Huh."

"You don't understand. It's not that easy."

"Sure it is. You put money in the slot and you punch in the number."

They stood slightly apart, tension vibrating between their bodies.

"Let me start over," Brian said softly. "You look beautiful."

Robin smiled and cocked her head to one side. "Yes. I know."

"I've missed you, Robin. I really have. Can I take you to dinner?"

She waited a moment, weighing her decision. She was furious with him; she was desperate to see him. Her toughness had faded, somewhere along the way, about the same time that she had fallen in love with this man.

Robin turned from the door to get a coat, and Emmie looked up from her spinning. "Are you sure about this, Robin?"

"No. But I guess I'm going to find out." When she left and they walked down the hill to the Drift Inn, she was determined that she was only going to dinner. That's it, nothing else. Just dinner. Afterward, they left the café and strolled down the street, down to the sea wall park, just below the businesses, at the water's edge. Reflections of Christmas lights danced on the water. They could smell the salt in the air.

The breeze off the water was cold, and Brian put his arm around her shoulders and pulled her close to him. "I've missed you so much, Robin. I've been miserable without you."

All her resolutions dissolved, pooling into the sand at her feet. She had missed him; she was glad he was back. At ten, she called her mother and told her not to wait up. And then they climbed the stairs to Brian's bedroom. For the next week, they spent every night together.

On New Year's Eve, they went to a party at Stephanie Spencer's house. Her parents were gone, and Steph was quick to put out word. It was the usual crowd, many of them Brian and Stephanie's age, home from college, but also a few of the current seniors. Jim Butler, Robin's friend from art class, was there, drinking a beer and watching everything like he could hardly wait to put it in his sketchbook.

For the first half of the evening, Brian stood with his arm around Robin's shoulder, sometimes hooking his elbow around her neck to pull her head in close to him so he could nuzzle her hair and kiss her temple. Stephanie watched it all, a beer in hand. She started the music, and a few couples, and even some singles, started dancing across the living room.

When Robin came back from the restroom, Brian was dancing with Stephanie, both of them teetering slightly from the beer. Robin stood in the doorway, watching them, until Jim appeared next to her. "What do you say, Robin? Want to dance?"

She nodded, and they swung out onto the floor.

When the song ended, Brian reached for her arm and pulled her in close to him again. He stood with his arm on her shoulders, glaring as Jim Butler made his way over to the kitchen. "You been seeing that guy while I was gone?"

Robin turned to him, incredulous. "What are you talking about?"

"It's just a question, Robin. All I want is an answer. Have you been seeing that guy? Yes or no?" He pulled her in closer to him.

Robin yanked away from him. "You have a lot of nerve. I don't hear from you for four months, and now you're pulling this shit? I'll do what I want, and it's none of your business. You don't own me, Brian Carter. I don't need your permission."

"I take it that's a yes?"

At that very moment, the voice of Stevie Nicks cut into the room, "Rhiannon" blaring through the speakers. Without turning to look away from Brian, Robin could hear the voices of Steph and her friends in the kitchen, joining in that same juvenile version of the song.

Brian smirked. "Have you been spreading the magic around, Ro-ah-bin?"

"You asshole."

Robin turned away from him and pushed through the crowd of dancing bodies. She found her coat on a chair by the door and left. Brian followed her outside, and a few of the partygoers watched through the living room window as the two of them stood outside on the grass, in the rain, obviously arguing. Brian leaned over her, and with his index and middle fingers, tapped her on the chest, as if he were trying to make a point.

Inside the house, the music ended at exactly that moment, and several people heard Robin's words, cutting into the night. "Don't you ever touch me like that again." She turned and headed down the road, into the darkness.

THIRTY-TWO

Alex unlocked the door and ran inside the entryway, trying to adjust her eyes to the darkness inside. She pulled her hood down and stood for a moment, letting her heart slow after the run uphill. Outside, the storm was raging, branches slapped against the roof and walls; wind whistled down the pipes and rattled the window frames.

She took a deep breath and removed her jacket, reaching for the hooks in the dark. She took her glasses off, shaking the water on the floor. Lightning flashed, and for one brief second, she thought she saw the face of a young woman flash in the mirror next to the coatrack. It was a face she knew, although she couldn't remember how. The woman was young, with long dark hair. Her hair was soaking wet, just as if she had been out in the storm with Alex. The room went back to darkness, and Alex took a step backward, her heart hammering.

Behind her, she heard soft sounds of movement. She turned slowly, listening as the lock in the back door clicked. She could hear the sound of the doorknob turning. The door creaked; cold air rushed in around her. It was too dark to see anything.

She put her hands out in front of her, feeling her way toward the kitchen, toward that open back door and the cold air rushing into the house. Halfway across the kitchen floor, she stopped.

She was not alone. She could hear someone breathing, someone standing nearby in this room.

"Happy New Year, Alex."

She started to step backward, unable to see in front of her or behind, still feeling the cold air blowing through that back door. "Daniel?"

He laughed. "Were you expecting someone else?"

She could hear him moving in the darkness, heard the creak of the wood floor as he placed his feet. Alex continued to move backward, her hands just behind her hips, feeling for the wall of the front room.

"It's one of the things I've always found so interesting about you, Alex," Daniel continued, still moving slowly. "The way you think you're so smart. The way you think you're smarter than I am."

"Daniel. I . . ."

She didn't know where he was; she could still see almost nothing. But even through the pounding of the storm, she could hear his voice, coming down the hallway, not far away from her. She kept sliding her feet backward, one soft step at a time. Retracing her path, back to the front door.

"You're not as smart as you think you are. Did you really think you could leave me? Did you really think that I would just let you go?" He laughed softly, not more than a few feet away from her. "I'm the smart one, Alex. I prepared for this a long time ago."

She took another step backward.

"You ever heard of those tracers? They're tiny. The size of a watch battery. So easy to stick onto something. So easy to put one almost anywhere. Your mother's car, for instance. Just in case. Just in case you got some crazy idea, and I needed to find you."

She shook her head. She said nothing.

"That was a hell of a fight, that last one." Daniel chuckled. "I had no idea you could be such a wildcat."

She could hear his breath, coming a little louder.

"But nobody hits *me*, Alex. I don't stand for that kind of thing."

His fist exploded in her face, and she fell backward.

"You're not nearly as smart as you think you are, you little bitch."

Alex had dropped to her knees on the floor; she held a hand to her face. Blood poured from her nose. She knew Daniel was above her somewhere in the darkness, though she could see nothing. *This is it*, she thought. *He's going to kill me.* The thought was not as dark, not as terrifying, as she had always imagined. For the past eleven years, she had been resisting, trying to imagine a way to escape from this madman and his uncontrollable anger. She had no resistance left, no more will to fight. No more will to keep running.

It was in that exact moment that she realized she was no longer afraid of him. She was no longer afraid of death. She was no longer afraid, period. She didn't care what happened, she only knew that she would never go back to live with him, ever again. She pushed herself up from the floor and stood, her feet planted just slightly apart to give her more stability.

"You want to kill me, Daniel?" She took a step sideways, still trying to gauge where he was from the sound of his breath.

In the darkness, she heard him laugh softly.

"Well, go for it. Kill me, if that's what you need to do. But I'm not running anymore. I'm not hiding anymore. I'm not cowering in fear anymore." Alex threw out her chest, her back as straight and as tall as she could make it. "I'm not doing it anymore. Go ahead, Daniel. Go ahead. Do whatever you need to do."

The back door slammed against the wall. They heard the crack of thunder. Another branch fell, somewhere just outside.

There was a clicking noise, like the hammer of a gun locking into position.

"Hold it right there, mister. I've got a .45 on your temple. If you so much as blink an eyelash, I'm going to blow your brains out." There was no mistaking Maggie's voice in the dark. "And don't think you can hide. I can see exactly what you're doing with these night-vision goggles."

None of them moved. The only sound was the sound of breathing—Daniel somewhere in the darkness of the kitchen; Alex standing in the hallway between the kitchen and front room, her hand on her bloody nose; Maggie somewhere in the darkness.

Lightning flashed in the sky, and Daniel dove to the floor. A second later, the thunder roared.

The front door flew open, and Emmie Porter stepped through, her white hair almost glowing in the darkness. "Alex? Are you okay? I thought I saw a light in the trees."

They waited in the darkness, unable to see where the others were. Except for the soft glow of Emmie's hair, nothing was clearly visible.

The next moment was a madness of movement. Alex felt Daniel's arm as he reached out and grabbed her, locking his arm around her body, half dragging her toward the back door. She struggled against him, kicking and yelling, "Leave me alone!"

There was the sound of a shot being fired, and suddenly Alex was free of his grip, dropping to the floor.

The back door crashed against the wall, and the sound was followed by loud thumps and bangs on the back porch. There was a thud, as if something heavy had fallen.

"Got him! I nailed the bastard!" Caroline's voice rose in triumph from the back porch.

Another voice sounded in the darkness. "Caroline, is that you?" David turned on the headlamp that he wore on his forehead. He tipped his head back to get a good look at Caroline, in fighting stance, standing over the body of Daniel Frazier.

"Coldcocked him!" Caroline said, raising her eyes to David's and then immediately raising one hand to shade her eyes, blinded by the glare of his camping headlamp. In the other hand, she held a bottle of champagne.

"What did you do, christen him?" David asked, his headlamp moving up and down.

"It was the only thing handy when I ran out the door."

The noises on the back porch were immediately followed by the crash of the front door flying open again. Grace's voice came from the darkness. "Alex? Emmie? Are you okay?"

Grace turned on her own headlamp and focused on Alex, huddled on the floor of the kitchen. "Police are on their way," Grace added as she went to help Alex up from the floor.

They both turned to see Maggie, slumped in a kitchen chair. Her skin was gray; her eyes were enormous. "Oh, God!" she whispered. "I wasn't sure where that bullet went. He hit my arm, and the gun went off. I didn't even know the thing was loaded. That gun belonged to my uncle George. It hasn't been fired in fifty years. Scared the hell out of me. I was afraid I might have shot you. Are you okay, Alex?"

Alex nodded. She raised a hand to her cheek, the one that had absorbed his fist just a few moments before. "Yeah. Yeah, I'm okay."

Caroline's voice reached them from the back porch. "Hey, Maggie? You want to point that gun at this no-good stinking vermin? Just in case he wakes up?"

Maggie rose to her feet and stood at the door to the back porch, swaying slightly, her gun wavering as she aimed at Daniel's back.

"I got this," David muttered. "Just don't shoot me, Maggie, okay?" He stepped over Daniel, lying sprawled on his stomach, and pulled Daniel's hands behind his back. From his pocket, he whipped out a long cord and began tying Daniel's hands together.

Caroline examined him in the bouncing light of his headlamp. "What are those? Knitting needles?" She looked at David's face. "What were you going to do? Knit him a sweater?"

David finished tying Daniel's hands. "Addi turbos. Solid steel. Circular. Forty-seven-inch cord. Quite practical, actually." He looked at her, and she shaded her eyes from the glare of his headlamp.

Caroline watched him as he finished wrapping the cord around Daniel's hands. "It might appear, to the casual observer, that you have practiced this hand-tying-with-knitting-needles maneuver in the past."

"Don't be a smart-ass. It was the only thing I could find when I was running out the door." David stood and released a long breath.

They heard the wail of a siren, and the room was lit with the flashing red and blue reflections of the lights on the sheriff's vehicle.

The deputies came in from both the front and the back, yelling as they stepped into the room, their flashlights scanning the crowd. "All right, hands up!"

"No need. We've got the perpetrator all trussed up," David said. But he held his hands in the air anyway.

Daniel was just regaining consciousness.

Maggie lowered her pistol and leaned against the kitchen counter. Her voice was breaking, as if all the wind had been sucked out of her. "Oh my God. I want that man out of here. Breaking and entering. Assault." She pointed her nose toward Alex, sitting on another kitchen chair, a bag of ice on her cheek and Grace kneeling nearby. "If I'd known the gun was actually loaded, I would've killed the son of a bitch."

The deputy exhaled and nodded. "Almost wish you would have. Tons of paperwork, either way. But now the state of Washington has to host the animal." He helped maneuver Daniel to his feet and steered him out the back door, toward the sheriff's vehicle. They could hear him, reading Daniel his rights.

The other deputy scanned the group with his flashlight. "I'll need to get statements from all of you. But first, is everyone okay?"

David and Caroline had joined the group in the kitchen. They were nodding, the light from David's headlamp bouncing up and down, and there were several murmurs of reassurance. Grace knelt in front of Alex, trying to help her stop the bleeding from her nose. Maggie had slumped into a kitchen chair.

The deputy took a deep breath and said, "Thank God. We could hear that gunshot as we were coming up Main Street."

His flashlight swept through the front room for one brief second, and then came back to rest on Emmie Porter. She was leaning against the wall by the front door. Her eyes were glazed and unfocused. Her right hand was across her body, holding on to her left side. Her skin was gray in the weak light. Something dark was seeping through her fingers, dripping down her side and onto the floor.

"Ms. Porter?" the deputy asked, walking into the front room. "Are you all right?"

Emmie slid slowly down the wall and crumpled on the floor, her head falling forward onto her knees.

Behind the deputy, Grace Wheeler screamed. "No!"

She ran into the front room and crouched next to Emmie, pulling her friend's body close to her. "No. Emmie. No."

THIRTY-THREE

"Good morning, Brian. Happy New Year." Emmie waited a moment.

Brian Carter was still half-asleep. "Morning, Emmie. Same to you."

"I'm sorry. I wasn't thinking. Did I wake you up?"

Brian's voice came through, still coated with sleep. "Yeah. I was out pretty late last night."

"I'll let you go back to sleep. Can I talk to Robin?"

There was silence on the line, and Emmie felt as if she were in a large, quiet room, waiting for a pin to drop. Everything went a little off-kilter.

"Uh. She's not here. I thought she was at your place."

Emmie swallowed. "No. No, she didn't come here last night. I thought she was with you."

Brian sounded as if he was now awake. "No. No, she's not here."

Emmie felt a shiver. "Could you check and make sure? The couch, maybe? Or one of the spare bedrooms?"

"Hang on."

Emmie could hear him, laying the phone on the table, walking through the house, calling, "Robin?" She swallowed. Her stomach had the tiniest cramp.

Brian picked up the phone. "She's not here, Emmie."

Emmie made a sound, a small leak of air. "I ah . . . umm. Huh. I thought you went to that party together." In her head, Emmie tried to tick off any of the other possibilities for Robin's whereabouts. The café, maybe? Was it open today, on New Year's Day?

Brian cleared his throat, now fully awake. "Yeah. We went to that party at Stephanie Spencer's house. Pretty good crowd, you know. Most of the kids home from school. The old high school crowd."

Emmie swallowed again. "Didn't Robin come home with you?"

There was a small beat of silence. "Uh. No. No, she didn't."

Emmie waited, her heart beating faster. She felt as if Brian were responding in slow motion, and she wanted to grab him by the shoulders and shake him. "Why not? What happened?"

He let out a long exhale. "We had an argument. She left before I did. Said she was going to walk home. I thought she was headed to your place."

Silence buzzed through the telephone line.

"Emmie? Maybe she went for a swim."

The words struck Emmie like a cacophony of discordant notes, a jangle of clashing sounds. *A swim? In the middle of the winter? In the middle of the night? In the middle of a storm? What the hell did he mean by that?*

"A swim?" Emmie repeated.

"I don't know. Maybe. She did some crazy shit sometimes."

Emmie could not breathe. By the time she hung up the phone, her sense of time passing had completely warped. Every second seemed like a lifetime.

Finch stood in the kitchen, a cup of coffee in his hand. "What's wrong?"

She raised her eyes to his. "Robin isn't at Brian's house. They went to that party, but he says they had a fight and she left before he did. He doesn't know where she is."

Finch stood up straighter. "Huh. Okay. Let's figure this out."

Emmie looked up the number for Stephanie Spencer, who answered with her voice clouded in sleep. She couldn't remember exactly what time Robin had left, but she knew that Robin was mad at Brian. She couldn't say when Brian had left the party, either. "I can't be exactly sure, Ms. Porter. I had a little too much to drink."

Finch sprang into action. He called Grace Wheeler to come down and sit with Emmie. "Come up with every name of every person at that party last night. Let's call every one of them. Maybe Robin went home with someone else."

Grace nodded and sat at the kitchen table with paper and pencil and phone book, starting the list.

Then he called Doc and Kate Taylor, and together with Grace's husband, they went out, spreading around town, looking for any sign of where Robin might have gone. They walked the route from the captain's house to Stephanie Spencer's house, north of town a short distance. By one o'clock, when they had still not found any sign of the girl, Finch called the sheriff's office.

They sent a deputy, who took a statement from Finch and Emmie. "So she's only been missing for what? A few hours now?"

Emmie sat on her sofa, stunned at the question. "Since last night. Since shortly after midnight. That's the last time anyone saw her."

The deputy shook his head. "I'm sorry. I can't really file a report or anything. Can't start a search. Not yet, anyway. Not until she's been missing for twenty-four hours."

Emmie's eyes went wide. "What? You won't start looking for twenty-four hours? That won't be until the middle of the night."

"That's the law, Ms. Porter. They make us wait. I mean, she's what? Seventeen years old, you said?"

Emmie nodded.

He took a breath, as if he'd been through this exact scenario a million times and was completely bored by the whole thing. "So she's not a child. She's old enough to know what she's doing. This is exactly the age when a lot of young girls run away. She could be anywhere. Maybe she went to the bar. Maybe she met someone. Maybe she's at a hotel in Sea Rose Harbor. Or sleeping it off somewhere."

Finch stood up, his arms rigid at his sides, fists clenching. "I would appreciate it if you would not throw your dirty ideas on my daughter. Robin isn't like that."

The deputy nodded. "I'm sure she's not. It's just that . . . they really won't let us do much. Not for twenty-four hours."

They were silent for a few moments. "Is there a boat or something? Could she be sleeping on a boat?"

Finch met Emmie's eyes. He and Grace's husband headed out the door, down to the marina.

It was the beginning of a storm. Wind ruffled the water. Pine needles shivered in the breeze. Just a breath of dread, just a shred of fear.

It was Finch and the Taylors who organized the search. The sheriff's office joined them the following day. They interviewed everyone at the party. Several of the young people remembered that Brian and Robin had been arguing, off and on throughout the evening. No one really remembered when Robin left, and most were very fuzzy about what time Brian had finally left. No one could say whether Brian had been at the party the entire evening. There'd been way too much drinking.

Jim Butler was so distraught that he could hardly speak. "I should have gone outside. I knew Brian was mad at her. I should have given her a ride home."

They checked the ferries running out of Sea Rose Harbor, asking everyone who worked that night if they had seen this young woman, Robin Porter. They checked hotels and motels all up and down the island, and on the other side, in Anacortes, where the ferry emptied onto the mainland. There was nothing. No sign. No trace of Robin Porter.

Before cell phones, before everything was on computer, before bank cards, there was little way to trace movements.

They searched for a week, with a smattering of help from a few people in Copper Cove. Most of the kids who had been at the party did not contribute to the search. A handful of adults, those closest to Emmie, combed every piece of woods and farmland, every stretch of beach. No sign was found.

They tried to get the sheriff to do a search of Maggie's house, the one where she and Brian had been staying together for the three weeks of Christmas break. Maggie was furious.

"What the hell are you trying to say, Emmie Porter?"

Emmie shook her head, tears filling her eyes. "I'm not trying to say anything, Maggie. I just want to make sure we cover all the bases. I want to make sure we're not missing something. Maybe there's some clue, some . . ."

Maggie refused. "You just want to smear dirt on my son."

The sheriff did manage to get a search warrant, two days later, but it turned up nothing. They found Robin's purse, in the parlor downstairs, and Brian insisted that she had left it there before they went to the party. But nothing else.

For most of that week, Brian had very little to say. He helped with the search, but he was quiet and withdrawn, and he quit after only an hour or so of looking. He didn't wring his hands; he didn't show any emotion, any fear, about what might have happened to her. He didn't act like a man who had just lost the woman he loved. He didn't sit with Emmie and Grace, trying to figure out what might have happened.

A week later, he left to go back to college. He never came back to spend a holiday with his mother. He never came back for summer break, choosing instead to find a job in Seattle. He never came back to the island again. He never again spoke to Emmie.

The sheriff's office brought dogs, two days in, but by that time, with the storm on the night of New Year's Eve, and the rains that had followed, there was no trace of scent anywhere. The law pulled out after a week, about the same time that Brian left to go back to school. The case was marked, "Missing. Unsolved."

Every time the phone rang, Emmie jumped. Every time a car pulled up in the yard, she felt her knees buckle. Her hair went completely white, almost overnight. She wandered the streets at all hours of the day and night, often in the pouring rain, talking to birds and trees and sky and water. *Where is she? Have you seen her? Have you seen my daughter?*

Finch took a leave of absence from his job, just so he could stay by Emmie's side. They looked everywhere. Over and over and over again, they walked that path, from Stephanie's house to the captain's. They walked every trail, every street, every tiny little deer trail they could find.

Almost a year later, Finch found Emmie in the cemetery one night, soaking wet, her teeth chattering with cold. He wrapped a blanket around her and pulled her close to him. "Let's go home, Emmie. Get you warmed up."

Emmie looked at him, her eyes filled with hopelessness. So much of Emmie's light had dimmed in the past year. Her hair was white, her skin was pale, her eyes were cloudy. Her voice cracked with emotion. "She's dead, isn't she?"

Finch took her hands in his, kissed each one. He looked in her eyes. "I don't know."

Tears flowed down her face, lost in the rain. "I want to believe she's still alive. I want to believe she's out there, somewhere." She met his eyes. "But that's not the way it feels. She would never just leave and not tell me. She would never just leave and not try to contact me.

"I keep thinking about what Brian said, about how maybe she went for a swim. It felt all wrong, those words." Emmie's voice drifted for a moment. "Did he hurt her, Finch? Did Brian hurt my baby?"

She buried her face in his chest, sobs racking her too-slender frame. "How could I not have known? I always knew. I could always feel it. Whenever there was an animal hurting, I felt it. How would I not have known? How could I have missed the pain of my own daughter?"

Finch pulled her body next to him; he wrapped his arms around her, his chin resting in her now-white hair. His own tears flowed. He swallowed. "I don't know the answers. I wish I did. But I do know this. No matter where she is, Emmie—you can still talk to her. Talk to her like she's right here with you. Like she's still living here in town with us." He waited a moment, holding her close to him. "The same way you talk to the animals and the trees. Talk to Robin's spirit—wherever it is. Whatever form it might be in."

He guided her up the hill and back to their little home, across the road from Maggie's. They lay in the bed together all night, holding on to each other. Finch never went back to his job with the tribe. He moved into the house with Emmie, and he was the rock she leaned on for another twenty years. He died of a heart attack, in 2010, just a year after Grace Wheeler lost her husband.

That night marked the turning point for Emmie, the place where she started to come back from the edge. She started talking to Robin constantly, no matter where she was or what she was doing. When she went for a walk with the dogs, she talked to her daughter. When she wandered through the stones of the cemetery, she talked to her daughter. When she stopped to admire the pink buds of the cherry trees in the spring, she talked to her daughter.

A couple of years later, there was a baby born to the J Pod orcas. A female, at first called J28. It wasn't until the baby was almost a year old that she was given a name—Polaris. Emmie was out walking the dog, wandering through the stones of the cemetery, when she heard the whale bell ringing in the park down below. She looked out in the water and saw them—several members of J Pod, swimming past in a group. The baby was in the middle, popping up to the surface with what looked like absolute joy on her face.

And that's when Emmie knew. Robin was with her orca family now.

THIRTY-FOUR

They were sitting in a circle at the old Hadley house, David, Caroline, and Alex, listening as Grace finished telling them the story of that New Year's Eve, thirty years before. Every person in the room was flooded with tears, with the heart-wrenching pain of what Emmie had been through. Of what Robin had been through.

Grace took a Kleenex from a box and wiped her nose. She passed the box on to Alex. "Emmie knew, last night. She knew something was wrong. We were just getting ready to sit down to dinner when the power went out. I was looking for a candle and matches. Emmie walked over to the window, and she stood there, staring at the captain's house across the road. You can't actually see the house, just that big group of trees. Once in a while, if there's a light on inside, you might see the glow. But mostly, it's just darkness."

Grace took a shuddery breath. "But Emmie stood there, staring out into the dark, shaking her head. 'There's something wrong,' she said. And then she grabbed her coat, told me to call the sheriff and meet her at the captain's house. And she headed out into the storm."

"I knew it, too," Caroline sniffed. "Alex went running out of here, into that storm. And I stood there at the door, watching her go up the hill, and I just had this weird feeling. I told David that something felt really off."

David grabbed one of the Kleenex from the box that was circling the group, and nodded. "We grabbed the nearest weapons we could find and headed up that hill. But of course, Caroline beat me. She is a little younger."

Grace blew her nose, and then put a hand on Alex's shoulder. "Alex? He's in jail right now, waiting for the judge to set bail. And hopefully, bail will be too high for him to get out right away. But you know . . ." She paused, as if she didn't want to say more.

Alex nodded. "There are no guarantees. I know that."

"He might be out tomorrow, for all we know. And of course, you can get a restraining order, and you should, but . . ."

"That's no guarantee, either. I know that." Alex slumped in her seat for a moment. "All these years, I stayed. Afraid that he would hurt someone else. Afraid he was going to hurt my mother."

She shook her head. "But I can't live like that anymore. Whatever happens . . . whatever he does . . . I can't go back again."

Grace put an arm around her. "We don't want you to."

Alex wiped her nose. "But what about Emmie? I didn't want anyone else to get hurt."

"Alex, this is not your fault. And I know Emmie would much rather put herself in harm's way than let anyone else suffer. She's been like that her whole life. At least as long as I've known her." Grace pulled back and looked at Alex. "Emmie always wondered what would have happened if even one person at the party that night had gone out to help. If even one person had volunteered to take Robin home. Would she still be with us, if that had happened?"

Grace wiped her eyes. "And I feel the same way. I couldn't live with myself if I sat at home, safe, while he was trying to hurt you. If I can help, you know I will."

"Me, too." Caroline blew her nose. "Turns out I'm pretty fierce with a bottle of champagne in my hands."

"Well, I don't like to brag," said David. "But I'm pretty good with a pair of knitting needles. Anytime. Anywhere."

"Grace?" Alex's voice was soft, almost too quiet to hear. "They never spoke, in all these years? Maggie and Emmie?"

Grace shook her head. "No."

"Did Emmie hold it against her? Against Maggie?"

Grace took a deep breath. "I think maybe at first, she did. She was hurting so much. But you know Emmie. You know how she is. I asked her about it once. If she blamed Maggie. This was . . . I don't know . . . maybe five years after it happened? And Emmie just said, 'Brian could have been my son. Robin could have been her daughter. Whatever happened that night was not Maggie's fault.' She's right, you know. Maggie has suffered, too. Maggie lost her son, that night."

Grace sniffled. "It's Emmie's greatest gift. Being so sensitive. Being able to see all the different sides to a story. Her greatest gift. Her greatest torment."

"So Brian never . . . was never brought to justice?" Caroline asked.

"For what? As far as anyone really *knows*, as far as anyone can prove, there is no crime. No body. No evidence. No crime."

They were quiet a moment, all of them lost in their own thoughts.

"For a while, it was all anyone in town could talk about. What happened to Robin Porter? There were a lot of people around here who figured she just ran off. Went someplace else."

"Without her purse," Caroline sputtered.

"Without ever contacting her mother," Grace said quietly. "Which is not something I believe Robin would ever do. I can't imagine Emmie's pain. Never really knowing what happened. Never being able to say for sure if her daughter was alive or dead. Never being able to mark her life in any way, like she could if there had been a grave." Grace was quiet. "Robin Rose Porter. May 10, 1970, to December 31, 1987."

Alex lifted her head, felt a sharp gasp of breath. *Rose? Her middle name was Rose?*

THIRTY-FIVE

On a chilly morning in mid-January, Alex sat at her table in Maggie's cabin, the computer open in front of her. Maggie sat at her desk across the room. She had not had much to say in the past two weeks, since that night in the storm. But it had not been lost on Alex that Maggie was quieter than normal, that her hands shook slightly when she poured her own coffee. Though she had not specifically mentioned anything about Brian and Robin, Alex felt certain that it was on her mind. How could it be otherwise?

Alex had not been able to forget the sound of that gun going off. She had not been able to forget the awful story that Grace told them. She had spent many hours thinking about how quickly things can happen. How there are times when everything comes crashing down around us, despite the best intentions. Maggie would never talk about it, Alex was certain of that. But she could see it in Maggie's eyes—the questions, the doubts, the regrets.

The sound of the whale bell rose up from the streets below. Alex moved to the window, looking out into the gray. Maggie stood beside her. Neither one could see much of town below them, but they continued to hear the ringing of the bell.

"Let's go," Maggie said. They grabbed their jackets and started down the hill toward the park.

"I had a notice in my e-mail this morning." Maggie panted as they hurried down the hill. "It's in all the reports coming out of the whale research center. There's been some bad news."

"Oh?" Alex whispered. She kept her hands in her pockets.

"This is part of J Pod, going by out there," Maggie said, tipping her head toward the gathering of people lining the overlook. "But two members are missing."

Alex forced a swallow. "Missing?"

"Missing. Presumed dead," Maggie said flatly. "They were last seen over two weeks ago. J28. Polaris. Born in '92 or '93. And her baby, Dipper. One of that group of babies born in the last year or so."

Alex stared out at the gray misty water, along with several other people from town. *Missing. Presumed dead.* The words looped in her head.

Maggie continued, "Polaris had an older daughter and a sister. People have seen them catching salmon, trying to feed Polaris and the baby."

Alex wanted to collapse in a heap, right there on the pavement.

"She had been showing signs of malnutrition for the past few weeks. Peanut head, they call it. Their bodies start burning their own fat reserves when they can't find enough salmon.

"And that's when it gets really bad for the babies. All those chemicals in the water? The PCBs and fertilizers and pesticides and every other stupid chemical we use on our lawns and parks and in every part of our lives? All that stuff washes down into the water and absorbs into every living thing. Including the orcas."

Alex nodded.

"That baby was drinking mother's milk, laced with poison." Maggie swallowed hard.

Maggie turned and looked Alex in the eye. "After Polaris went missing, the sister was seen trying to push the baby up for air. Trying to help it breathe. Now the baby is missing, too."

They had arrived at the deck, just above the sea wall and just beneath the whale bell. Several people had gathered at the sound of the bell, but the crowd was subdued. Most of them had read the reports in the morning edition of the paper.

On Alex's left, a small group of spinsters was gathered. Grace and David and Caroline all stood quietly, watching the orcas. Caroline was wearing big fluffy dog slippers, like those designed for children. They nodded at each other, murmurs of "hello" quiet and subdued by the gloomy news.

Maggie looked back to sea and crossed her arms over her chest. "I don't know if I can bear to watch much more of this."

Alex blinked back tears. *Missing. Presumed dead.*

The orcas passed by in front of the onlookers. "That's Polaris' family out there. Her mother, her two sisters. Her daughter, one brother. One nephew. It's like watching the family at a funeral, isn't it?"

Everyone on the observation deck was quiet. Somber. The mood was black, completely opposite of the excitement in the crowd not that long ago, when they'd been standing out here to look at one of the new babies.

"They're starving." Maggie stared at the blackfish, heading down the coast. "And unless a whole lot of people start caring a whole awful lot?" Maggie turned and caught Alex's eye. "We'll be seeing a whole lot more of this."

They stood quietly watching the orcas as they headed south in Haro Strait. There was no sound from the crowd. Some folks continued to stand quietly; small groups of two or three broke off and headed back home.

Maggie sniffled and took a deep breath. "There's a meeting tonight, down in Sea Rose Harbor. It's the Department of Fish and Wildlife, taking public comments on the removal of those old dams on the Snake River. The Save Our Wild Salmon people will be there. I think I'll go. Put in my two cents, for whatever that's worth. May not do a bit of good, but not doing anything sure isn't helping. Want to come along, Alex?"

Alex turned and met Maggie's eyes. *Missing. Presumed dead.* The words vibrated in her head. "Yes. Yes, I would. I'll put in my two cents, as well. For whatever that's worth."

Maggie raised her eyes to Emmie Porter, standing on the other side of Alex, surrounded by the spinsters. Her left arm was cradled in a sling, still recovering from where she'd been hit by Maggie's stray bullet. "What about you, Emmie? Want to join us?"

Emmie swayed slightly, two rivers of tears flowing down her face as she watched the orcas. As she searched for the ones that were no longer there, for all those that were missing. Emmie's voice was barely audible, and she did not turn to look at Maggie when she spoke. "Thank you, Maggie. I believe I would like to go."

Alex sensed Emmie's swaying body, as if she was fighting to stay upright, and she stepped closer and put her arm around the woman's waist. Emmie leaned into her. After a moment, Alex reached out and put her other arm around Maggie, who stood rigid and unbending, but did not move away from the embrace. Alex held them both for a moment. The spinsters, these two women—they were her clan now, her pod. They could lean on one another.

AFTERWORD

All the stories about whales included in this book are based on true events, recorded in published accounts. I changed the timing, to make all of it fit in one story.

For more information about domestic abuse:

National Coalition Against Domestic Violence
www.ncadv.org

For more information on killer whales:

Center for Whale Research
www.whaleresearch.com
Orca Network
www.orcanetwork.org

To listen to killer whales on hydrophones:

www.orcasound.net

Movies about orcas:

Blackfish, 2013, directed by Gabriela Cowperthwaite
The Whale, 2011, directed by Suzanne Chisholm and Michael Parfit
National Geographic Killer Whales: Wolves of the Sea, 1993
Lolita—Slave to Entertainment, 2003, directed by Tim Gorski

Further reading:

Death at SeaWorld, David Kirby
Of Orcas and Men, David Neiwert
The Grandest of Lives: Eye to Eye with Whales, Douglas H. Chadwick
Listening to Whales: What the Orcas Have Taught Us, Alexandra Morton
Beyond Words: What Animals Think and Feel, Carl Safina
War of the Whales, Joshua Horwitz
The Cultural Lives of Whales and Dolphins, Hal Whitehead and Luke Rendell

IN MEMORIAM

Most recent deaths in Southern Resident Killer Whales, as of date of printing:

Sonic, J52
Deceased, September 2017 (age two years)

Skagit, K13
Missing, presumed dead, August 2017 (age forty-five)

Granny, J2
Missing, presumed dead, January 2017 (age approx. 105 years)

Doublestuf, J34
Found deceased, December 20, 2016 (age eighteen years)

Dipper, J54
Missing, presumed dead, October 2016 (age ten months)

Polaris, J28
Mother of Dipper
Missing, presumed dead, October 2016 (age twenty-three years)

Samish, J14
Missing, August 2016 (age forty-two years)

Nigel, L95
Found deceased, March 2016 (age twenty years)

Unnamed baby, J55
Missing, January 2016 (newborn)

And

Sherry
Missing since August 1987
Age thirty-one years
Unsolved

ACKNOWLEDGMENTS

Stories have so many helpers, and there are numerous people to thank for supporting me with this one. First, to my agent, Alison Fargis, who believed in me even when no one else did. To my editors at Lake Union Publishing, Danielle Marshall and Christopher Werner, for their guiding hands and support throughout this process. I especially want to thank Jenna Free, whose keen eye helped make this a much better manuscript.

After a three-month visit to the Puget Sound area in 2012, I could not get the smell of cedar and salt water out of my mind, and I returned here to live in 2014. Learning about this area, after a lifetime in Colorado, completely inspired much of what you find in this story. It is a magical place.

A few of the business names in this book were borrowed from actual places, although none of them are in the same town. Here's a nod to Brewed Awakenings, in Allyn, and Turnip the Beet, in Port Angeles. Moby Dickens was the name of a longtime independent bookstore in Taos, New Mexico, that went out of business in 2016. For years, that place was one of my favorites, and I especially appreciate Willie Wood, with all her wonderful recommendations.

I did a massive amount of research for this story, and many of those sources are listed in a separate page. I also read Buck Brannaman's *The Faraway Horses* and watched the documentary about him called *Buck*.

There are so many ways to deal with animals (and humans) that are amazingly kind and gentle.

I want to particularly thank two energy healers who allowed me to observe their work: Jan Gillander and Dixie Golins—you are both amazing. I am also indebted to the Orca Network and the Center for Whale Research for their dedicated love of orcas and whales and the massive amounts of information they have accumulated. To my children, who inspire me always, and particularly for Ho Hos and vegan cookie dough. To the village, for teaching me to spin and for adding important information at several key stages along the way. In particular, I want to thank Marcia Adams and Heidi Dascher, at The Artful Ewe and Ewe II, who took me in when I was a stranger in this wet world. And to my friend Kathleen Reid, who listens to me rant and always finds a way to make me laugh.

BOOK CLUB DISCUSSION QUESTIONS

1. Emmie Porter, the "village witch," talks a lot about the effects of trauma, including loss of memory of the actual event, and the way that memories of the event can be triggered. She says that "the body remembers," in dreams or in physical conditions. Have you seen examples of this type of thing in real life?

2. Emmie has learned a gentle approach to working with animals, based on empathy, understanding, and sensitivity. Describe some types of therapy or energetic healing work that take this approach. (Examples: Reiki, acupuncture, massage, yoga.) Have you had experience with any of these types of therapy?

3. At one point, Alex explains to her friend Rachel why she has not left her abusive husband. Alex has a better situation than many abused women. She is educated, has a good job, and does not have children. What are some of the reasons that a person would choose to stay in an abusive relationship? Can you imagine situations in which the abused does not believe he or she has a choice?

4. Compare the society of the Southern Resident Killer Whales to modern American society. In what ways can you see examples of empathy, or the lack of it?

5. What examples of the sensitivity of animals have you experienced?

6. Discuss issues related to domestic violence. What things can you imagine that might improve this situation?

7. In what ways is *The Music of the Deep* an appropriate title for the story? What are some examples of different activities or aspects of the story that would fall under that description?

8. Have you ever had a "ghost" experience? Discuss the idea that trauma can leave a mark, not just on humans and animals but also on places.

9. What are some of the issues facing the orcas that seriously threaten their survival?

ABOUT THE AUTHOR

Elizabeth Hall, bestselling author of *Miramont's Ghost* and *In the Blue Hour*, is a former teacher, communications consultant, and radio show host. She resides on an island in the Pacific Northwest, where she indulges in the fiber arts and keeps an eye out for whales.